Trust

Taryn Harvey

BALBOA.
PRESS
A DIVISION OF HAY HOUSE

Balboa Press books may be ordered through booksellers or by contacting:

Balboa Press
A Division of Hay House
1663 Liberty Drive
Bloomington, IN 47403
www.balboapress.com.au
1 (877) 407-4847

Printed in the United States of America.

ISBN: 978-1-4525-1326-3 (sc)
ISBN: 978-1-4525-1325-6 (e)

Balboa Press rev. date: 3/6/2014

Acknowledgement

Thank you to my family and friends for
your unwaivering support and love.

Also I'm grateful to Nicola O'Shea for weaving
editorial magic and breathing life into my cathartic musings.

Contents

Part One

Stumbling
Upon Utopia

Prologue

Monday morning came around far too soon, bringing with it another bout of nausea that hit me with such force I thought I was going to pass out. But I wasn't about to let a small case of nerves get the better of me; determined to go through with this crazy idea. Many of my friends, if they knew, would consider my choice to be completely out of character, but this only added to the appeal.

With fingers that no longer felt like mine I did up buttons on my new emerald silk blouse which, matched with a black David Lawrence suit and some pearls, looked superb. Taking one last look I raced out the door. Just breathe and forget about everything else for a while, I told myself. Let's see what happens.

My feet took their usual route to the train station, but my body knew it was heading in a new direction. I sat there in the carriage, surrounded by commuters, wondering what they would think if they knew where I was going. To combat the denial playing out internally, I continued to pitch this as another temporary role I would only do for a month. Nobody would ever have to know.

As I got out at my usual stop, I had the distinct impression that people were staring at me. Maybe they were; at some level I hoped so. My black stilettos echoed on the stairs, seeming to proclaim that soon I would be entering a completely new world.

It was a fine spring day in Sydney; a glimpse of the ferries moving under the bridge, disappearing into its vast shadow as I made my way to the Victorian terraced houses by the water. Turning into a side lane where the main entrance of this establishment was located, I looked up at the balcony where double French doors were slightly ajar, a hint of lace curtain gently swaying in the breeze.

Nervously I pressed the door buzzer, my eyes fixed on the broken entrance sign stuck to the glass pane. A minute passed, long enough for my mind to flood with fear and doubt. I took a deep breath, my heart racing as the door opened. Another swift dose of nerves hit my belly with a vengeance – this time I would be sick for sure.

"Hello, I'm Sherri," said the woman standing in the doorway. "Daphne's on the phone so she asked me to greet you."

Sherri looked like she'd just stepped out of a Parisian history book. I guessed her to be around fifty, with black hair gracefully clasped up in a French roll. Glasses were perched on the end of a little nose, but it was her eyes that I liked immediately. A rich, dark brown, they twinkled with warmth and kindness.

"Do come in. We've all been looking forward to meeting you. I'll take you through to the girls' room, where you can make yourself comfortable."

Sherri's words sent my heart rate soaring. Here I was, on the threshold of a new way of life, about to meet the women I'd read about on the establishment's website. How would I fit in? Steeling myself, I walked through the doorway into a room furnished with two white leather lounges displaying beautiful floral throw rugs dangling over the arm rests. Three faces turned to stare at me and their chatter stopped.

My body turned to ice. *Oh my God, I can't do this!*

They were all elegantly dressed in gowns, making me feel like an idiot for having chosen a suit. But that was what Daphne, the owner of this business, had suggested I wear on my first day when she'd interviewed me last week.

"Okay, girls, this is our new lady beginning with us today," Sherri said. "Jewel, this is Amber, Kelly and Ashley. Lilly's with us today too, but she's already busy."

Each girl smiled at me.

"Hey, Jewel, come and put your things down over here," Kelly said. "First day, hey? It's okay. We'll help you with any questions."

"Um, okay, thanks," I responded awkwardly, finding it strange to be introduced under an alias.

"Here, hun. Put your bag down here." Kelly pointed to the space beside one of the lounges.

"Thanks," I said again, careful not to make too much eye contact. This was uncharted territory; almost like the first day at school as I wondered who it was safe to befriend.

I took a seat next to Ashley, who was inspecting her fingernails. The whirring sound, a clothes dryer, confirmed the smell of damp laundry mingled with hair spray I had encountered when entering the room.

"Jewel, if you need to get changed or anything, just slip through the back – that's where the shower is," Kelly went on, pointing to a doorway. "And grab yourself a towel from that cupboard there. Pick your favourite colour and that'll be your towel for the day."

I shuffled around the coffee table until I reached the cupboard under the window and grabbed a red one, not my favourite colour at all, but it was on top and I was keen to get back to my unobtrusive corner spot as quickly as possible.

"Ashley, Peter's here!" Sherri called.

"Okay, thanks," Ashley answered, hopping up to scurry out.

Within minutes, Sherri was back to inform Kelly that her appointment had arrived. Amber sat deeply engrossed in a nurses' training manual, not paying much attention to the chatter around her or to me.

Sherri popped in again a while later. "There you are, Amber. Your 10.45 is here."

"Okay," Amber answered.

When she stood up, it struck me how tall she was, like an Amazon. She had long, lean legs and big, square shoulders holding up bountiful breasts. Her blonde hair was short and curly. Even though it was still early, she went over to a fridge in the corner of the room, pulled out some beer and put it on a tray with two glasses.

I sat there quietly, staring at the A3 poster on the back of the door that said *No Divas Here, Thank You!* Sherri came back into the room.

"Jewel, are you ready?" she asked, looking at me carefully.

The surge of fear swept through my body again. "Oh, sure," I stuttered, not really sure at all.

"Mike's lovely and so looking forward to seeing you," Sherri said, smiling at me. "He was booked in for ten, but we moved him to eleven to give you time to settle in."

I tried smiling back, but couldn't.

"We're here if you need anything, Jewel," Kelly reminded me again.

I wondered if she would come with me, to show me what to do. Come to think of it, where was my training session? I'd never had a job before where there hadn't been some kind of orientation process.

"Right, okay then. Bye." My voice trailed off, sounding rather pathetic.

As I headed down the lengthy corridor toward the front of the house, I felt like Alice about to enter a strange new world. I came to the door of the meeting room where inside a man called Mike was waiting for me; a man I didn't know. Was that even his real name? All I really knew of him was that he was a stranger who was about to pay for the pleasure of my company and probably to have sex.

Grasping the brass knob, I turned it and opened the door. It felt odd, but at the same time I had come to a junction; an acceptance that my life as I knew it was over. I was no longer that little girl with big dreams of happy ever after. I was a woman, wounded and exhausted. This was my safest and most secure option, and I hoped it was a smart move.

Chapter 1

An Intoxicating Life

I *was* smart. It's just that somewhere along the way to adulthood, I failed to develop confidence. When I was a little girl growing up in Adelaide, it was my intention to become an actress; the appeal being a glamorous lifestyle and the freedom to reinvent myself. However, this was soon abandoned due to a fear of public ridicule. Being the firstborn on both sides of our family, I was the first to go through puberty, hence absorbing occasional off-the-cuff remarks that stayed with me for years. One uncle pointed out that I was "robust" for a teen, and an aunty commented when she saw me in bathers, "Gee, haven't *you* developed big hips and thighs? Solid, just like your father."

My dad, a fitness fanatic and vegetarian, made it quite clear that my weight gain was cause for concern. Such scrutiny was intimidating, convincing me that I had failed them all. Why did I have to grow up to have breasts and a body I didn't want? I was confused, becoming adept at disassociating from my physical form by practicing what I discovered to be transcendental meditation.

I was eight years old when the sensations borne from controlling my breath and body made me inquisitive. Experimentation taught me how far I could go before blacking out, floating through an alluring realm between heaven and earth. The tingling in my fingertips and the euphoric blanket of peace enthralled me for years, drawing me away from everything else that had me less inspired. I would sneak away into my bedroom to enjoy this magical space where no one ever bothered me.

The only person with whom I ever felt safe with was my dad's mum. Dad was extremely close to her too, having grown up with an absent father—also an alcoholic. When my parents both worked nights, Grandma would look after me, taking time off from nursing, changing shifts only when it was holiday time, so that my cousin Tina and I could stay over. Grandma was easy to talk to whenever I had big questions to ask without feeling stupid or afraid like I did around Mum. Ashamed of her alcoholic mother, who had taken up with a much younger lover, Mum felt betrayed for the judgement she endured from Nan when falling pregnant with me. Nan's lover bore the brunt of Mum's violent rage, sending me into hiding whenever they rocked up uninvited and drunk. Much of this fury stemmed from her disappointment, claiming Nan was a hypocrite who had kept secrets—her older sister was fathered by a different man, and the younger one was adopted, the baby of a friend who was apparently a prostitute.

My young, fertile mind sought clarity around all this. At the same time, I was battling to accept my body's changes whilst observing jovial high school friends with hourglass figures exuding confidence and looking carefree. It didn't take long for me to conclude that there was clearly something wrong with my life and my family.

A few years later, when I was sixteen, a schoolyard accident that nearly killed my cousin, Tina, changed my future plans. Tina, who was touted as the smartest one in our family, spent her early teenage years in rehab, making us all very aware of how quickly our assumed destiny can be denounced. My dad, an emotionally passive man, in sharp contrast to my aggressive mum, drank even more than usual to cope with the tragedy his brother was facing.

I idolised my father when I was a little girl, even though he wasn't around much, given this battle with the drink. His absence was tempered by the wonderful gemstones he often presented me with. Aware that I was mesmerised by their shape and colour—purple being my favourite—he had an amethyst necklace made up for me. Later, when I was to observe his struggle to sober up before work, my contempt for him grew. How could he possibly love us and yet keep behaving in this way?

Mum threw herself into community welfare work, where she looked after seriously ill Aboriginal children, generations affected by cancers and genetic heart disease that stemmed from radiation contamination. Bomb testing had taken place in the Outback decades earlier. One young boy became part of our family. Mum brought him home to play during his stints of chemotherapy, but he died on my birthday at the tender age of four.

My late teenage years were spent watching my parents distract themselves from the pain, leaving me to take care of my sister who was five years younger and oblivious to all the drama unfolding that made me feel extremely tense.

Around this time, an uncle committed suicide. He was alone in a hotel room in Sydney's Kings Cross where he shot himself. My mother, who was close to her stepbrother, one of four, was devastated. An avid traveller, my uncle had always sent me postcards from exotic places, knowing I was keen to experience the wider world. Mum said he was a lonely, solitary man who never drank, yet suffered quietly from unrequited love.

These events shunted me along a different path, one where bouts of manic exercise and self-imposed starvation became my way to cope. I nurtured a new belief system in order to function with a sense of control. The world didn't seem fair nor was it safe. By the time I attended university, the anxiety and panic attacks had set in. Assemblies or shopping-centre crowds sent me into overwhelming claustrophobia, gripping me with fear. This is when running in the morning and three-hour walks in the late afternoon helped me build resilience.

Reinventing myself became possible when a neighbour introduced me to Weight Watchers. Soon I gained a sense of how to control my body. The more I could cut my food intake while monitoring my exercise and food regimen constantly, the happier I felt. As my physique changed, so too did everyone's attitude. When they commented on how good I looked, it fuelled the desire to be more stringent with my routine—proof I was on the path to success.

I felt secure and powerful until there was a glitch in the plan, like if my parents were home together, sitting at the dining table, where it would be impossible for me to turn down food. This made me restless, slightly abated by counting to a certain number, which helped me evade dark thoughts. These obsessive compulsions irritated me until I found comfort by drowning out the noise with alcohol.

During my last year in high school, a girl I became friends with coaxed me into going out to pubs. We were only sixteen when we sneaked into the city to drink and dance for hours. Already earning a good income on the weekends working with an aunt at a local nursing home, I could afford to pay for my own drinks.

Just before my eighteenth birthday, Mum decided to leave Dad. When I woke him up to prepare for night shift, he asked me to sit for a moment as he cried, telling me the news. I felt nothing, even when he began attending AA and Mum gave him another chance. Taking on more shifts meant I wasn't around much anymore to care.

In the meantime, my cousin's slow, traumatic rehabilitation due to the brain injury inflicted by a foolish schoolyard prank motivated me to develop significantly greater goals. Healthcare became my focus, and although I wanted to study medicine, this was not an option for someone who couldn't make sense of chemistry and maths. However, I was good at doing research and did love to write. Choosing journalism with a major in psychology seemed like the right way to proceed, as I opted to study a communications degree at the University of Adelaide.

On orientation day at university, I met a couple of girls with whom I became quite close, but fearing that they would notice my binge-eating behaviour, I averted spending any time with them. That first day, as we sat there chatting, all I could do was focus on the donuts in the middle of the table. There were five assorted ones and only three of us. Who would eat one? I wanted all of them but wouldn't allow myself to have any. It became so unbearable that after we parted, I walked for twenty minutes before finding a deli where I knew I wouldn't be seen. Buying and eating a selection of cakes ushered in a sense of relief; however, the ensuing anger and guilt were overwhelming, driving me into despair as I grappled with the notion that I had failed to maintain control.

Fearing my behaviour was becoming more difficult to hide, I chose to spend very little time with anyone, avoiding any event or function where there would be food or alcohol. Binge drinking had already begun when I was left alone at home. Stumbling upon my dad's hidden stash, I was taking swigs of vodka from the bottles found at the back of the linen cupboard, refilling them with water.

I couldn't stop myself, enjoying the pleasant lightness that alcohol provided. A routine was crucial at this point, helping to ensure that I could pull myself back from the brink of getting drunk. It was already a fine line, having accidently drunk too much gin one afternoon, left over from my eighteenth birthday. I could hear our phone ringing but was unable to reach it before it woke my father. Stumbling back into my room, I listened carefully, waiting for him to shower, dress, and leave for work before I emerged, feeling a little dizzy with eyes that could barely focus!

When I began to go out every weekend with Abbey, a girl I met while working at the nursing home, I got my first taste of freedom and more opportunity to drink. Somehow I managed to justify that the drinking curbed my binge eating, convincing myself that at least I wasn't acting as obsessive anymore. This gave me a false sense of security, believing I finally had complete control. Excited by this level of discipline I had in place, I ramped up the physical activity; running, plus six sessions of aerobics every week at the gym. I loved earning money, taking on extra cleaning shifts whenever anyone called in sick, quickly saving enough to afford a new car and holiday within that year.

Excited about the prospect of travelling overseas, I decided to take off more time given that Europe and the UK were so far away. Besides, I had become thoroughly bored with University life where I felt so out of place. The subjects were quite dull, leaving me with too much time to think about my next binge eating or drinking opportunity. This was when I made the decision to work full time and put my degree on hold for at least a year.

Staying on at the nursing home on weekends, I began working for an advertising agency during the week, finding it far more creative and rewarding than university. Looking into this further, I took up part time study in advertising at a local college few nights during the week, which also helped to keep me distracted from drinking with friends.

A few years later when I was twenty one I met Becky who was working in the same building as me. Drawn to her gregarious nature and optimism, we had a lot of fun, sharing intimate facts about ourselves over copious amounts of wine. Life moved along incredibly fast during these years. I met my future husband, then shortly after Becky moved to Sydney followed by my sister who moved to far North Queensland for a year. When my sister returned I was already separated and barely coping, just as we received the shocking news that our grandma had been diagnosed with lung cancer, only to die within six months.

The impact of these crises sent me spiralling out of control. I lost twenty kilos which reduced my 164cm frame to 45kg in a matter of weeks, worrying my parents and friends. This same year I had begun working at a television station where the partying lifestyle was an expectation, helping to hide my drinking which masked unbearable grief. Bouncing between one media launch to another, trying desperately to stay focussed so I could build an advertising career, eventually I moved out with a radio announcer who had been living next door to me and my sis.

Jessica was such a wonderful, observant friend. Concerned about my self-destructive behaviour she was capable of pulling me up on it. Whenever I came home after a big night out, she would calmly introduce me to her music industry friends then discourage them from giving me a drink.

"You've had a great night, I can see!" Jessica would say. "How about we go to your room and you can tell me all about it."

I was well aware that my drinking was becoming noticeable but no-one ever questioned me, not even after I stumbled into work straight after an all-night drinking binge. Part of my role was to entertain clients at corporate events, so it was easy for everyone to let me continue sashaying through the fog. Of course my mother noticed I had a problem on the occasion that I ever popped back home for a Sunday afternoon roast.

"You're an alcoholic, just like your father!" she'd scream.

And she was probably right. Even when I promised myself I'd only have one glass, by the time I had three the lines were well and truly blurred. I would be desperate for another one. I wanted to stop, but I just didn't know how!

During the years that followed, Becky invited me to work with her team in Healthcare PR. It was 1998 and news of life changing blockbuster drugs was constantly infiltrating the media, making this a lucky break into the industry for me. Moving to Sydney I began working on the launch of Viagra for Erectile Dysfunction. In the meantime, my sister had since got married and was already expecting her second child – another boy. I fell in love with my nephews, and felt the pull at my heartstrings each time I would visit and then leave.

I was already thirty three years old with no intentions of settling down again. It was a good thing that my career began taking off, helping me to diffuse any feelings that I wanted a family of my own.

Success was my baby, and I would give it my full attention, this career move an opportunity for a fresh start in every way.

Post Viagra launch there were new, exciting accounts to keep me busy as I mastered the Sydney media. With the help of a mentor, one of the Account Directors working with us, I was encouraged to be more ambitious and expand. Registering with a specialist health recruitment agency, I landed a consultancy role with a global agency.

A year later after experiencing what was one of the most spectacular Olympics in history Sydney gleaned the spotlight, only to later reel from the pressure to continue with such a positive vibe. Australians never seemed to learn that after every party there is a hangover, and as the year ended our company began to feel the heat, with big clients moving their business to smaller, more competitively priced agencies. Longer hours were spent preparing pitches to pharmaceutical and nutritional companies. I was getting tired, and to combat this I was drinking even more, partly due to the constant celebrations held in honour of winning a new account.

There was a social aspect to this new life, just like the old one I had tried to leave behind. New friends invited me for a drink after work. However, I would carry on well into the early hours, having only eaten a sushi roll mid-afternoon. The next morning always came around far too quickly bringing with it the unavoidable acceptance that one needs to get up and gets one's arse to work, no matter what condition the body was in.

"Oh, no, I can't do it!" I bitched, dragging myself off the mattress, slinking into the shower long enough to remove yesterday's make-up and a stale odour that managed to encase my skin.

Within minutes I managed to exit the apartment looking fresh and well dressed as usual, hence my optimism would return. Too soon I was packed into a tin can, fighting a primal urge to scream. My heartbeat ticked over at a higher than usual rate, creating more effort to stay calm as we came to a sluggish standstill. Leaning against the cool metal door temporarily eased my desire to claw through the gap. I was trapped; I needed to breathe and not panic at that point. No-one moved or said anything for fear of wasting any air.

Time stood still. The short journey was excruciating every day. Wheels expressed their relief at the same time as doors popped open to allow us throng of commuters spill out onto the packed concourse. Humidity engulfed the carriage, making it even more difficult to breathe, encouraging occupants to burst out quickly like bubbles rising to the surface in search of air. Free to make my way to the exit, frantic to escape the especially potent mix of bad breath, overwhelming perfumes, hair spray and toxic subway fumes violently stinging my nostrils, I struggled to carve out a route for my own feet through the arid space. With my hearing intensely heightened, the clip clopping of shoes was inscrutable, along with an overhead announcement about some train that wasn't about to arrive anytime soon.

By contrast, my purple coat swung elegantly as I stealthily climbed the stairs. Poised, commanding attention whilst managing to contemplate the occasional two steps at a time, I still wasn't used to the pushing and shuffling of city dwellers making their daily pilgrimage. I was feeling a little flat that morning; a legacy of one too many drinks which also contributed to my idling capacity to function. My brain really felt sore. Receptors enhanced by an overwhelming desire to over-ride biology, I wasn't about to let a little hangover get the better of me. Taking in a few deep breaths to accelerate my heartbeat again, I prepared to push through the crowd.

There was no denying my body was a servant, reacting instinctively to a rush of oxygen which, in turn, increased blood flow. Aware of bodies being sucked out through the exits, the hasty lifestyle of working humans curtailed any reason for intimacy here. Suddenly this realisation was too shocking to ignore. These were other beings sharing my space but there were no familiar faces.

Anxiety sat in the pit of my stomach. Stuck there under the city wondering how on Earth I'd coped before, I only knew I couldn't afford to panic. *Oh God, I'm not going to make it.* Looking up to focus on the light taunting me. I held my breath.

My feet tripped onto the grooves of the wooden escalator as I leapt forward to escape. Traffic noise filtered down to greet me, filling my body with a mix of relief and assurance. Another two minutes and I would be alongside Darling Harbour. As I took up the pace there was something more sinister about this particular morning's commute, making me very unsettled as I realised the previous night's melancholy hadn't faded with the dawn.

An aroma wafted through the air, greeting me warmly like a lover. At last, coffee would be my reward for surviving the journey into town. Arriving at my desk on the tenth floor, I barely registered my enviable harbour view. *Was it so enviable?* Sitting there behind thick glass in a tall, monolithic symbol of man's prowess, it occurred to me this was just a piece of concrete and I was only doing a job.

Looking down at the ripples on the water's edge, it was hard to recall ever seeing the little boats there before. Well-crafted and anchored by the Quay, they rocked gently on the tide.

"What's wrong with me?" I whispered.

As that year ended and a new one began, stress really began to take its toll. The city became frightening, heightened by the devastation that took place a few months earlier in New York. I was already feeling fragile thanks to a going no-where, not really a relationship with Greg. Drinking no longer helped. Not since the fatigue set in. Weariness had enormous impact on my capacity to function on all cylinders which, as Senior PR Manager, I needed to do in order to remain switched on. It was increasingly clear by mid-year that I could no longer ignore the signals - my body was crashing under the strain.

Looking up on the card index file, I found Doctor Patterson's phone number and rang to make an appointment that afternoon.

"Could I have HIV?" I asked him nervously, thinking this would certainly explain a lot given the level of exhaustion I'd been experiencing. The Aids campaign of the 80's had really made an impact and I *was* having unprotected sex with my current partner Greg. Who's to say he wasn't cheating just like my ex-husband did. The knot in my shoulders twinged.

Dr Patterson's face was so friendly, his big grey eyes transfixed on me.

"Maybe you need to relax a little. Anxiety isn't good," he said. "Here, let's do some blood tests then, shall we? I doubt that you will have HIV, but we will test for everything. Can you tell me more about your other symptoms?"

He tightened the tourniquet around my upper arm. "Pump your hand for me, please?"

Blood moved into the middle of my elbow as a huge vein revealed itself. I watched as he pushed the needle in, blood quickly filling up the syringe.

"Mainly fatigue," I responded. "And this sinus problem, it's driving me nuts! Everything, the smells are so pungent in the laneways, burning my nostrils so much they bleed!"

Taking out the needle, he pressed a cotton bud onto the dot.

"Your immune system is struggling. You're not getting enough rest, then. Maybe you need a holiday?"

"Yes of course you're right."

I felt stupid. With all the banter about terrorism these days, hadn't we all experienced extra stress? Maybe I was just run down and not able to cope anymore? Added to this, although I daren't say anything, I probably should go home earlier instead of staying out and drinking so much!

Blood test results negated such things as HIV or cancer. So I was going to live. But why did I feel so bad?

It was at a Holistic Health Centre where I first met a naturopath who diagnosed my symptoms as Adrenal Fatigue. Barry did eye scans as he talked to me about the deficiencies that were reflected in my retinas. Certain marks and lines pointed him toward asking questions about my energy levels, and how my kidneys were going. Then to my surprise he began to ask me about my family. My relationships seemed irrelevant but the more he questioned me, the more I flinched when reflecting on all the drama I had experienced as a child.

I explained to him how I could barely walk for an hour without wanting to lie down, so he encouraged me to continue with moderate exercise which would help reignite adrenal function. He also provided a dietary outline to support greater protein intake, recommending I rest throughout the day without settling into the weariness. His manner was reassuring so I continued to see him for a few months, taking on board his recommendation that I delve deeper into the source - but I wasn't quite ready for that.

After another year worse symptoms began to appear. I would wake up with such a dry tongue that drinking more water wouldn't fix. Research pointed me toward a specialist naturopath who informed me that my amino acid level was compromised due to the lack of protein in my diet. My body was no longer absorbing any nutrients, inhibiting saliva production. From that moment on, supplements became mandatory three times a day with food.

Rehabilitation took a great deal of commitment, but I soon noticed an increase in my function and energy. Feeling good again was such a welcomed relief, it was addictive. And as such, I made it my mission to focus on changing my lifestyle completely. Eating more and living within easy access to natural outdoor spaces became a must so that my system could flush out all the toxic waste and pollution that the big city produced. I avoided walking along main roads and stopped using chemical cleaning agents which had become so highly potent, making me violently ill. Even absorbing minor levels were enough to leave a lingering bad taste in my mouth for days.

Adrenal Fatigue was not something well documented on at that time. I researched it, learning that it was triggered by a lifetime of constant stress. I was getting sick so easily with sinus infections. Bouts of hypoglycaemia kept me from socialising anymore. One glass of wine could prompt heart palpitations making me instantly drop to the floor. The inexplicable timing of such reactions scared me, but what was even worse was trying to explain my condition to anyone. The best analogy I eventually came up with was this.

"Imagine your body is a brand new car. You're in the car and the fuel gauge shows that the tank is full, but then after travelling for a short while it begins to feel sluggish. You know the car is finely tuned so there can't be anything wrong. Heading home, suddenly the car begins to stall at the end of your street and yet there's still plenty of fuel in the tank. Will you make it home?"

Where my body was concerned, this was when I panicked. Not having any idea if and when it might crash, when my limbs suddenly became heavy I knew there was a window of about twenty minutes to get home and lay down. Of course this didn't make sense to anyone, so I stopped going out at all.

The only other focus in my life was my sister and nephews.

A return visit to Adelaide at Christmas to check in on my sister and the boys had been a real strain. Trying to stay up with her into the evening and chat was near impossible, I was bottoming out around 8pm. When we went to the park one afternoon my father was amazed at my lack of energy. After an hour playing by the river with the boys I had to lie down and take a nap.

"That's not like you?" he said, looking at me slightly perplexed.

I knew that, but how could I explain? How could I suggest that it was serious when I didn't have any proof? It was imperative for me to listen to my body and improve my long term health, so much to the amazement of friends and colleagues I chose to leave my career for a long term sabbatical trek around Europe.

Walking around some of the most stunning places along the Mediterranean coastline inspired me to live differently. I no longer saw the purpose in pitching the power of life saving drugs when there was more value in preventing illness in the first place by being stress free - a revelation that had me contemplate my next career path.

Months later when I returned to Sydney, I began freelancing in PR whilst landing an opportunity to work as a health coach, mentoring others toward achieving better health at a leading women's city gym. This was a move that didn't work out exactly as I had planned. Women from local offices would rush past in a hurry to secure a spot in the lunchtime pump class. It was madness, and far more stressful than I had imagined, having been shoved into sales during staff shortfalls, such was the revolving door due to low pay. I needed more money. My sister, newly divorced, had relocated to Queensland once again to begin a new life for her and the boys.

Not having the financial freedom to help out made me feel anxious. I had to get back on my feet fast but needed to avoid the stress of full time PR. What was I going to do?

Sitting in a tiny bistro in the heart of Sydney's CBD, I was on my lunchbreak quietly observing my fellow workers scurrying to their eatery of choice. Sometimes I wondered what it would be like to have simple needs. I seemed to crave so much more stimulation, working at the gym barely getting me through, but at least I got to chat to the members and my bills would be paid. How could I earn more and avoid the stress of working long hours? I thought about expanding my freelancing contracts, possibly write another magazine feature. With this in mind, I continued to flick through the newspaper someone had left behind.

"Ladies, do you want to make more money than you've ever seen and be pampered in the process?"

A nice, demure caricature of a woman's face seemed a little over-the-top. It certainly didn't scream anything wrong or naughty. She simply looked nice, like me. I sat there wondering for a moment if I was? What's nice anyway?

"If you know you deserve the very best, then why wait? Don't hesitate. Please call for a discreet discussion about our unique service."

Interesting, I thought. Ideas formed in my mind as I contemplated what it would be like to be free to have gratuitous sex and be paid for it. Feeling somewhat more invigorated by this idea, I continued to read the paper. Flicking the pages, I ended back onto *that* page – the one with a column waving some cheeky little title at me.

"Ad-ult Seeervices."

My mind began racing. It fascinated me to think that there was little support or awareness of the need for sexual freedom for women; a topic that was conveniently avoided even amongst my friends. To be sexual was to be called a slut, or worse – a whore. I cringed, continuing to stare at the ads, shocked to see ones listed under 'Women Meeting Men', with many offering their company with no strings attached. I sure as hell knew I wouldn't be giving it away again.

Clearly I was jaded about romance. Wouldn't there be more reverence and emotional safety in being desired and hired as opposed to screwing around with unrealistic dreams of 'happy ever after' ever again?

This scenario sounded a whole lot more like my idea of the perfect relationship. No crap, no expectation and definitely no more late night booty calls along with many cancelled dinner dates. Men had always disappointed me, so why shouldn't I be independent and enjoy sex without the emotional baggage?

I began scrawling sums on the paper, calculating the potential earnings. I mean really, what *would* a girl get for an hour; surely around a thousand dollars or more?

For the first time in a while I had butterflies in my belly. Signs of life at last, remembering this feeling and welcoming it as visions of grandeur placed me in spectacular James Bond style situations; flying high with successful businessmen paying to spend the day with me. My imagination was the only thing keeping me sane.

There was also something else I found rather exciting, written in smaller print in the next paragraph.

Escorts also needed.

"What did that mean?"

Sitting back, a smile stretched across my face as I envisioned sleek, well dressed women in stilettos. I remembered as a child admiring ladies who worked at David Jones, wearing streamlined stockings always with a seam so neat and so perfect, a vision of impeccable and cool demeanour. I imagined this kind of woman must surely be contrite and masterful at… well, I didn't really know so there was only one way to find out!

I nervously dialled the number and waited. Listening to my heart beating in my ear drum, I waited some more. About to give up, someone answered.

"Hello, Scarlett's House. How may I help you?"

"Um, yes!" I responded, jumping out of my chair.

The woman's voice was friendly, strong and surprisingly direct. Suddenly a little nervous, my hands began to sweat.

"Hello?"

A wave of fear tore through my body, proposing a threat to my already delicate ego. I got cold feet and yet my voice was responding on its own accord.

"I, ah yes, sorry! My name is, um. Sorry."

Feeling stupid, sick and at the same time aware of this constant thud, thud thudding in my chest, my head begun to swim and I nearly hung up for fear of collapsing. The last thing I wanted was for someone to find me passed out, holding my phone with this number dialled on it.

"That's ok dear. Take your time."

"I might call back," I said.

"Are you considering this work for the first time?"

A mature woman for sure, she spoke articulately with a slightly raised tone, probing for me to respond. Picturing a madam with big buxom boobs and large, outrageous hair I couldn't help but think how crazy this all was - and loved every minute of it.

"Ah, yes actually."

There was silence as she waited for me to say more, but I didn't.

"Yes, I'm sure we can, dear. Do you know about our business?"

"Yes. I think so. I liked your ad."

That was another pathetic thing to say. Why did my mouth always have to work faster than my brain?

"Excellent. How old are you, dear?"

I had expected this question. Who was I trying to kid? I was far from being model material, and at thirty eight was way too old anyway.

"Twenty seven," I answered. People were always commenting that I looked so much younger for my age.

"Ok then. Yes, yes we have the most wonderful and adoring gentlemen who would so look forward to meeting you! Can you come in and…"

This was all happening too fast. "Oh, aah… I'm not sure if I am really suited. I'm… ah – I'll call you back."

"Oh yes, please do call back then, darling. Let me tell you, you would not regret this opportunity. My girls make an excellent living. This is a most wonderful, wonderful life - for the right girls, of course. Sorry what was your name again?"

Frozen, juggling the perilous idea of giving my name versus the will to simply hang up, the cafe walls were closing in; a passer-by seemed to be staring at me. Was he that perving smart arse I temporarily worked with a few months earlier?

"When you're ready then, just give us a call back my dear. Bye for now."

The woman hung up. Somewhat relieved I put the phone down and sank back into the booth, trying to come to terms with how stupid I felt. My mind had gone completely blank. Had I given her my name? Did I get hers? Oh for God's sake, what *was* my problem?

Returning to the gym I tried to eject the whole episode from my mind, reminding myself it was just another one of those moments of curiosity. As I strolled into the gym foyer, I noticed my client, a young girl with low self-esteem, sitting unattended. Asking my manager who was in her office chatting with her friend, if anyone had spoken to the girl - she retaliated.

"Do you mind? I'm busy, don't be so rude!"

I was stunned. Aware that the personal trainers were scattering in all directions, I tried to contain the situation without any further embarrassment. It was awkward but I was in the firing line and not happy at all about her approach.

"Sorry? I'm just aware that she…"

My manager stood up, coming out toward me. "If you have a problem with how I run things, maybe you should leave!"

This made things perfectly clear about where I shouldn't be.

After my hasty departure, I sat in much nicer Italian bistro further down the road and dialled the number again.

"Hello, Scarlett's House. How can I help you?"

"Oh, yes hello. I phoned you earlier?"

This time I breathed slowly, my voice steady and focussed on asking questions.

"Oh, yes! It's so nice to hear from you, dear. Glad you called back! So, you've given it some thought and now let's meet, shall we?"

Within minutes this Madame had me booked in for a meeting the following Monday.

By the time Monday morning arrived, I was more than ready to find out what went on behind the doors of Scarlett's and, if anything, finally put this whole idea to rest so I could get on with my life. Dressing in my best black Donna Karan trousers matched with a close fitting baby pink cotton blouse intentionally buttoned to the base of my push up bra, I chose to wear a long strand of pearls in the hope that the smart seductress look was a winner.

Overall my average height and personality was never anywhere near what one would term 'seductive', so this outfit was the best I could come up with. Anyway, how did a girl dress when going to such an interview? I'd also dyed my hair a warm blonde, part of my complete make-over from an otherwise contained appearance; rich auburn waist-length locks usually pulled back in a tight ponytail. This new look made me feel so much sexier. I had also noticed on the website that there was only one other blonde; a Swedish girl with D cup breasts of all things, therefore I needed to avert attention given my bosom wasn't so full.

Arriving at a very old terrace in Milsons Point around 9.30am, with my shaking finger pressing the buzzer, I was aware of a shadow behind the glass which soon greeted me as the door opened.

"Um, hello?" A short, mature woman prompted cautiously.

Standing there before me with blonde hair cut in what could only be described as a 1920's bob, her trousers were smartly tailored and a cream tweed jumper didn't hide the fact she was also blessed with ample bosom. After an awkward silence I was about to introduce myself when the penny must've dropped.

"Oh yes! Hello, hello dear! Please come in! This way," the woman prattled excitedly, showing me through the door as it swung open. Allowing me to step inside, I caught a glimpse of the long hallway leading to a stairwell, the wooden floors covered in bright rustic Persian rugs. I followed a waving hand toward the first door on the left, watching as she proceeded to walk around the old oak desk where she sat in a gaudy leather maple arched armchair.

"At last! Come here, a little closer and take a seat."

In the lesser appealing wooden chair opposite, I sat down, all the while trying hard to fathom this eccentric woman. There was no mistaking her gaze at my blouse as she continued to scour my body from head to toe.

"Hmm, well my dear, you have a great body. Simply lovely. Lovely! My men are going to adore you!"

Mesmerized by the animated behaviour of this woman, who seemed more enthralled with herself than anything I had to say, I marvelled at the surreal picture this made, theatrics working well to intrigue me even further.

"Um," I paused, thinking she would introduce herself.

She didn't. Her little pale blue eyes still staring out at me from her round face were waiting for me to continue.

"So, what's involved then?" I asked more confidently, catching a flash of a female naked body as it ducked through the side door; a rather alluring vision to say the very least.

My senses were also heightened by a tantalisingly flavoured aroma, the fresh hint of Lavender mist hanging in the air. L'Occitane bottles were lined up on the mantel behind reception, leaving no doubt effort had been made to ensure this place resonated luxury and sensuality.

"Oh yes, yes of course, Jewel! I'm going to call you 'Jewel' from now on. You look like something special; shiny and new like a sparkling diamond," she cooed.

I raised my eyes a little. "Oh! I was thinking something like Bella or..."

"No, no dear. We have Bella's, Ella's and Stella's aaaall the time." She threw back her hands and chuckled like a schoolgirl. "We need you to be unique; something different, yes?"

"Ok, sounds good, why not?" I responded, not wanting to sound too naive.

"Oh and I'm Daphne, okay, just let me get this paperwork out and we can talk through the..." she prattled on, a little distracted, still eyeing me constantly. "Ok, here it is! Let's say that we arrange for you to meet a gentleman." Daphne stood up and pointed. "You sit in that lounge over there, and if it's a comfortable meeting then of course you can wander up and choose a room to your liking."

She pointed to the large chaise lounge over in the adjoining room. The decadence didn't escape me.

"Oh, yes. We do have marvellous antiques and works of art here. Many of our clients over the years have happily donated a treasure or two as a gift to their favourite girl. Often the gift ends up staying, but of course the girls tend to run away eventually with the man of her dreams! Not good for business, but what can you do?" she admonished.

"Ah, excuse me Daphne, can you tell me more about the procedure then? What about cleanliness, what should I expect training wise? And also the money would be good, too."

Awkwardly my eyes opened wide with part fear and part innocence, knowing my words hadn't come out right, but at least Daphne, smiling politely at me, had understood exactly what I was getting at.

"Yes of course, dear! You will be in demand and become very wealthy in a very short time. No don't you be concerned at all, dear."

My head tilted, unsure if I got all the answers, still expecting to go through some formal procedure when Daphne quickly hopped up, mainly to escape the buzzing of the phones which seemed to frazzle her, and secondly to skip me along on a tour. Dutifully I followed through the doorway, wondering what exactly I would have to do 'in the room', and how do I 'do it'. I wasn't a virgin, but this was a profession right? So, there must be some kind of professional workshopping, right?

Further along the corridor and up the stairwell past many images of nubile nymphs and reposing women, it was clearly a very intimate place. Ornate and prestigious with luxurious bedrooms filled with more antiques and original Norman Lindsay paintings.

"Yes, we have six rooms, Jewel. Come through here we have three upstairs and three downstairs and here's the bathroom which everyone uses." Daphne pointed as I leaned over her to see. "But of course the girls go downstairs," she muttered before turning back down the hall. "And here's our Emperor's Room which has a nice view of the harbour."

Looking at the wooden four poster king sized bed I imagined the passionate activity this room must've witnessed over the years.

"You would be right at home here," she smiled, ushering me back downstairs to the office where the phones were going mad.

"Ok, what do you think? You can come in just once and discover for yourself what a wonderful world of pleasure it is! Be totally spoilt and treated like the Goddess you are! Hmmm, yes let me see." Her eyes scanned the open book on her desk. "Ok, we have an opening on the roster for next Monday and I know for sure that we can have you booked for the day."

Her directness once again caught me off guard.

"I can't make it Monday," I said, working out in my head what my excuse could be. "I have commitments."

"Oh no, dear, trust me. Start on Monday and you will wonder why you ever waited so long." She smiled, patting my hand ever so gently. "From one business girl to another, you deserve to do this for yourself."

My heart was racing again. I would do it. Just for a little while until I got back on my feet and worked out which direction my career was going. I liked the idea of having the freedom to explore my sexuality in a nice, secret exotic place where no-one would judge me, nor wish to form a relationship.

"Yes, ok then. I will see you on Monday," I responded.

"Ok, Jewel, it's a ten am start so be here by nine!" Daphne came alongside me, staring at me up and down in the way that she did, as we began to walk toward the side door. "And you look absolutely divine, so please, do dress like this again."

Before I could answer, she had ushered me out the back door. Standing there in the narrow laneway I wondered if this event had ever taken place. I was numb and intoxicated by the whole thing, reminding myself again no harm was done. Besides, Monday was another seven days away and it was too crazy an idea to even contemplate any further, so I wouldn't.

Seriously, I had seen more than enough to know this wasn't the place for me.

Chapter 2

My First Time

I entered the meeting room to greet my first client.

"Hi Michael, I'm Jewel."

It was surreal. I watched as Jewel extended her hand, just like I used to only a few years earlier when meeting corporate clients. My eyes slowly took in Michael's face; he was old and it took nerves of steel not to flinch with distaste. A soft-looking patch of white hair covered most of his head, and his pale blue eyes were framed by drab reading glasses. He leaned back on the Chesterfield sofa, his long gangly legs extended to full stretch.

"Daphne you always know what I like," he said, turning to glance at her. "She's lovely, and you're right about those lips." He smirked as he looked at me again.

Trying not to quiver with revulsion, I stood firm and put on a fake pout, almost a tease, knowing there was no way he'd be kissing me!

"Very sensual and tempting!" Michael said. "What a lady!"

My belly felt a rumble of resistance, but I knew also that I could change my mind about seeing him at any time. I wasn't afraid of anyone here, and felt completely within my rights to leave. Raising an eyebrow teasingly I leaned forward to touch his arm. His eyes followed my every move. I knew it was imperative not to flinch as my fingertips caressed the bumps of his aging, sun-damaged skin.

"Michael, you're a cheeky one, aren't you?" I said. "Come on, let's go upstairs."

As he stood up, he winked at Daphne, making me squirm as I reminded myself that I only had to do this once and then leave. In fact I didn't have to do it at all – I was in control.

Michael chatted away, oblivious to my feelings as we went up the stairs. "I've been looking forward to meeting you. The girls are all so lovely. I look forward to my time here every Monday."

I was barely listening, not wanting to know anything about him.

"Come in," I said nervously, when we got to the room. I handed him a plush white towel and he began to unbutton his blue chequered cotton shirt. When he was naked, he wrapped the towel around his waist.

"I'll be right back," he said.

I just stared blankly at him.

"Just relax Jewel, I promise you we can just talk if you like."

He left the room to go take a shower, leaving me there a little startled by his comment. Sitting down on the bed, grateful for the extremely high ceilings that gave me ample space to breathe, I became little more relaxed. Next, folding the heavily braided burgundy bedspread I placed it on one of the winged green velour chairs. I'd just sat back down on the bed when Michael returned.

"Can I take off your blouse?" he asked.

I stared at him, trying not to look horrified.

"It's just that you look a little too prim sitting there and I don't want to get your clothes messed up," he said softly.

Of course it made perfect sense to get undressed. He'd paid for me to do so. For a moment it seemed funny, until he sat down next to me. I sat upright, determined to co-operate but struggling with where to start.

"Sorry, it's my first day," I said. "I don't really know what I should be doing exactly."

He leaned back onto the fluffy satin paisley pillows and tried to put me at ease by chatting as I took off my clothes.

"You know, it's hard getting old," he said. "I look at your youth and beauty and feel so grateful to be here. Oh, you are a sight to behold, young lady, extremely fit too! The only exercise I get these days is walking with Kate. Every morning we go for an hour or so…"

"Kate?" I asked, feeling a little uncomfortable. Was he talking about his wife? Poor woman, I thought.

He gestured for me to lie next to him. "Come, let me look at you," he said, smiling as I moved closer. "We can talk more easily then. Yes, Kate, she's my dog!"

I relaxed a little, moving tentatively into the middle of the giant bed, determined not to touch him. I caught a whiff of his foul breath and it threw my body into turmoil.

"You are such a beautiful woman, Jewel. Thanks so much for seeing me."

His compassion stirred something in me, a kind of sympathy. But who was it I felt sorry for - him or me?

Lying back on the plush cushions, I stared at the ceiling, focusing on the intricacy of the plaster circles around the chandelier. My head spun as I wondered yet again how I'd managed to get here.

"Hey, are you okay? I hope I'm not talking too much – I'm a little nervous." Perched on his crinkly elbow, Michael was staring at me with a look of concern.

"I'm fine. It's just that I'm a little nervous too… I'm not sure what I'm doing here, to be honest."

Part of me felt that if I told him the truth he may not try to pursue sex, but I didn't want to put him off. I still wanted the money.

"Yes, well Jewel, sometimes I ask myself the same question." His eyes met mine, showing no pretence. "You're probably wondering why I'm here? Well let me just say that I adore my wife and so I would never ever hurt her by having an affair. But you see, for most of our married life she was never interested in sex, especially after our fourth son was born. That was thirty five years ago! And so, seeing a lovely lady like you allows me the opportunity to indulge."

He showed no guilt at all, which for some reason made me feel better. I was grateful and surprised he felt so comfortable to share his personal history.

"So tell me, Michael, what's it like being the father of four boys?"

It was the right thing to say; a look of pride appearing on his face. I listened while he talked, believing things were going well until he turned the tables on me.

"Jewel what about you? I bet you have a lovely, adoring boyfriend."

I froze. Jewel – that wasn't my name. Again, I tried to tell myself that I wasn't really here. Michael lightly tapped me on the arm, bringing me back to the moment. "Hey, look at that – the drapes!" He pointed and my gaze followed. "They're allowing the most intense ray of light to shine through. Look how it's bouncing off the marble over there."

I looked over at the marble mantelpiece that took up most of the far wall. Sunlight was slipping through a gap in the red crimson drapes and spearing the white marble, creating a mist of colour that exploded into tiny star-like fragments.

"What magic, hey?" Michael said, turning to watch me. "Reminds me of so many wonderful things, like when I was a boy. And let me tell you," he continued jovially, "That's a long while ago! They look like bright stars. What do you make of it, Jewel?"

He touched my arm, startling me. The string of pearls that I was rolling between my fingers broke; scattering, bouncing everywhere.

"Oh no!" I cried. I knew it wouldn't take much for me to break at this point too. It was part to do with letting go of that delicate dream. I only really wanted to be with one man, in love forever. But why kid myself anymore?

Michael leaned over in an attempt to catch some of the pearls, but I held his arm to stop him.

"Don't worry, they weren't real," I said.

"You looked so distant. There's a lot going through that mind of yours, isn't there?"

I didn't respond. Inside, I was struggling to adjust to being this new person – Jewel.

"I thought I'd lost you for a moment," he went on. "But I loved watching you. Like a child, you were. What could you see?"

Feeling exposed, I quickly made my expression neutral.

"Well, the light was so beautiful on the marble." I hesitated. "It reminded me of a dream I used to have."

"Go on," he said, encouraging me with warm eyes.

"See there? It looks a little like a unicorn, don't you think?" I pointed to the spectrum still bouncing along the white marble.

"You know what, I think you're right. Isn't that a lovely sign?" He smiled tenderly and leaned back, getting comfortable. "Do you know the story about the unicorn?"

"Well, I know that they don't exist. It's a myth," I responded, surrendering to his game.

"Ok, yes, it's a myth, but an enchanting one. I'll tell you, if you like?"

I figured it best to play along. Besides, listening to his story would be a good way to pass the time.

"I'm ready," I said, settling back onto the pillows.

"Did you know that the unicorn's horn was deemed to have magical powers –um, an aphrodisiac, if you like?"

"Really?" I said, wondering what kind of crap he was going to come out with next.

"Yes, really," he responded with a hint of playfulness. "Apparently the horn also had healing qualities, especially if one drank from it. The most wonderful and magical thing about unicorns, though, was that they were able to determine whether or not a woman was a virgin!"

He raised an eyebrow to acknowledge this scandalous idea, but I didn't react.

"And the most interesting thing of all was that only a virgin could mount a unicorn; no-one else could get close to one. Apparently that's why it's impossible to find one these days."

Michael's grin stretched into laughter as he observed my expression.

"Oh, I get what you mean," I said. "Very funny! Maybe I *am* a virgin as of today!"

I laughed with him, but then to my surprise he ran his hands over my belly. I gasped, wanting to tell him to get his hands off me, but then he stunned me again by gently rolling me onto my back and moving down between my thighs, slowly kissing parts that hadn't been touched for a very long time.

"I love that you have such thick pubic hair, it's so beautiful," he whispered, before disappearing again.

At first I felt tense as his tongue probed at me, then shocked that I liked it. He continued to lick slowly.

"Tell me if it's okay?" he said. "I want you to feel good, Jewel. That will make me feel good."

I couldn't remember any man ever asking me how I felt before.

"Mike, you don't have to please me," I whispered, hoping he would ignore me and continue what he was doing.

"I want to see your body quiver with pleasure," he said. "You are such a beautiful girl – you deserve this, my dear."

A few moans were all the encouragement he needed to continue licking my swelling clitoris.

"Oh my God!" New, warm sensations filtered throughout my body. My head was swimming. Why hadn't I ever felt like this before? Was it because I'd always been under the influence of alcohol with men in my past?

"Here, let me do something for you!" I said, trying to lift my body up.

Michael began fondling me with his fingers, causing my hips to arc up and my legs to open further.

"Enjoy, my darling," he said soothingly.

Warmth ignited my skin, sending shock waves down to my clitoris as liquid formed like beads along its peak. He plunged another one of his little fingers delicately, which prompted louder moaning from me. "Oh yes!"

There was no turning back now – his continual stroking had certainly reached the spot. A wave of orgasmic vibrations engulfed me; my body soared without any further consultation with my brain. I grabbed his arm in case he stopped. I was so close to something big, I could feel it.

"Oh no. Oh my God, yes. Don't stop," I shouted, and meant every word.

My eyes were closed and there were no longer any thoughts running through my mind; just an overwhelming desire to ride this orgasm out, aware that I needed to check where his penis was. It was an effort to reach for it and roll on the condom already in my hand, just as he lurched on top of me. With a quick thrust of his hips, his body jerked and he moaned, "Oh, ohhhhh!" again and again.

My orgasm dissipated. I focused on making sure his body didn't touch mine as he shuddered for moments afterward, finally rolling onto his back as we lay side by side, saying nothing. I couldn't help but feel disgusted at myself. How could I have possibly enjoyed it? Slowly I edged away from him.

"I'm sorry it was so quick," he said, sounding a little self-conscious.

"There's nothing to be sorry for," I answered reassuringly. "Are you ready to have a shower?"

"Jewel," he whispered.

Now I understood why we had alternative names as I chose not to respond, turning around to offer him a towel. Reluctantly he rolled off the bed.

"I'll see you when you get back," I told him, as he peeked into the hallway to check it was clear.

While he was gone, I stripped the bed and replaced the coverlet, my head still buzzing– blocking the memory, pleased it was quick and counting the easy cash. When he returned, I watched patiently as he slowly did up his shirt and at last we were ready to leave. We took the stairs down to the back door where I'd come in only hours ago. Ushering him out with a polite kiss on the cheek, he held my arm and looked into my eyes.

"Thank you so much again, Michael. It was a pleasure," I whispered into his ear before closing the door.

He was forgotten as soon as I entered the lounge area again. The other girls looked up at me cautiously.

"Hey, how's it going, girl? All okay?" Ashley asked.

Looking at the board, I saw a row of names filling my column and felt the adrenaline kick in.

"Absolutely fine," I responded. "Okay, who's next?"

Embracing the euphoric rush I felt, it occurred to me how easy it was to indulge in my body's craving for pleasure whilst harbouring a fantasy in my head. I had always wanted to be an actress; it was only sex and I was pleased with my stellar performance, keen to prepare for more. I felt there was no limit to what could be explored with the aid of willing parties, and it hadn't escaped my ego that I was also getting paid so well!

I soon learned what Daphne didn't tell me at my interview or on the first day. Firstly, my experience with Mike was as good as it was going to get for a while and secondly, being the new girl on the books was an invitation to all the perverts who were keen to check me out. Resentment of men fuelled my desire to have one upmanship at all times, hence whenever an idiot thought he could whip me onto my back or head fuck me with words I would surprise them with strength to hold my own. These few weren't going to topple my newly made plans to earn a fortune within a limited amount of time.

I had decided to ride it out for at least three months, having just signed up at college to undertake two diplomas at once; one in coaching and one in counselling. If I could make enough money to pay for these, I would be clear of any debt, making it easier to slide into temp work to pay for everyday expenses. Then set up my own clinical practice immediately after graduating. Just like the girls here, I discovered that this lifestyle made it so much easier for study. Soon we're comparing notes and offering support. We all had our reasons for being there and as such there was no judgement, only a few obvious discrepancies. For example, when I conducted my initial research by checking out the website for this place, Ashley was listed as a Meg Ryan lookalike. I couldn't see the resemblance. With a mane of tangled blonde hair and thick thighs squeezed tightly under a very short denim skirt, she was quite rough looking compared to most of us. Ashley had moved into night shift in order to rack up the deposit for a house she was buying out West with her truckie husband. He was supportive of her being here to make their dream happen.

I struggled with the concept of a man being happy to allow his wife to do this work, but realised it was simply banging up against all of my beliefs that had been moulded since I was young. What were those beliefs, I wondered? And where had they stemmed from?

Raven haired Kelly was another friendly Aussie with a rich, deep tan that matched her spirit. She loved the flexibility that working here afforded her, having just come back from a Vipassana retreat in the Blue Mountains after a taste of meditation in India six months earlier. A tantric teacher, she was quite experienced in many areas that I had yet to explore. For example, she was quick to enlighten me about the basic procedures in the bedroom after we were booked for a lesbian double, witnessing my lack of expertise. I had never put a condom on a man before working here. Nor was I going to be giving oral, which was what I observed her doing on our client - much to my horror.

One very busy lady that I never really got to chat to because she was squeezing in study during her breaks, was Amber. It was hard to pick her age, and as most of us were in the practice of not divulging too much, I gathered that she was in her mid-thirties given that she was a practicing doctor before marrying an Australian and settling here. But when they divorced, she couldn't practice with her overseas credentials, therefore had to begin studying all over again.

Not all of the women were academic or married with short term goals, of course. There was Lilly, whom I briefly met during a whirlwind break when she raced down to scoff a sandwich between clients. I had watched her enthusiastically as she ate in a way that I found extremely sensual. Added to this, her voluptuous womanly body and sandy hair that swayed just above her shoulders was captivating, but the most astounding part was her personality and energy. No wonder the men were lining up to be with her. Lilly was crossed off the board as fully booked.

Wearing no make-up and only a t-shirt pulled over her c cup breasts, Lilly's clients apparently adore the motherly type and she adored the money which, for a single mother with five kids, came as no surprise. She only worked three days and was buying a house, proving that this work was certainly paying dividends not to mention saving the welfare system; something the government would probably never know or appreciate!

These girls soon answered many of my sex work questions once they realised I was a stayer. They shared with me that there was no point in bonding with new girls in the first week because many just don't have what it takes. It's not actually that glamorous and it's not about being loved if one is needy for praise or attention, which I wasn't, making it easier to ask more questions about how the place runs.

They informed me that day shift is 10am to 5pm; night shift 5pm to midnight. Health checks were required monthly with a certificate required or we weren't allowed to work. As for the tools of the trade, all condoms and lube was supplied. Once we were in the room, all men are asked to show their penis if we request it, awkwardly holding their limp manhood under a lamp for investigation of any lumps or bumps. A colleague can be called upon to double check any questionable bits and if he refuses he may be asked to leave.

It took a while to get used to the general shuffle of a working girls' day, but it basically began like this. When a client arrives, he gives the money to the receptionist or duty manager (Sherri or Daphne) who then takes him into the meeting room next door. Then we would be called upon to grace his presence, one by one, so that he could then make a choice.

Once this happened and one of us were given the nod back in the girls room (where we waited eagerly, tallying up the day's takings if we were to be successful) we would then take him into an allocated room, give him a towel and direct him back down to the shower whilst we went back and got our little bag containing condoms and lube. I was dead curious as to why these men, who were more often extremely wealthy, self-made entrepreneurs or corporate CEO's, chose to spend so much time and money on us? The girls informed me that these were often highly stressed men looking for an escape from responsibility to enjoy a little fun. I still didn't have the answer I wanted. Why couldn't they do this with their wife? I would love to be spoiled like this if my husband were so inclined.

At the end of shift, the receptionist/duty manager handed over an envelope containing half of the earnings which for a day in 2003 was approximately $500. Not bad when the average hours were between 10am-4.30pm - remembering this was a split share.

Key Services included in the fee usually consisted of the following:

1. Sex with a condom in any position that is possible - within reason
2. Oral with a condom
3. Massage

Extras were usually charged at a premium and could include;

1. Fantasies (i.e. dressing up in a nurse's uniform)
2. Kissing

3. Doubles (we're not talking tennis)
4. Lesbian Double (two girls getting it on in front of the client; authenticity soon becoming highly demanded e.g. the girls didn't use a piece of rubber – dental dam – protection to cover one another's vagina. The more real the experience, the more a client got off.)
5. Golden Shower (a girl peeing on a client)
6. Other

Given my naïve understanding of this work, thinking that it was as simple as just having sex with a condom on, I soon have to establish boundaries when any of the above activities were asked of me. It wasn't expected, and Sherri was quite happy to know what she could and couldn't pitch to a caller. Unfortunately no-one talked to me about oral being mandatory and as such I didn't do it. Management also knew I didn't want to kiss, so if a caller asked specifically, I wasn't offered up which meant soon my clients began to taper off. Good thing I had a healthy enthusiasm for sex, passionately tapping into a resource which was my sexual energy, exploring my own sensual depths and experimenting whenever a client allowed – which was often!

Having feelings, or should I say emotions, were not part of the equation at all, which was why I fitted in so well. Simply put, this work was purely a physical and mental transaction, with the following attributes catapulting me toward success. Emotional Intelligence (life experience), good self-esteem because I was able to *act* like a Goddess (although in the real world I had felt insecure) and a wicked sense of humour (vital when a client was the moody type) all worked well. I was also highly sexed which I soon understood had always been part of me. This had become repressed due to lack of passion felt for my first lovers, plus lack of awareness about my own sexual needs.

There were some unusual idiosyncrasies I'd never have known about had I not entered this place. I'd found it rather amusing to hear about the fantasies men have, although being an upmarket North Shore establishment there were very few variations. Generally the criteria included;

1. Lingerie and suspenders
2. Multiple orgasms for you
3. Lasting erection for him
4. Two women
5. Talking dirty
6. A discount
7. I tell him he has the biggest I've ever seen (and I would know) *
8. Spanking him (rare – I discover there are places for Fetish and these are cheap bastards trying to get an extra)
9. It was good for you too (I've heard this often, whether professional or not)

*The 'how big is my penis' question correlated with the 'how big is my bum' question for women. Kelly constantly reminded me to have a mantra ready from this selection so that I got repeat bookings; it's normal / it works for me / It's huge / I love it!

It goes without saying, given the lucrative nature of such work, the girls finally share that there's no fine print when applying for a position as profoundly seductive as this. The bottom line was that if I worked hard I could earn well, which translated as 'the more sex you have, the more money you make'. This was a similar mantra for the duty managers; the more bookings they got, the bigger their commission. Whilst Sherri was efficient, she always put us first, making sure to match personality with client, unlike a new girl Jana who was more motivated by getting us all bookings regardless of the scenario.

With only six of us there, I quickly embraced the prestige, accepting my body as a tool to be utilised for the pleasure of others and very rarely mine. I realised there was a great deal of personal sacrifice involved and in order to stay disciplined my lifestyle changed completely, but it was changing quickly for the sake of my health anyway. I watched what I ate more carefully and worked out regularly like an Olympic athlete. Overall the rewards were worth it, and I began to have fun – especially given that some of the clients were such weird and wonderfully entertaining men!

There was very little warning of these types except for the tell-tale behaviour of my colleagues when they saw a name scrawled on my list. Someone would smirk, or look away seemingly relieved not to have been marked with the booking, which taught me to be on high alert. A few weeks after my arrival I met Ken, an odd looking Japanese guy with his face polished white with tattooed eyebrows, like a doll. He came in asking to see someone who could be a little bit more broadminded. Being the ambitious type, I stepped up to the plate believing that I was as broadminded as anyone could be. To say I was wrong is an understatement, much to my humility.

"Can you do this for me?" Ken asked, carefully scanning my face.

I watched as he began wrapping up his penis tightly with nylon thread.

"Yeah sure," I said, with no expression before taking the thread from his fingers.

Slowly I began wrapping the thread around his balls.

"Can you do it tighter, if that's okay?"

I hesitated, noticing a strange sensation stirring in my body, a tingly lightness.

"Hey, um, I don't know if this is working too well," I explained, noticing the blood gorging into the tip of his penis.

"Here," he said, taking the thread and pulling tight, making his balls swell. His face contorted as they looked like they were about to explode.

"This is good, Jewel," he said, to appease me. "You okay?"

"Yep." I answered, remembering I was paid to lie.

Squatting over him in my gorgeous new red lace underwear that clashed with his crimson tip, it was hard to comprehend what was going on this young man's mind. How on Earth could he find this sexy?

"Ok good, just pull tighter. Here, here tighter okay?" He pointed to the base of his balls where I took hold of the cord, fumbling for control.

Needless to say I fainted, and by the time I regained composure Kelly and Sherri were leaning over me. Ken was sitting on the edge of the bed looking rather embarrassed and yet concerned. The girls downstairs all got a good laugh and would remind me of the incident for months to come.

"These are called fetishes, love," Kelly informed me. "They should go to a fetish house but if they can't get in, they come here."

It took a little while longer before I realised they got a better deal, given that fetish was charged at a much higher rate!

Surprisingly some of the kinky behaviour seemed rather tame for us to be paid so highly at all. For example there was Roger, an overweight Englishman with an underwear fetish. Each time he returned to the UK, he would purchase a new pair of big bum women's undies from Harrods then come in here requesting I watch as he put them on then wanked. Dressed in a short skirt I played with myself too. It might sound like an easy session but sometimes it's hard to stare at a grown man wearing a huge pair of women's knickers and trying not to laugh as he mumbles "I'm such a naughty boy!"

I also met Hank who liked to be placed over my knee and spanked.

"Don't hit me, please don't hit me!" He screamed, as I beat him hard. It was great therapy, giving me opportunity to release remnants of stress from my past life, but I couldn't do it again. I hated violence.

To know that these men were wandering around with no-one ever having the slightest idea about their quirks, made me question the world further. They were masked behind such prestigious positions of patriarchal power, often savvy in appearance which is why I was shocked when I met Dr Humphries. Struck at first by the height of this lanky old man standing there with a briefcase, his thick, long white hair falling across his forehead it was his piercing baby blue eyes that made me feel uneasy.

When we were naked in the room, Dr Humphries looked so sullen and vulnerable. But he wasn't. I noticed he had something dangling from his right hand.

"Jewel, if you don't mind, when I fuck you can you bite my nipples and then put this clasp on them?"

Blinking back the disbelief, firstly at the crude language I had not expected from this dapper looking man, it was hard for me to not look at him cynically. Seriously, I thought. Bite his nipples; was he kidding me?

"Is that ok?" He asked me again, holding out this strange metal contraption.

No it wasn't a joke, which explained Daphne's avoidance tactics when I asked more about him earlier.

"Yep, sure," I lied.

I knew he wanted a regular girl, so it was imperative to disappoint. Taking his nipple in my mouth I bit, but couldn't do it. So, as disgusting as it had at first sounded, I used those metallic pincer things. My arms ached from holding him up off my chest until he was finished and flat out next to me on his back. It was a while before I realised he hadn't made a sound. Turning sideways, it was clear he wasn't moving. There was no response, not even signs of breathing which had me paralysed with fear. Putting my hand up to his nostrils, I felt nothing. My heart raced as next steps were being rehearsed in my head. I'd sneak down to reception and say he's having a shower and I needed to move my car, but of course I'd keep on driving, collecting a few things in my suitcase along the way.

"Ah Jewel, you're amazing!"

I jumped up in shock, more disappointed he liked me but glad he was alive.

I was enjoying my time at Scarlett's.

Already I was learning from the many men who paid to entertain me in between the occasional reciprocal provision of sex. That was the reason I was there, of course. But it wasn't a requirement to always have sex, and hard for management to uphold this. Within weeks I became successful, attracting like-minded types who indulged their ego by bolstering mine, which of course worked well for the agency as my bookings had increased.

Sex wasn't always on my client's mind, yet money was always on mine.

However I gained so much more than money thanks to the calibre of gentlemen who frequented this high end place. One in particular was Mr Gem, a delightful gentleman with whom I could relax with a little. An austere and rather forthcoming man in his eighties, he gauged my craving for meaningful conversations, filling a deeper void.

I never forget the first time I saw him plonked lazily amongst the plush crème woollen cushions spread out along the sofa on the mezzanine level.

"Hello, how are you?" I asked, thinking he look rather well.

Plump, like Garfield the cat, a bow-tie at his neck portrayed a man of incredible eccentricity, one who seemed very comfortable in these surroundings.

"Good morning Jewel," his voice purred. He nodded at me Professor-like. "I'm extremely well, thank you. Now, let me see your flesh. Yes, yes, lovely," he cooed, eyeing me up and down. "Just like a Norman Lindsay painting; yes. What a piece of art you are!'

Soon he was playing an integral role in bolstering my confidence, also preparing me for the curve balls that came with this game. He showed me how to be gracious and not overreact when confronted by sex and porn language, but most importantly he showed me the value of my own judgement.

Mr Gem's regular visits, which sometimes were purely for our conversations, confirmed that having the gift for communication and intelligence was a great skill to have, along with my sexual power as a woman. He became my mentor, the first of many to validate that this experience would pay off

After a session we would loll about for ages as he admired the Norman Lindsay paintings above our bed. He would ask my opinion on art and together we would ponder the world's affairs, discussing philosophy and psychology, often disagreeing at times. If it weren't for him sharing his vast experience in marketing and early studies on Jung, I would never have entertained such grand ideas of running my own healing business.

Mr Gem was the epitome of patriarchy; providing support that I'd not received from men I was supposed to trust, his wisdom highlighting this discrepancy as I reflected upon my recent past. Prior to coming here, I had been approached to take up a director's role within a PR healthcare team, but the GM asked that I sign non-disclosure declaration waiving maternity leave in order to be awarded the role. Of course I turned it down. Women taking time out had cost him thousands in leadership training, he explained.

Here I was at Scarlett's being my own boss, working a third of the hours whilst learning more about men's needs and discovering my own. It was a win-win situation – one I had always craved.

Chapter 3

Work/Life Balance

With a New Year approaching I was aware that if I chose to study again, then this was the time to enrol. I met with a Life Coach to see if she could help me map out my goals and make the next decision. It was through this process that I decided coaching would be a good subject to undertake.

An alternative health college in North Sydney offered the best Life Coaching curriculum. Attending an open day in January where I met with course advisers, they helped me make the decision to undertake few subjects to start. Transformational Life Coaching diploma subjects included Introduction to Life Care, and Holistic Counselling 1A and Life Coaching 1A – an intensive weekend scheduled later that term.

Half way through term one I was ready to enrol, also deciding to take on the Diploma in Holistic Counselling and Life Care. We students were challenged to discuss our own direct experience of feelings as they unravelled, and deep personal processes began surfacing to be explored. One lecturer practiced and taught Gestalt whilst another embraced the teachings of Jung. Then there was the lead facilitator Simon who had studied shamanism, which he integrated into some of our core studies. This was all new territory for me, so I was tentative at first until I began experiencing the transcendental process of change for myself. Soon I was surrendering, undergoing visualisations and enduring powerful insights about my life. I began to understand so much more about the human condition, understanding my capacity as a child to manifest 'out of body' excursions through meditation.

I discovered Maslow's Hierarchy of Needs; a chart making great reference to fundamental elements in man's evolution - a stark reminder of my own subsequent arrival at this junction in my life. According to Maslow, we are all vying for truth, goodness, beauty, unity, transcendence, aliveness, uniqueness, perfection, justice, order and simplicity. He called these "B-values'; part of humanism and basic human needs which, when fully functioning in a healthy way, allow us live balanced lives.

His theory was presented in a basic pyramid; at the base we see values along with physiological needs. Next is our need for safety, often more experienced by children; third is love and belonging; fourth relates to our self-esteem. At the peak is self-actualisation whereby we become more aware of the greater need to have a cause upon which to base one's meaningfulness in life, building upon the notion of authenticity as preamble to feeling joy.

Discussing these studies with Mr Gem helped give me perspective, finding the courage to let go of my otherwise conservative mindset. He fascinated me; surprised me even, telling me that he was a trained hypnotherapist and fan of alternative streams, making me curious enough to explore modalities like astrology and tarot. I loved that he listened intently when I shared my experiences of shamanic journeying and totem animal manifesting, not once making me feel ridiculous when I told him my totem was an owl. Two arrived on my balcony one night after meditation class!

On the subject of owls; on a quiet Wednesday afternoon I was introduced to a timid, tall man with long and hairy eyebrows, an odd strand of grey strutting out from the sides and a thin beak-like pointy nose. He projected wisdom and yet said very little, meaning it was up to me to lead.

"So, tell me, what do you like?" I asked, waiting patiently for his reply.

He sat staring at me blankly, making me feel uneasy.

"What kind of things do you like to do?" He finally asked me, taking me by surprise.

Did he mean here in the bedroom or, what?

"Well, I love to explore your body." I started, moving my hand on his left thigh.

He flinched, sitting more upright.

"Oh no, no. Not what I meant!" He apologised, making me feel uncomfortable. "Not yet Jewel. Um, would you mind if we just talk? What do you like to do as in travelling, visiting museums?"

My astonishment was obvious but a slow smile spread across his face, finally put me at ease.

"Well," I started. "I've travelled throughout Europe extensively."

"Where to?" he asked, his eyes looking more alive.

After this gentle interlude he became my regular. Every Wednesday he greeted me with an excited smile and gifts.

"What are these?" I gushed, looking down at the David Jones bags by his feet.

As usual he said nothing.

"Are you going to give me any clues?"

Wandering up to the room he would continue with this game then pull out delicately wrapped packages. First was a little white box wrapped in gold ribbon.

"What is this?"

His eyes were dancing wildly, enjoying the fun.

"Open it and see." Was his short response, but at least he had spoken!

The ribbon fell away quickly as I fumbled with the box lid, peering in to see layers of finely decorated chocolates. 'Godiva' was lightly inscribed on some.

"What's in this one?" I asked, pointing to the other bag. He lay out a crisp, white tablecloth, suggesting I sit back and observe.

After many months of being spoilt like this, I was keen to see him again when I came back from a Christmas break.

"Well, don't you look good young lady?" Sherri said, greeting me with a hug.

"Yes and I feel fabulous!" I laughed, hugging her back. "How is everyone?"

A couple of new faces looked up at me nervously when we wandered into the girl's room. Turning around to stare at the white board, I made a mental note of what to wear before realising my column looked quite bare. Turning to Sherri before looking back to the board, my eyes skirted along the names written across the top.

"Kelly, Ashley, Bianca - oh, she's back? Jewel, Olivia, Pamela…"

There were a few bookings scribbled under the first names with more blanks than usual, but things had been getting quiet; and then I saw it.

"What's this?" I asked Sherri.

Sherri grimaced as some of the girls quickly made out they were busy.

"Ok, what's happening?" I asked again, walking up to the board for closer scrutiny.

Sherri bumped me out of the way and promptly tidied up Mr DJ's name written in Olivia's column. The blood drained from my face. I believed this High Court Judge to be a loyal regular, but he had moved on. It made sense that he would love her company while I was away. Sherri's eyes met mine as she spoke directly.

"Well, Jewel. You *will* go away at a crucial time. You *know* these men are flighty!" Her lips pursed as they always did when berating one of us. "They expect attention. That's what they're here for, and why they pay so well!"

I wasn't happy. Thinking I was special proved to be a costly mistake. Shrugging my shoulders, I let it go. Accepting my lesson as we laughed, I glanced over at the sign;

No Diva's in here, please!

It didn't take me long to pull my head in and get on with it, embracing the benefits of living such a lifestyle with wonderful flexibility. But this didn't mean I wouldn't be occasionally tested on the merits of sex work.

A little nervous about stepping into night shift, fearing drunks and men behaving badly after attending their work events, I was surprised to discover these clients were more amenable, meaning they were less likely to be sad, old married men who wanted to rescue me. In the evenings I saw bored bachelor boys who were lonely, often on the same wavelength. One in particular was to become my best friend and confidante.

"He's here!" Sherri had asked me to hang around for a 9pm booking.

"Ok thanks!" I said, struggling to get off the couch. It had been a quiet few hours which was good for studying in preparation for college the next day.

Wandering into the waiting room, my new client was standing there flicking through a magazine.

"Hello!" Offering my hand, my eyes did their usual scan. A twenty something young man, he put down the magazine, turning toward me to smile.

"Hello indeed, young lady! I'm Jay."

His response was light-hearted, making me smile. His deep brown eyes were warm and friendly.

"Ok are you ready Jay? Let's head upstairs."

Directing him ahead gave me a better view of this short, bald man.

"Hey, how about we just stop here?" he asked, just as we entered the loft mezzanine lounge.

"But the room is up these stairs…" I began to say, watching as he pointed to the couch.

"Relax young lady, here. Take a seat."

His gesture caught me off guard but I sat down anyway.

"Would you like to go have a shower? I can take off my dress here if you like…"

My voice hovered with its usual seductive inflection, again interrupted by a cavalcade of excuses.

"No girlfriend, don't go doing that! Please!" He feigned disdain, making me laugh, towering over him in my stiletto shoes.

"What are you doing!? Don't you want to get undressed and play?"

"Yeah yea, no. Actually not yet. Can we talk?" His eyes were wide, humour again present in his friendly round face.

From that moment I liked him. We didn't seem like strangers at all.

"You're a funny man, aren't you? I said, watching as he carefully sat down next to me. He did look rather familiar. "Hey, you're not that guy from the Kumar's are you? What's his name?" Framing his face with my hands, the resemblance was uncanny. "Sanjeev isn't it?"

He made a face. "Aagh, caught out, but don't tell anyone!"

We laughed again, no sexual tension present at all.

"Yes that's better," he spoke animatedly, enjoying that I had become relaxed.

And he relaxed too, extending the booking for another two hours with clothes never being removed. Our sessions continued like this for months until finally I broached the subject of becoming acquainted outside. It only seemed right, given I felt so guilty for taking his money. I needed his company just as much. Soon we were meeting up at our favourite restaurants, me telling him about my coaching studies as he asked for business guidance between jokes. Jay could talk to me about his fears and business plans, and I bolstered his confidence. His self-esteem was low, which I figured was the reason behind his need to be funny all the time.

There was no judgement either way. For me, having Jay as a friend was good timing as he provided me with an ear; making me feel appreciated and heard, just like Mr Gem always did.

The magnitude of course topics, some of which were beginning to place heavy emphasis on mentoring, never once provoked me to acknowledge the existence of my alter ego. I was turning forty that year, so any masking of reality was a good distraction from having to face this particular milestone! Even as I began the journey of transpersonal psychology and healing, not once did I reconcile with my past. It was during a compulsory therapy session held as part of Introduction to Life Care, a subject that crossed over into the Counselling diploma, that my lecturer pointed out I may have certain 'issues' with my parents. He made it clear that if they weren't dealt with I would not make an authentic practitioner.

I resisted such notions, believing the relationship with my parents was good but we just weren't close. They were in Adelaide and I was here in Sydney. No problems at all! However, given that I loved the various topics and insight this training was providing, I began taking my lecturers comments more seriously, committing a little more of an open mind.

It was not my intention to do two diploma streams, but they complemented each other superbly, and as a high achiever I could see the advantage of having a psychological platform upon which to deliver my coaching more effectively to future clients. A year later during a three day Vision Quest retreat (part of the coaching), Simon took us on a drum beating, spiritually challenging journey. While many of my fellow students wept, I found it easy to remain detached. My mind wandered elsewhere, disengaged from any resurgence of feelings. Years of silently retreating on my own were paying off, or so it seemed.

Later when we all huddled around candles, incense and a fire, a few students were traumatised by their ordeal; being alone forcing up issues they hadn't wanted to face. For me it was quite the opposite, I loved chilling out under the trees. It was an escape from thoughts, feeling nothing but safe and free. I was a master at keeping secrets, even from myself, learning through this process that to shut down my mental and physical faculties was my way of deflecting pain, giving me complete control over my internal and external environments. Recognising how this behaviour had become my survival tactic helped instigate my healing process, at the same time making me understand why I had embraced sex work so easily.

One evening during my second year at Scarlett's, Sherri booked me for a 9pm outcall close by. Escorting usually combined my two greatest passions; exquisite food and good company that paid! Unlike in-house clients, who were extremely important for their regularity, escorting was more likely to be a one-off or at the very least a monthly affair with no strings attached, and much fewer questions about my personal life.

When the time came to leave, Sherri stopped me.

"Wait! There are a few more things you need to take. He wants you to bring candles! Here, grab these."

Two glass candle holders were placed into my hands.

"Matches! I'll need matches then."

"No Jewel, just bloody well go, will you! There's always matches in the hotel room, come on hurry, and here's some more info."

Before she could finish I was out the door, running up to the hotel thinking it was sweet that the client wanted candle light. It wasn't until I entered the lift and checked the note that I realised there was more to it. Scrawled on the paper, it read;

Dominatrix Fantasy; 'John' wants to be pushed around and tied to the bed so that you can melt candle wax and drip it onto him. Slowly.' love Sherri (hehee!)

"Oh bloody hell!"

What am I going to tie him up with?

The lift opened, just as I was congratulating myself for an idea. Slipping off my black Tina Liano shoes, I removed a stocking and walked barefoot to the door, summoning my inner S&M Bitch before knocking.

"Come in," a slightly shrill voice called out.

Slipping shoes back on, gently I turned the handle as the door swung open easily.

"Hello?" I enquired cautiously, tiptoeing to the middle of the room.

Standing there by the King sized bed was a timid looking little man with light brown hair stuck across a bald spot. Pale blue, his eyes looked a little more fearful than I had anticipated. The poor thing, it takes all types I reminded myself.

"Get on the bed!" I screamed.

His face froze at the steeliness of my voice. I stared him down as he slowly backed away, the corner of the bed catching under his knee, tripping him backward where he crawled into the centre of the quilt. He observed me closing the door. Spotting some matches splayed out on a small table I plucked them between my fingers. Leaning over him, my bigger torso must have seemed intimidating.

"Move over!"

I loved feeling powerful as I watched him fumble, nodding as he slid his body along until there was nowhere else to go. He flinched under my gaze.

"Get your fucking clothes off now!"

His trembling fingers began the task of unbuttoning his shirt and trousers. Grabbing his belt, I gave it a tug then slapped it down hard on the bed. He flinched again, huddling up against the bed head. By this stage I had dropped my jacket to the floor. Standing back over his body, slowly I pulled of my other stocking from underneath a tight, black skirt.

"Put your hands up over your head! Hurry! Don't fuck with me here."

With long blonde hair and decked out in black, I projected my best Madonna impersonation. Managing to tie his hands together, I maintained domination.

"Who the fuck do you think you are? You've disappointed me!" I screamed, wrenching my arm through the sleeve of my blouse, flinging it to the floor. Unzipping my skirt, I slithered out, which was not easy given I was trying not to laugh. At last my black lace underwear was on show, but I knew it wasn't going to be appreciated.

"So tell me, have you been a naughty boy then?! I teased him with my eyes.

"Can I touch your breasts?"

What the...?

"Don't you *dare* talk to me! Shut up and wait!"

"Sorry!" he said, squirming again.

Defiantly I struck a match, holding it to the wick of the tiny candle until we had a burning flame. Straddling him firmly between my thighs, I could see he was hurting. Squirming beneath me, I made him wait until the candle burned down to a glistening liquid. Slowly, slowly angling the glass, a fine drop of wax spilled out over his body. Wailing in pain as the heat smacked his chest, fine hairs recoiled in shock.

"Is that enough for you, hey naughty boy?" I growled at him again.

His face was contorted. Continuing this for another five minutes I noticed he looked a little too horrified, so I stopped. A nanosecond of silence was disconcerting, forcing me to think and I didn't like what popped into my head. Something didn't seem quite right - not normal. Jeez, who was I kidding? None of this was! Awkwardly leaning back to look at his face, I had to stop and ask.

"Um, are you ok?"

There was no response, just a glazed stare although I was sure I saw a few tears. This made me panic.

Oh fuck! Don't tell me I'm in the wrong room?

"Ahh, um, look, I'm not sure this is going well. Are you Mr MacDonald?"

He said nothing, just lay there staring up at me. What was I going to do now? Lifting my knee off his chest, still he remained silent. This was not looking good; my heartbeat was almost deafening.

How am I going to explain this to him?

As I was preparing some wonderfully creative explanation, he spoke.

"Yes, yes. You're doing great, its fine; keep going," he said, nodding to assure me.

Staring at him blankly from my overhead position I felt empty, stuck somewhere between S&M bitch and the real me lamenting this ridiculous job. I wasn't sure who was being tortured here. More likely it was me.

"Good," I said, fighting back sarcasm. "You really had me worried there for a minute."

"Sorry!"

His impish apology did nothing to fuel my flagging S&M persona, although now I was ready to whack the living daylights out of him. Drizzling hot liquid wax over his meek looking apricot tinged furry nipples, I enjoyed every minute as he screamed, my acting no longer necessary as his body shuddered with an orgasmic release.

"Oh, thank you," he cried, hopping up like we'd just had tea.

I jumped away, keeping a clean and clear space between us.

"I'm off for a shower, if that's okay?" he asked, rolling off the bed to leave me there.

I sat down on the edge of the bed before getting dressed when Mr Macdonald came back into the room, sitting down opposite me.

"Thankyou so much, Jewel. You were superb!" he remarked.

It was all too bizarre. Superb at what, I had to ask?

"Why do you like being treated like this? And how can you see this as sexy and fun?"

"Well, I'm highly strung. You can probably tell," he said, scratching his arms nervously. His thin mouth smiled as his eyes darted away slightly self-conscious. I felt sorry for him.

"So can I ask then, what do you like about being abused in this way?"

Who would want to be emasculated? I found him quite sad; pathetic actually, as I thought about was how great an opportunity this was for me to hone my listening skills. He explained sporadically, like a five year old excited to have someone paying so much attention, as I took mental notes for one of my subjects; Attachments, Addictions and Wholeness.

"Well, I have lots of sisters." His speech was robotic which was quite off putting. "And my mother, she was so hard. They all were. I was the youngest."

He smiled occasionally, glancing at me to confirm he had permission to continue.

"Fascinating. Tell me more," I prompted, hoping this would make a good assignment topic. I wasn't quite sure how I would justify the research but would work that out later.

"Ok, yes well then I'm also married to a woman who pushes me around," he announced rather proudly, pausing for effect.

I waited for him to go on, although I was beginning to think it would have been wiser not to ask, but it was too late.

"And I love it!" He was beaming. "It makes me feel needed, like I always did when my sisters vied for time to play with me! One would dress me up, another would slap me around and make me cry but it was fun!"

Sitting there quietly, nodding occasionally, I thought back to my own childhood. Sure, I hadn't experienced anything bizarre as such, but I had never felt the same compulsion to embrace the anger vented toward me. I was a child for fuck's sake! How can any child be expected to observe rage and absorb the belief that this is love? But sadly, people like Mr MacDonald did just that.

After another twenty minutes off the clock I finally departed, grateful for the quiet, insular personal life I had built up around me. Occasionally confronted with other people's torture gave me a new benchmark regarding life.

Mine was normal after all.

Chapter 4

Hierarchy of Wants versus Needs

In second term I began the compulsory therapy sessions that were mandatory to complete the Counselling Diploma. I wasn't concerned about anything too painful emerging, believing I had nailed my alcohol problem since relinquishing my PR career and social life. Jewel was also well hidden – a separate entity.

The workshops were formatted in a way that had us safely held by within a therapeutic space. Each week one of us would plunge into shadow aspects of our nature, all of us bearing witness as strongly held beliefs became threatened, possibly deconstructed once exposed by the lecturer during experiential play. We students soon became tethered to one another within this classroom, as it became clear we were undergoing a life changing transformation. We watched as resistance would initiate further scrutiny, tears becoming a sure sign our fellow student had underlying issues surging through. To observe someone undergoing a breakthrough of epic proportions was quite confronting at times; overwhelming when it triggered something in one of us sitting there.

When it was my turn I didn't crack. Not once did I ever cry. It was when my lecturer Simon took me through a focussing process that something finally stirred. Gradually he talked me through, asking me to close my eyes and envision my inner child. Aware of his voice, I was amazed at just how quickly my body began responding uncomfortably. If I twitched nervously at a question about my family, he asked me what thought or feeling had come up. I thought about my drinking behaviour when I was young. Successfully I put the brakes on any more questions being asked, just as the pain began to well up inside. Simon was picking up on this, informing me at the end that we would delve further during our scheduled one on one the following week.

"Ok Taryn. Let's start, shall we? Firstly, how are you?"

"Good thanks. Really good," I responded, hoping it was enough to convince Simon to go easy on me. I followed his gesture for me to sit down. Priding myself on being able to read body language, I was already preparing responses for his onslaught of personal enquiry. Deflecting attention had become a standard tool from an early age.

Few candles glowed, evenly spaced along the bookshelf in this clinic room located off campus.

"Ok that's good. So let's start, shall we?"

I smiled, not really keen to start anything.

"Would you like to pick up from what happened in the class recently? I was aware of your resistance when the topic of your parents came up, and that's okay. It's more private here. Know that you are safe."

I smiled, a little twitchy. Did we place the same meaning on this word? I didn't think so therefore I would be sharing very little about myself. This shamanic stuff was all still a little too 'out there' for me, and as far as psychodrama went, I really believed I'd experienced enough drama in my life to ever allow myself to become that vulnerable again. Although I was beginning to think that if I managed to survive this course I may seriously need some therapy - but not now.

He was waiting for me to start.

"Well, no not really," I said.

I smiled, more like a grin, as I rolled my eyes. Simon smiled, matching my body language as I leaned back into the chair.

"Ok then, how about you tell me more about yourself as a child. Remember we did the focussing meditation, talking to your younger self in class?"

Yes I remembered. I turned to my younger self in that meditation and couldn't believe how long it had been since I saw her. It was me at five. Dark, deep set eyes, a furrowed brow.

"Okay I can see you're reflecting on this now. Just sit comfortably there and allow those thoughts to become words. Allow those words to flow. What is it that just came up for you?"

Oh Geez, here we go! I twitched nervously in my chair.

"I can see at your throat," he put his hands up to his. "You are gulping down words. Sit with this for a moment. Give these words permission to form and speak when they're ready, whatever they are. It's okay to take your time and express yourself freely here."

Was I just feeling tired from all the juggling of clients at Scarlett's or were the classes becoming too much for me? I felt a little fragile, too exposed there in the chair opposite a man who suddenly seemed able to read me. I wanted to run.

"I see your eyes are darting toward the door, Taryn. You can leave at any time. It's okay. You are safe."

I took a deep breath and folded my arms, seriously considering doing just that.

"Taryn. You do know I'm not here to make your life difficult, but if you leave I cannot allow you to continue in this course."

Raising my eyebrows, our eyes met. He held me, not in an aggressive stare but with eyes that looked like he really did care. To my surprise I liked this man. I liked his strength. He gave me boundaries, a choice and opportunity to speak. Inhaling deeply, relaxing back into the chair, I took a chance.

"I don't know what to say, really?"

Simon scratched his head.

"Okay." He leaned forward a little. "How about you close your eyes for a moment and open your palms up on your knees, take some deep breaths. Centre yourself and breathe. That's it. Relax and feel at peace."

The aroma of incense danced in my nostrils. I loved the warm smell of sandalwood. I softened. My heart slowed. I did feel at peace. Slowly Simon guided me back into the past, asking me to reconnect with myself as a child. The little girl appeared again, but she didn't want to turn around. I couldn't blame her. Who'd want to look back into the past? Not me, that's for sure!

"Where are you, and what feelings are coming up?"

I sighed, ready to surrender.

"I'm at home when I was young, and I'm remembering that my mother always used to say that I should be seen and not heard."

Opening my eyes, I laughed conspiringly. Simon didn't move. His face didn't show any conspiracy at all. My laughter abated, eyes lowered to hide my shame.

"To be seen and not heard was such an old saying back then, wasn't it?" Simon said.

I looked up.

"Yes. I guess it was."

"What did that really mean to you when you heard this?"

My body shifted. A deep breathe steadied me. My throat constricted some more, so I closed my eyes to ease the discomfort.

"Well, I always heard that she never wanted me."

I didn't open my eyes and Simon didn't speak.

"This is my earliest memory; a constant thing I heard when I was growing up."

My shoulders lurched forward, the realisation upsetting me more than I anticipated.

"It's okay. Take a moment to allow these feelings come up. How do you feel about this?" Simon asked.

"I was confused. And my mum was always angry so if I ever said or did anything that upset her she would slap me hard across the face. She didn't want to hear from me. It was like she didn't want me to exist!"

Where did that all come from, I wondered?

"What was she angry about?"

All the memories came flooding back. "The stories my mother used to tell me about her mother not welcoming the pregnancy and calling her a whore for not being married. She didn't feel accepted by her mother. So I guess she took it out on me."

The feelings stirred quickly, much to my surprise. Had I been holding to all this anger all these years?

"She took it out on you. Do you have a good relationship with your mother now?"

My attention came back to Simon.

"Um, yes we're okay I guess. You know, the same as most people. I'm here and they're in Adelaide and we find common ground talking about my nephews."

"They're in Adelaide. Are you talking about both your parents? Are they still together?"

"Yes they are. They stuck it out." I rolled my eyes.

"You don't think this is a good thing?"

I didn't have to ponder this one too long.

"Well, when I was growing up my dad wasn't around much. When I was little, say five, six or seven I can't remember exactly, he worked night shift and mum worked early morning shifts so I was home when he would walk in. He was usually drunk. Mum would scream at him then storm off to her job and leave him to fall unconscious. I used to hide in my room, hearing him stumble around until I knew he was asleep."

"Were you left alone?"

I tried to remember.

"No, no a neighbour would come over just as mum was leaving. She would get me off to school. My sister wasn't born yet. She came along a year later I think. Or mum would drop me off down the road at a cousin's place if dad hadn't come home. It's all a blur."

I was getting agitated. Memories were getting stuck somewhere between dreams and reality.

"I had a great imagination as a child," I said, opening my eyes. I smiled at Simon, this memory pleasing me.

"You had a great imagination. How did this help you, do you think?"

"Well, I could imagine being somewhere else. I was part of another family, but this wasn't the case sadly."

There was a long pause as I cast my mind back to how happy my younger cousins always were. By the time my sister came along, the pressure had eased. The focus shifted away from me so I was free to spend time locked in my room. I loved reading for hours on end, blocking my family out.

"You could imagine being somewhere else?"

Recalling the many books, one of my favourites was The Magic Faraway Tree. I loved the adventures these characters described.

"Yes. I knew that as soon as I was old enough to leave this place, I would! And I used to think that if my mum hated her life and dad so much, why didn't she just leave?"

I recalled my early years, the fighting and violence.

"My mum hated her family, especially when they started drinking with my dad. She hated alcoholics. She hated everything."

"Can I ask why you think she didn't leave?"

I took a deep breath.

"Mum said her mother always said it wouldn't work. The marriage, that is."

I looked at Simon. Was he keeping up? How did I get here, I wondered? I had not intended on talking about any of this. It was in the past. It was my mother's past, not mine!

"We get on fine, now though. I just accept that she's an angry person. Dad's fine, he stopped drinking when I was eighteen."

Hoping this was enough to appease Simon, I watched as he sat there quietly.

"You accept that she's an angry person. How does that really make you feel?"

I was furious. How dare he push me like this?

"I can see that this has upset you. Stay with these emotions and relax, let's see why shall we?"

"Well, you know. Her childhood was crap. What can I say?"

I sighed, crossing my arms.

"This is making you defensive. If you can, please relax a little and breathe. Close your eyes and give yourself a moment to process these feelings. What's coming up that makes you so angry about all this?"

Closing my eyes didn't help. I remembered more about my mother's rage toward me. Her abuse was constant. I was confused, never knowing what mood she would be in if Dad didn't come home straight after shift. Mum would sometimes disappear, leaving me to look after my little sister, hiding her when Dad stumbled in. I didn't want to think about all these things. It was so long ago. The tears came. I opened my eyes to see Simon handing me the tissue box.

"I was never good enough. I was a mistake. It was my fault for being born!"

This was not what I had bargained for. Sitting back, my knuckles clung onto the wicker chair.

"It's okay, really. I've got it all under control."

Simon didn't say anything, sitting there observing.

"You've got it all under control," he said, finally.

I nodded. "Yes."

"How did you get it all under control? Can you take me through this journey?"

Fuck! Not really, I thought. I was alright here, right now. No need to look back!

"Sit for as long as it takes, and visit that young girl again. Can you do that for me?"

I glared at him, with no intentions of going there. Slowly I relaxed, closing my eyes. I was tired of keeping Simon at a distance, unnerved by his patience. I was also aware that avoidance and fake compliance was an old tactic of mine. Struggling with the idea of admitting that I wasn't in control, a shameful voice hovered, confronting me like it did when I was a child. The incense filtered through, putting me at ease as I regained my power, reinforcing the same protective mechanisms I had come to learn and activate at will.

Summertime in Adelaide can be gruelling, the heat very intense when temperatures soar well above the forty degree mark. It was the 70's and fashionable to toast one's bare flesh for the sake of a tan. In my friend Julia's backyard, I lay stretched out on a towel.

"C'mon! Last one in is a rotten egg!" she screamed, dashing toward the pool.

"In a minute!" I yelled back, watching as she rushed toward the metal framed sphere containing gallons of water.

We were eight years old when we became friends at school. Now twelve, I envied her pubescent body, following every move as she ran around in a bikini supporting newly formed breasts that bounced wildly in a top that no longer fit. My body was still plump, laying there ready to welcome the calming sensation of sunlight. Stretching out, unfurling my stark white chubby limbs, I loved the feeling of laser like beams pummelling my skin. It was seductive, soothing even when an unbearable sizzle began to lure me into semi-consciousness, hovering between the realm of pleasure and pain.

"Hey! Come on, have a swim, silly. What are you doing?"

Her voice dissipated under the simmering chills welling inside, catapulting me further away. It was an easy thing to do. I hadn't eaten in over two days. Blocking out hunger pains filled me with a sense of achievement. The angry red flickering beneath my eyelids proved I was dangerously close to the edge. This was the moment I was addicted to; teetering between worlds wondering what was on the other side. The pain eased a little when unconsciousness swirled; endorphins rendering me into a state of suspension. It was a blissful moment where I could surrender to the energy vibrations lifting me up, floating lightly as I no longer felt anything at all.

This was how it felt not to be in my fat, white, ugly body that no-one ever loved. I would always be in control and could leave at any time. No-one could stop me.

I didn't share anything about my eating disorder with Simon. However, obscure thoughts cropped up during the weeks that passed as memories hovered near the surface, triggered by conversations; things that clients would say to me like, 'you're such a control freak, what's your story?'

"Okay let's get comfortable then, and see where you are today. How did you feel after last session?" Simon asked.

I sat down, ready to close my eyes and breathe in deeply, clearing my mind. Fragments of my past were given permission to reconstruct and flow. Gradually there was trust forming between us.

"Well, things came up. Some stuff that I had completely forgotten about, especially anything to do with my childhood but I know I've got one very painful experience to get off my chest still," I said.

Simon smiled, nodding. "Sure. Whenever you're ready. Relax and breathe."

"Okay," I said, quickly settling in this time. "I'm still angry about something my mum said once. It was when we were at my cousins wedding held six months after my divorce. She overheard me talking to my aunty who was teasing me about having a fling when I was away on holidays."

Stopping to take a breath, the annoyance was building.

"She turned around to us, calling me a whore in front of everyone. I was stunned!"

"You were stunned. Then what happened?" Simon asked.

"Well, eventually my dad spoke up asking my mother to calm down but this only fuelled her rage. Nobody, not even my own mother could see I was still in pain after the way my ex-husband left." Regaining my focus, I continued. "Her reaction was proof that she thought I was unworthy. Whatever I did it was never the right thing. She expected more from me."

Heaviness felt like lead in my belly.

"She expected more from you."

His repeating got my attention as I pondered the word 'expected'. *Was it her or was it me that expected more?*

"Hmm. Probably I did, I guess. I don't know, it's too much at the moment, I'm tired!"

My breathing intensified as memories resurfaced with such force, thinking about how shocked she would be if she knew about my secret life. *Was this a rebellion in some way?*

"I was so angry at her!"

"What's the anger about? It must be exhausting to hold on to so much for so long."

I looked at Simon. My whole body tensed. I wanted to scream.

"I'm angry at everyone, even my dad for not being around."

I stopped to think about this a little more.

"You know, all he had to do was come home sober. But that was rare! Mum would go nuts! Throwing stuff at him and screaming. I would lay there awake hearing everything then go to school so tired the next day. Once one of my teachers came hovering above me with a large wooden ruler and whacked me for not paying attention. It was humiliating, but I couldn't tell her why because I was afraid of everyone finding out about what was going on at home. The secrets. I'm angry I'm just so over it!"

Clutching myself, I began to cry.

"Where is the anger in your body, Taryn? Give yourself permission to be angry."

"Here. In my belly." A muffled voice whispered. "And I can hardly speak because of this lump on my throat. I want to speak up. I'm tired of caring about what everyone else thinks!" I yelled, a volcanic explosion of emotions pouring out.

"I am angry at my mum. I'm so angry that I was judged! How dare everyone abuse me?"

The rage would not let up, gently encouraged by Simon's persistence that I let it all out.

"Gosh she was so damned unhappy, that woman!"

Overwhelmed, I couldn't hold the tears back any more.

"What else is happening?" he asked, handing me the tissues.

Sitting there with this story unfolding, pieces of my childhood came together; the puzzle that was my mother's life making sense.

"Mum had a tough childhood," I said, remembering the stories. "My grandfather was an abusive drunk, so Nan had to constantly move, hiding my mum along with her sister and brother. Always attending new schools, they finally settled in Adelaide with an extended family – other people's kids."

I imagined the cycle; how awful it must've all been.

"When she was only sixteen she met my dad."

There was a long pause as I imagined this.

"She met your dad," Simon repeated, pushing the tissue box closer.

"Yes, but do you know what she always said to me?"

Simon waited, not interrupting.

"She said, 'I went from one hell, straight into another, falling pregnant! I had plans of escaping alcoholics but then I ended up married to one!'"

Saying this out aloud was an immense relief, followed by a wave of sadness I suddenly felt for my mother.

"What do you feel now?"

I dabbed my cheeks.

"Well," I said, smiling a little. "You know what? I actually feel sorrier for her. I really do. She was so young – and trapped, wanting only to be loved and to create a safe home of her own."

The relief was sweet; my body felt like it had given up a ghastly weight.

The clock ticked behind Simon, making me aware the music had stopped but he remained silent. Everything began to slowly sink in.

"I've never allowed myself to stop and understand my mother before. I know she loves him, my dad that is, but it was her mother that made her feel so ashamed. I remember her telling me how she couldn't enjoy her young married life."

Something shifted as empathy arose. I sighed.

"It's sad, really. But still."

"But still." Simon reflected.

There was a long pause before I caught my breath again. "I feel let down."

"You feel let down."

I nodded, relieved that at last someone heard me.

"You were let down. No-one stood up for you when you were a little girl. This has been a huge breakthrough, yes?"

"Yes, it sure has."

"Did you want to explore anything else in the last few minutes then?"

"Um, no!" I smiled, stretching my limbs. "I think that's quite enough for one day."

Hopping up, I leaned over to hug Simon, surprising me more than him.

"Thank you so much, I can't believe how much better I feel. I had no idea I was going to talk about all that."

"Yes, isn't it nice to let anger go?"

"Yes," I answered, picking up my bag. It had been a tough but enlightening session.

Once outside in the fresh air I felt unusually happy, like there was a chance I could start over. But what more was left to surface, I wondered? Was I ready to explore anything else? Deep down I knew it was time to challenge the status quo, and part of me was ready. I was beginning to like knowing myself once again.

It had been too long.

On the way home I thought more about my parents. My childhood hadn't been all that bad. There were treasured moments but they just didn't seem to have made the same impact; not enough fun stuff to erase the horrible things. Walking into my kitchen, searching the cupboards for some crackers I noticed a bottle Merlot, a gift from a client, hidden away. The need to appease such an emotionally exhausting day gave me an excuse to open it.

Pouring myself a drink, I put the glass down before wandering to my bedroom where I changed into comfortable clothes. Bending down to grab my leggings, I saw this little box under my bed. It contained a pile of memorabilia I hadn't gone through in years. Without thinking, I pulled it out, flipping open the lid. My clumsy fingers sent photos flying everywhere, and one picture captured my attention

My mother was standing with me and my sister dressed in costumes for our annual ballet school concert. There was no smile on my face. A lump formed in my throat as it always did when I remembered that particular day.

"Ok girls, you all look stunning. Now, remember, always look straight ahead like in rehearsal and focus on your feet; listen to the music and last but not least, have fun!" Miss Jane said. She was our dance teacher.

We all shouted in excitement, resuming our positions before the curtain was raised. I couldn't help myself, sneaking off to look behind the curtains, waving at my cousins sitting a few rows from the front. I ran back into the dressing room.

"My cousins are out there!" I shared with the other mums grinning at my enthusiasm.

There was a ringing in my ears, followed by a burning sensation and a deathly silence. Everything faded momentarily between shards of light, like stars through the fogginess as I regained vision, shocked faces confirming I had been slapped in the face.

Everyone was staring, but nobody moved. They only looked on as my mum's hand hovered above me, her mouth screaming as I cowered.

"Shut up and behave yourself! If I ever hear you carry on like that again you won't be going on stage at all!"

I wanted to hide but there was no-where to go, humiliation burning greater than the pain on my cheek.

"And if you cry I promise I'll hit you harder!"

Shoving the photos back into the box sent everything flying out, scattering beneath the bed. Only a few images were within reach, staring back at me as I tried desperately to pick them up without another glance. What was going on with me? I felt confused, not wanting to face unanswered questions.

"Fuck you all, I don't care anymore!"

My rage turned into a pain I could no longer deny. Then the tears came, my body shaking uncontrollably for ages. Breathing deeply, somewhat overwhelmed, I couldn't help but notice how much better I felt once they stopped. Leaning against the wall, I wondered if this was due to the emotional outpouring I had experienced during sessions with Simon.

This was all too heavy. I needed to relax more, get out and talk to friends. It had been far too long.

My head was throbbing like mad, making me wish I hadn't answered the phone which put me in the firing line of Sally's loud voice.

"Hi love, what's happening?" she asked, not giving me a moment to get the phone to my ear.

Sally and I had become close when working together in PR. An Indian-born Englishwoman with wild afro hair and thick pouty lips, Sally was what Australian's consider to be a fun, lovable larrikin. Her element of contempt for this world gave her voice compassion, gifted for being outspoken which made her one very successful media consultant and a close confidante during those late night drinking sessions we used to share at our local bar.

"Hello?" I moaned, still groggy, trying to sit up.

"Hello, you okay? It's me Sal. Remember, your friend? You left me a garbled message last night. Sorry I wasn't home to catch up!"

"Oh fuck. Sorry yeah, hi Sal, yes of course! How are you?"

"What's that, love? Fuck what?"

"No, not you, I just woke up," I said, slowly gaining some focus. "And it looks like I polished off some wine."

Wistfully noting the empty bottle, I cringed. And I had to stop swearing at everything!

"You okay?"

"Yeah yea," I quickly interjected, envying her energy.

Hearing me hesitate, Sally persisted. "Sure?"

"Well, maybe not really," I confessed, checking my watch. It was 10.15am. I was usually up by eight but the last few busy weeks had put me completely off balance.

"What, you're not? Do you want me to come over? Stupid bloody question. I'm on my way. Okay?"

"Um, yeah, that would be good actually," I answered, realising how much I missed her company. "Why don't you come over for lunch? I'm so sorry, Sal. We're way overdue for a girlie catch up, and God knows I need a hug, *badly*," I whispered, my throat constricting. "And Sal, maybe you can pick up Lucy and Cassie on the way if they're not doing anything. I'll give them a call now."

Sisters Lucy and Cassie were my flatmates when I first arrived in Sydney, becoming my second family.

"Oh sure, that's a great idea! Okay love, do you want me to bring anything?"

My reaction was immediate. "No that's fine, Sal! I've got it covered."

Although I knew her intentions were good, I didn't fancy a packet of Home Brand macaroni for lunch.

"Ok, love no problems. I'll swing by and pick up the girls, just send me a text if they're not coming, okay?"

"Thanks Sally that's great. Oh I feel so old, can't wait to see you soon then."

"Ok love, yeah we're all fucking getting old," Sally colluded. "Okay won't be long. Bye!"

I hung up relieved to have these few friends. Lying back down I was grateful for the lightness creeping in. It was amazing the difference that a quick telephone call could do. On that note, I thought about my sister who was settled in her new life in Queensland with the boys. I was so proud of her for having the courage to start again in a new state. It was a big move, but she was much closer up there so I could visit more regularly given it only took fifty minutes to travel by air. I cleared my head to think about what to cook for the girls. Looking at my watch, it was 11am. Could I have been reflecting on the past for that long?

"Oh bugger!"

Grabbing my mobile, I dialled, hoping it wasn't too late for Sally to pick the girls up on the way

"Hello?" A little voice answered.

"Hi Cass, it's me!" My voice was still a little croaky.

"Who?"

My mind began to spin. Did I just say Taryn or Jewel?

"It's me, Taryn. How are you?"

"Oooh, hey love, I'm good! Where in the world have you been?"

"I know I'm such a bad friend. Um, I'm sorry I'm going to have to be quick but, well, Sally is on her way over for lunch and I forgot to call you," I said, frantically trying to make sense of everything. "She can pick you and Lucy up on the way? I'd *love* to see you both!"

"Oh ok! I was about to go wander through shops in QVB, and Lucy's got a movie date so it's just me!"

"No problem. Ok Sally will be there soon; see you around midday then!"

"Oh? Ok, bye!"

I hung up and lay back down for a quick nap.

Squinting, I forced my eyes open to glance at the time. Another hour had quickly passed.

"Fuck, fuck," I cried out, jumping up.

Swearing seemed to help with the task of pulling a rebellious jumper off over my head as I stumbled into the bathroom. Where was all this rage permeating from? Nearly naked, I pulled my knickers down for a quick pre shower pee when I saw an intruder there. Petrified, a cold shiver ran down my spine rendering me motionless.

"Oh, you are fucking kidding me," I whispered, stopping my pee in mid-stream.

Sitting right beside me on the window sill was a Huntsman spider. What the hell was he doing there?

"Ok, you need to leave."

My voice was stern in the hope that it would encourage him to go, but obviously I was no-where near convincing. He didn't budge, so it was time for plan b. It was a simple plan, however a little more tricky to carry out given that my knickers were still around my ankles. Taking a deep breath I counted to three before pulling them up and racing to the laundry for a broom.

"C'mon, come on! Where are you?" I screamed, knowing I was running out of time.

Turning to look behind the door, I found my weapon.

"Okay then!" I yelled, acting like a warrior as I got into position, broom handle poised with bristles facing the hairy intruder. I was ready for battle.

"Hmm, okay you're not moving?"

His legs responded, scrunching up.

"Fuck!" I screamed, at the same time wielding the broom in his general direction.

"Get out. Get out!"

He went ballistic, running down the wall and back up by the toilet cistern where I lost sight of him. There was no way I could move from here now; not until I knew he was outside otherwise I would never sleep in this house again.

"I'm sorry pal, but I did give you options!" My panting had increased, making it difficult to speak. This little bastard had me on edge!

Carefully prodding the broom head down under the s-bend, standing firm before the next big battle, I saw a leg then three as he took off back up the wall toward the door.

"No you fucking don't!"

I notice my mind immediately race to psychoanalyse what this swearing must all mean. Was there no escaping my new revelatory path? Bashing the wall over and over again, I focussed on the murder I knew I had to commit, watching as he fell backward onto the floor, laying near the toilet brush holder probably playing dead. I whacked like he was a golf ball, but instead sent the container rattling behind the cistern.

"No more, no more, sorry… you… are… dead!" I cried out, watching as pieces of leg flew everywhere. Then with one final blow the broom head ploughed into his plump, furry body. He was crushed, I made sure of it. Guts oozed out into a messy spray, confirming his life was nearly over. Another few twists of the broom bristles and I was confident he had died.

Pondering this grisly scene, body parts still stuck to the wall, the nausea welled up inside my belly as I dived in for a quick shower. Just as I had the towel around my waist, I heard a knock.

"Hey gorgeous, it's little ol' me!" Sally's voice echoed through the door.

Oh my God! They're here already? Throwing on my leggings and a tee, I shouted back.

"Hello, wait I'm coming!"

When I opened the door, Sally was standing there first bearing wine and two bottles of champagne, with Cassie pottering in behind holding a big platter of food.

"Hello, at last!" I hugged the girls as they stepped into my lounge.

"Hello, hello! Sorry love I'm dying for a wee. Have to run through."

I froze, watching as Sally skipped toward to the hallway.

"Don't!" I screamed after her. Cassie walked past me more slowly.

"Hi lovey, what's wrong?" she asked.

Taking the platter, I ushered her toward the kitchen while still glaring at Sally standing there looking confused. They both looked at me like I was mad, and for a moment I was sure they were right, completely losing it as tears came back again.

"I... just don't go in there Sally." That annoying lump formed in my throat again. "It's terrible," I howled, trying to explain. "I couldn't do anything else; I'm just over it. It's all too much!"

"What love? Over what?" Sally asked, looking worried as she watched me fall limp onto a dining chair.

Cassie was searching the kitchen cupboards for champagne flutes.

"I'm just so fucking sick and tired of men, you know," I whimpered childishly.

"What? Why, what's happened now?" Sally moved closer to me, showing more concern as she dropped onto a knee.

"I've, it's ok Sal. Go pee! I've... he can't move... I had to, it's an awful mess I'm so sorry," I mumbled, struggling to regain composure.

"What? Sorry, who's a mess?"

Cassie poked her head out. "Jeassssssuus Christ! What are you trying to say?"

By now it was nearly impossible for me to speak.

"He, he was there and, came out of nowhere and I just couldn't help it. I just couldn't stop, Sal. I kept bashing and bashing..."

Taking in a deep breath I cried harder, realising how tired I really was.

"Who!" Sally screamed, hopping up. "Who came at you? Who is this prick, I'll kill him!"

I was hysterical, replaying everything I had shared with Simon in my head, realising I was barely able to tolerate men trying to get closer to me at work. Everyone wanted to know more about me and about my past but I didn't want to talk about it!

"No Sally I've killed him, he's dead, I was so angry, whacking him so hard, even his head came off!"

Sally's incredulous eyes stood out on her pasty face.

"Oh, it's ok love," she soothed me, putting her arms around my shoulders, her body shaking more than mine.

"I'm sorry Sal. It's all too much... I'm..."

"Don't worry about anything, you hear? If that bastard thought he could just pounce on you then serves him right. I'll work out how to get rid of that dirty fucker," she continued sporadically.

I looked into her eyes, recognising fear.

"You sure he's...? Okay, okay don't say another word. It's going to be fine. I can get friends to come and have a look... um, we'll work it out. Trust me. It's going to be alright. He'll disappear, and this will all go away. Ok?"

Sally wasn't making any sense. She continued rambling and jumping around looking for something, stopping still as we heard a disgusting noise echoing from the kitchen. Cassie was vomiting into my sink.

"You alright, Cass?" Sally asked.

My hand reached out to stop her from moving anywhere.

"Sally?"

"It's okay love," she said, placing her hand on top of mine. "Just breathe. You've lost the plot. It's all going to be ok. You're hysterical but that's normal. This is big, but we'll fix it, don't worry."

"Sal," I gulped, feeling a sudden impulse to laugh. "It was a spider. I killed a spider, *not a man!*"

I could see from her expression she was struggling hard to digest what I was saying. Gradually some colour returned.

"What? A fucking spider! Are you fucking kidding me?"

"No Sal, it was a Huntsman actually. A big, furry one!"

Raising my eyebrows, nodding, finally she started to relax.

"Oh fuck me! You do know I was going in there thinking you'd killed some poor sod and you're telling me I'm wetting myself over a frigging spider!"

"What are you both saying!?"

We both turned to see Cassie in the doorway, looking pale as she wobbled out with both champagne bottles in her hands.

"I cannot hold them glasses my hands are shaking so much," she blurted out in her best Irish twang. "I'm having a heart attack!"

Sally was doubled over.

"Go, go!" I screamed. "Don't bloody well wee on my floor!"

"You're lucky I didn't fucking *mess* myself on your floor!" Sally threw back at me.

A few seconds later we heard Sally screeching from the bathroom. "Oh Jeeesus! Fuck! Sure it's dead?"

Cassie screamed at the same time as a loud pop sent the champagne cork flying across the room.

"Cassie, it's ok," I assured her.

"Jesus," Sally laughed, waltzing back into my living room. "That was some massive furry fuck... Cassie what the...?"

Sally stopped to stare at our friend. "Here, give me that bottle and get down off that table, will you? Trust me, he's dead. The poor bastard never had a chance, by the look of it!"

"It's so good to see you both again!" I said, laughing hard.

My home felt warm. I moved over to help Cassie crawl off my table.

"Thank you, girls'. You are the best friends ever, you know that?"

"Well love, this could've been one of my last visits you know. I nearly had a bleedin' heart attack too!" Cassie said. "Here's cheers!"

"Yes cheers." Sally yelled, taking long swig from the Champagne bottle. "Aaaaaaah, fuck I needed that!"

Brushing away the tears, it took ages to settle down.

"So, on a more serious note," Sally started to say, trying not to laugh anymore. "Where've you bloody been?"

She proffered a fat strawberry over her ripe lips and I couldn't help but think she would be very popular at Scarlett's.

"Well," I said, choosing my words carefully. "I have some work, a few days that fit in between my studies."

"Yes tell me more! Natural therapies are the best!"

Cassie's interjection was sweet relief.

"Yes! Well, the coaching and counselling is great and I'm doing some introductory classes in energetic healing next term."

"And what about, did you say you've met some people at work?" Sally was fishing for more gossip so I took the bait, deciding to let her off the hook.

"Well, I've made some friends there of course," I answered, sharing a little more information.

"At work?" she asked me this time with more determination. I realised the difficulty in dodging such questions. I really *was* tired.

"Yes Sal, at work," I teased, waiting as the girls leaned closer. "I did meet someone rather lovely."

"Who? What?" Sally asked, looking from Cassie then back to me.

"Jay," I announced, pleased to see that mentioning a blokes name made any job outline null and void.

"Ooh, go on then. Tell us more, don't keep us waiting," Sally prodded, noting my distant stare.

I was mapping out the practicality of this person being in my life. Where to start, I wondered?

"He's a bit of a computer nerd but you'd like him, Sal."

"Well, I can't wait to meet him then," she answered, looking at me rather cheekily.

"You will one day. More Champagne Cas?"

With an interesting life to manage, my timetable was fused with an array of sordid interludes and spiritual learning both day and night. It amazed me to think how much had happened since we all caught up. How had I managed to avoid them for so long? It was hard to believe the weeks had flown, blurring into months until finally a year had passed. My life had become all sex work, lattes and study although not necessarily in that order. I hadn't banked on finding such a perfect life balance in a brothel, but there I was - having sex for a living.

This notion made me uneasy, fighting a sudden urge to cry, recalling the plan was to be there for only a few months but I liked this life so much more than my old one. These men booked in, paid and left without me ever having to think about them again.

But now it seemed that juggling two lives was beginning to wear me down.

Chapter 5

Pandora's Box

"Hi Taryn. Come in and sit down."
Simon pointed to the cosy looking little wicker chair with a tapestry cushion. It looked so welcoming, but I really didn't like it here anymore. Things inexplicably came up and I was running out of ways to avoid talking about the past. Why couldn't he just let me get on with my studies?

"How are you?" he asked, sitting down opposite me.

I sat, easing myself into place.

"Well, I'm fine," I said, finishing with my usual smile.

I was beginning to suspect that this gave too much away.

"Ok I can see that you don't seem too sure."

My face froze. He wasn't about to let up.

"So tell me then, how were you after our last session? Would you like to pick up from where we left off last time?"

Actually, I was feeling rather annoyed that I'd begun drinking a little more. *What was it that had been haunting me?*

"I can see there's something coming up. Sit for a moment with your eyes closed. Take some deep breaths and give yourself a moment to settle."

Closing my eyes, I hoped that the nervous twitches wouldn't chime in.

"Well, I should probably explore more about how I felt after my marriage ended, but, then there's my struggle with alcohol. Then I guess there's my so called relationship with Greg that probably pushed me over the edge!"

I rolled my eyes.

"Greg was your husband?"

I looked up, realising Simon had no idea where I was going with all this. How could he when I was confused myself?

"Oh no, sorry. Greg was someone I met when I came to Sydney years ago. Mitch was my ex-husband," I said. "In fact, if it weren't for finding Greg in bed with that girl, I probably would never have thought of Mitch ever again. Funny that!"

There was a silence. My body fidgeted uncomfortably.

"Is it funny, Taryn?"

Oh fuck. Well, here we go, I thought. But he had a point. It wasn't funny at all. Especially when Greg had chosen *her* to go away with after saying he couldn't take time off to meet me in Italy.

"I can see you're a little uncomfortable so let's just take a few deep breaths and settle into the energy of the room. That's right, close your eyes and breathe in."

Simon leaned back into the chair, prompting me to relax again. "Out and again in, and out, that's right."

With my eyes closed, sinking back into the soft cushion I caught a whiff of incense; Dragon's Blood. Its dewy fragrance soothed me as my mind desperately searched for an escape, anchored by this grounding process of breath and mindfulness. Gradually I became more aware of my body.

"Taryn, when you're ready. Maybe you would like to talk more about your husband Mitch first?"

I took in a deep breath when it should've been out. Where the Hell was I again? The room swam, or was it my head; dizzy, overwhelmed. I shook it off.

"No. Actually I would prefer to talk about Greg," I said, unsure why.

"I can see there's more going on. What else was happening for you at that time?"

"What do you mean?"

I was confused. *Wasn't I meant to be leading today's session?*

"Oh. Okay, well when I realised that my health was so bad, I decided to go wandering around the Mediterranean. You know, on a sabbatical."

I opened my eyes to see Simon still sitting quietly, patiently waiting for me to continue.

"What was so special about taking this trip? And where does Greg fit in? Please, close your eyes and try to relax. Just see where this takes you. That's right, relax. Breathe in and out."

I frowned. Good question.

No, actually, it was silly question. Greg began chasing me. He wanted to join me overseas and I said no. I needed space. The time away was important however I knew he was keen for me to return, and so I did – finding him there in bed with that girl. Now that wasn't a normal homecoming by any stretch of the imagination. I did feel like I was over him, so why did this scene still bother me so much?

"I can see you're not sure where to start, just talk about whatever comes up for you. What came to mind then?"

"Well, I thought it would be best if I left Australia for a while."

A lump formed in my throat. Now what, I wondered? I opened my eyes, taking in another breath, desperate for some sign. "Sorry," I stumbled over the word. What was I sorry about?

"That's ok. Take your time. What happened to make you take in a sharp breath? Was there something that you couldn't speak, maybe?" Gesturing to his throat with his long fingers, Simon reminded me of that comic Billy Connolly, with the same fleck in his voice. Scottish, if I remembered correctly.

We stared at each other momentarily and I couldn't help but be amused – like an eyeballing contest. Simon won; his deadpan face not allowing me to deflect.

"Why did you choose to leave Australia?"

Staring past Simon, I was convinced this counselling crap was nuts.

"Taryn, I know this is hard, but I can tell there's a lot more going on behind that look. Your shoulders, the way you're sitting upright, that's defensive. I'm not trying to hurt you."

Stunned, I sat back. What the fuck? Prick! Why were all these men in my life demanding so much from me? But then I thought, actually they weren't. It was me who demanded more. I wanted to be noticed. To be heard. And this was clearly my moment to speak up. Part of me was beginning to understand how important this all was.

"I know," I responded calmly.

"Good. Close your eyes and just let your body rest again. Take your time to consider your reaction to what you said, and ask your body to let you know what it needs. Can you do that?"

"Sure. Ok. Well, you see this trip overseas." I sighed, sinking into the past. "It was magnificent just living day to day, surviving on the basics without the pressure. No stress."

Where was I going with this?

"I hear you saying words like 'survive' and 'no stress'. What does that mean for you?"

This reflection helped; everything began to flow.

"Well, after my holiday, or what was going to be an open ended trip, I came home but I knew I felt different. Something changed and I realised that I couldn't live in the same way I used to. Even Greg didn't matter."

There was a moment's silence as this sunk in.

"Greg didn't matter," Simon repeated.

That sounded right. He didn't matter. None of it did; my career, success. And would I have had the courage to end it with him?

Probably not.

"You're smiling."

"Yes. I'm smiling because I'm pleased that I could let go of my old life. Drinking, partying. I was over it. It was like I broke a pattern at last, even though it wasn't what I call a great way of discovering this about myself. That morning, it's like fate had stepped in."

The words came more easily now that I could make sense of how I felt. My eyes opened, staring up at the ceiling, darting past Simon.

"It's like something was screaming loudly for me to get out, like my body had to crash under the pressure of juggling everything and I just couldn't do it anymore!"

Simon copied my posture, watching my flailing hands carefully then leaning forward as I had. I began to remember everything I'd endured in the past few years.

"Gosh. No wonder I was so exhausted." I smiled again, looking at Simon.

"What do you mean?"

"Well I guess something deep inside me was screaming to be heard ever since my divorce from Mitch."

My eyes were still locked with Simon's. I felt silly. It was hard to describe such things, but Simon was patient.

"Even with him I stayed because I was tired, but then when he no longer wanted me I felt rejected. I had no idea who I was."

The tears welled; a lump formed in my throat.

"Just take a few deep breaths. I see you're holding your stomach and looking a little stressed. What else is happening when you remember this?"

I could feel the tightness in my brows as they furrowed at the notion of me going back there.

"I don't want to say," I whispered, a glimpse of the shame too much for me to continue.

"We have time. Just sit with this. Okay?" Simon's voice was soothing, making me less likely to bolt out through the door. I had a choice; I could leave, temptation stirring as I peered closely at the handle. But this time I no longer desired to run away. How could I? Running away had never worked before. I smiled more, almost hysterical with the realisation that by being still I could finally escape.

"Okay you look like you're in a good place with this. What's happening for you now?"

My smile was wiped away by a sudden urge to cry. My arms moved forward as I clasped my hands together between my knees then up to my belly as I tried hard not to wail.

"Let's see if your inner voice within the region your belly, has something to say. Maybe something will come up and speak for itself?"

My heart was having palpitations. Anxiety was kicking in again but this time I was ready. Turning my attention back to Simon I breathed in, noticing that something did want to speak up.

"Yes there is something," I shared nervously, the tears abated. My heart began to beat faster again, making me a little nauseous. "Well, after finding that girl at Greg's place, I couldn't stomach food for weeks. The humility of it all was too much. Like when Mitch left me to go live with that girl – I was so shocked!"

Everything came out, anger regurgitated.

"The shock? Is this Greg?"

How ironic that both homecomings had shattered my illusion of what it meant to be loved. How could they have loved me when they treated me in that way? Was this because of what I had witnessed in the relationship between my mum and dad?

"Both actually, would you believe? But I'll start with my ex-husband. Sorry to be all over the place!"

Simon smiled. "Go on, it's okay. Soon it will all make sense."

I was twenty years old when I met Mitch. Working as receptionist with his sister Mandy, she had wanted me to meet her boyfriends' brother, inviting me to a party where he was hovering around acting like an idiot. I wasn't interested in either of them at all, but in the end it was Mitch who wore me down. When his sister invited me to sleep over, he greeted me each morning with a cup of tea and a smile, afterward pursuing me relentlessly. Exhausted with juggling university and working weekends, then Monday's 9-5 I had no energy for boys at all.

A few years earlier when I was seventeen an older man had ended our third date by seducing me in the back seat of his car. Pressured into having sex, it was quick and disappointing just like this man turned out to be. He stopped calling, leaving me very confused until I bumped into him with another girl by his side. It was awkward to say the least.

By the time I was confronted by Ian a year later I'd become an expert at knocking back the vodka, deeming any sexual encounter ambiguous and liberal. This in itself created chaos when he insisted we were meant to marry. The sex with him was great, but settling down and having kids was not on my agenda at all. Who was he kidding? We had nothing in common and I had plans for a career and to see the world.

Mitch made it known that he could see what was going on, which had me intrigued. How could he possibly know when I had hidden that relationship so well? Conveniently he would show up to visit his sister at our work, always available to keep me company and listen to my woes over a drink. Eventually after a year of his merciless pursuit, I rendered myself to him under a cloak of tequila slammers, although he tried to resist. We both weren't after the sex, it was intimacy and belonging we both craved – the one thing we had in common which was more than enough for me. But then he wanted more. He wanted a relationship so I ended things.

Sadly he didn't take the breakup too well. Volatile, his father threw him out of their home. A while afterward when we began bonding as friends, his parents moved interstate. This was when he began calling constantly, begging me to take him back otherwise he would kill himself. This seemed like a ridiculous notion, so I stood firm, only seeing him again when admitted to hospital for emergency surgery on his eye.

Upon being discharged, I tried to find appropriate post care accommodation, but there was nowhere for him to go. What else could I do? Near blind he needed a nurse to bathe and apply drops which I was experienced at administering, therefore we were suddenly living together which is when he bought me a ring. There was no proposal, only his need for stability and acceptance from his mum who was Catholic, threatening to disown him if we weren't in a serious relationship.

A few years later when twenty four I was tired, my body already beginning to rebel. In the lead up to our wedding which I had pushed back for as long as I could, bouts of stomach problems were diagnosed as stress related. During this time I got to see just how unpredictable my future husband was. Throwing our lives into chaos, our weekends were wasted with arguments that were never resolved. We spent four toxic years like this, splitting up then getting back together every time he made me feel guilty and afraid that he would do something stupid, like kill himself.

When I was fifteen there was a boy who attempted to take his life when I wouldn't go out with him. He survived but that episode had left its mark on me.

Mitch and I eventually bought a house up in the hills, giving us something to focus on as the wedding loomed. Our lives were interspersed with holding dinner parties for friends on the weekend, to working hard during the week. For the first time in years I thought we were going to make it after all, and added to this my career in advertising was slowly taking off.

"Hi sweetie, I'm home!" I slurred, barely able to walk through the door, my face still flushed after six or so drinks, but who was counting?

Giggling with this realisation, tumbling into our bedroom I heard another noise from behind. Without any prior warning, Mitch had grabbed my arm, forcing me to fall onto the bed, my shoes flinging off with the impact as his face came within centimetres of mine.

"It's 9.30pm Taryn!" he screamed. "Your promotion was just an excuse for you to go out and party, you fat bitch!!"

Shocked, staring up at my future husband who looked like he was about to murder me, I was momentarily terrified. This man was never going to let me be happy so it was time for me to stand up and fight.

"Excuse me!" I yelled back in his face. "How dare you speak to me like that?"

It was bad enough I was worried about telling him I would be home late. My body trembled, pent up anger gushed his way.

"I'm *sick* of it; I'm sick of *you!*"

He didn't move. I waited for my words to slap him, knowing they would enrage him more.

Mitch yelled back at me louder, mouth wide and ferocious. "You said you'd be home after one drink! I expected you home at 8pm! Do you hear, idiot!!"

His face contorted, frightening when in full flight like I hadn't seen in years. With this in mind, predicting my inherent danger, I pulled him down onto the bed so I could pounce onto his lap. Grabbing his shirt collar I leaned forward, my eyes boring into his.

"Listen *you* idiot, I'm a grown-up okay! I'm home now so calm down!"

Shocked at my move, he retaliated twice as fierce.

"You fucking whore! I know you've been with someone, haven't you?!"

Mitch was hysterical, swinging me around with the strength of ten men, pinning me down and completely freaking me out. This time surely I was going to die, but at least it would all come to an end. I was over it, living like this. The shaking in my body began as I stared into those manic, accusing eyes.

"I said get off me, you fucking idiot! If I had found someone else, why would I bother coming home to you? I've had enough!"

I hated this man, my future husband.

"I feel *nothing* for you! You are *nothing to me*!" I said again with more conviction.

"What did you say?" Mitch yelled louder, his face close to mine expecting this would intimidate me further, but it didn't. Something had shifted; I was no longer the same person.

Getting away from his grip, I raced down the hall into our neat, tiny kitchen, aware he was in pursuit. My eyes scanned for something to use for protection, making me feel disgusted even more.

"Get back here!"

Lunging for my throat as I turned away, it was too late to grab a knife. The idea of killing him wasn't too far off. Realising what I was looking for, Mitch grabbed each wrist with his large hands, squeezing hard to cause pain.

"Get off, will you!" I screamed, pushing back into his groin with my bum, our arms up above our heads as he held my wrists even tighter. Managing to get one hand free, ducking underneath to turn around and come face to face with him, he pushed me harder up against the sink, his hands moving down firmly onto my shoulders.

"Let me go!"

My heels fixed beneath the cupboard door to give me leverage, rising to meet his 6 foot frame, making it difficult for him to keep me pinned. My solid build contained strength plus I was much fitter than he.

"Yes, go ahead you cowardly fucking pig. *Hit me*! I want you to give it your best shot, I'm over it!" I shouted, my body shaking with rage.

Any moment he would break, I knew it.

"C'mon. Get it over with!"

We were deadlocked; staring each other down, waiting for the other to crack. Like a possessed woman, my eyes flared at him. He grabbed my upper arms in an attempt to take back the power.

"Kill me you fucking coward!! C'mon!" I taunted, no longer recognising this person I had become.

Then suddenly Mitch hurled backwards, his stunned look mirroring the horrific vision he was witnessing. I could feel my face stretched, veins in my neck so tightly strung I thought they were about to pop. He backed away, leaning against the sideboard adjacent me before taking a deep breath and slumping to the floor. My heart was thumping, my breathing long, deep and erratic as I prepared to flee.

"Oh my God, what have I done?" he sobbed there on the floor. His body jerked, tears falling uncontrollably as his arms fell by his side. I didn't take my eyes off those big, menacing hands which only moments earlier had tried to strangle me.

Mitch looked anything but dangerous.

"I never wanted to hurt you," he cried out, not looking up.

It was ugly; he was ugly. I no longer cared at all. Keeping vigilance, the clock above our fridge read 9.52pm. Only twenty two minutes earlier my day had ended well, with news of a promotion now tarnished as I stood watching him moan and cry like a baby. Clinging onto the bench I felt nothing; survival mechanisms in full swing keeping me safe and secure there.

Slowly this strange room began to look familiar again as adrenalin dissipated in my bloodstream. On the ledge of our pine sideboard, where Mitch lay crumbled on the floor, I could see our engagement cards stacked up on the note pad I was using to send everyone 'thank you' notes. The digital clock showed 10.38pm. Mitch's eyes were closed. The fridge whirred, reminding me how exhausted I was. Slowly I set down onto my heels before walking into our bathroom where I observed a hand – mine, reach for the shower tap.

I moaned under the welcoming caress of hot water as it hit the ache in my shoulder, easing it slightly. This was where he had pinned me, trapped like an animal fending for my life. It was 1am when his snoring confirmed it was safe for me to head off to bed, grabbing a blanket to throw over him along the way. Six months later the wedding went ahead.

The morning after our wedding was the day I tried to forget. Mitch's parents informed me of his massive debt that was to become my responsibility. Astounded by his parents' admissions as we stood there blinking in shock, he could see I was wounded, listening on as his embarrassed mother tried not to meet my eyes. I cried all the way to our honeymoon, a small B&B where I ended up keeping the waiter and cook company, leaving Mitch alone to return to our room where he was crashed out drunk like on our wedding the night before.

During those five days we didn't fight, we didn't have sex. We barely smiled at each other, too stunned to comprehend the reality. What had we done? He knew the shock of his financial news was too much for me to bear. He tried being nice, but something had changed yet again. Making things worse, when we returned home I was confronted with another surprise. A policeman was on our doorstep to issue Mitch with a summons for DUI (drinking under the influence) meaning he could no longer work as a sales rep on the road.

This was to be the end of our very short marriage but we weren't to know that yet. I had more important things to worry about, such as how would we pay our mortgage? Already doing well at the agency, I didn't want to take on a second job again. But I had no choice. Mitch had to stay at home while I worked in the city at an ice creamery to make the extra cash. Our relationship was dead. He became reserved, passive and depressed while I became more aggressive and angry. Shortly after, a friend of his came up with a job offer for him to work at a video store. The downside was that the hours were from 6am to 3pm meaning I had to drive him there, leaving the Adelaide Hills at 4am. We no longer saw each other. His guilt for my dilemma making me disillusioned and tired all the time, soon reclusive from friends and family.

After the year was up, he finally got his license back but it was clear that he was distracted by other things. I knew something wasn't right, asking him to talk to me as I prepared to call it quits.

Then another event changed our lives. He was landscaping our three quarter acre block when I heard an explosion. Racing outside I could see the fumes surrounding his body, his eyes blinking back in surprise. Then he got up and raced around screaming, I could see an outline of the heat from an invisible flame.

"What happened?" I screamed.

He had thrown petrol onto the pile of logs and leaned too close when lighting a match which ignited up into his face. Bringing him inside to the bathroom where I filled up the sink with cold water, we both watched in horror as his face began to melt. I called an ambulance but they said it would take too long, so I drove him down to the burns unit where he was admitted immediately.

After he was discharged a week later, I was once again undertaking his care. Bathing the peeling flesh and lathering his face with medical cream, after a while the scabs formed and peeled away revealing tender new skin. This was an extremely difficult time for us, but one that I believed had brought us together. His ordeal made him grow up, and I saw a different man. Once recovered, he became more involved in the video store business saying he wanted to earn more money so that we could have a proper honeymoon and start again. I truly wanted to believe that he was up to the task. After all, wasn't marriage tough and challenging for everyone?

Some days he was working later than others. There were many occasions when he was not around at all. It was becoming increasingly difficult to communicate with him anymore. Asking him questions only made him respond with a passive self-blaming dialogue.

"I've been such a bad husband, you deserve so much more. Don't worry. I'm going to make this all up to you, I promise," he said.

A few weeks later when I came home, the house was extremely quiet. Looking around, I called out.

"Hellooo?"

There was no answer. Mitch wasn't there. This was weird. Something was wrong. Scanning the long hallway down to the lounge, I thought maybe he had crashed out on the sofa. Wandering down, the room looked unfamiliar; our lounge, everything was gone! Realising we may have an intruder, I quietly moved back through the house, prepared for a possible attack. Backing up to the front door near our bedroom another fear arose. Was Mitch bashed to death on our bed?

I gasped; my heart pounding. Nothing could've prepared me for what I saw next. Our bed was gone. I tried to make sense of the scene, rationalising that maybe he was out buying us a new bedroom suite. But Mitch knew better than to spend money given his debt. I felt sick, looking up at the mosquito net dangling from ceiling that only this morning had covered our bed. Paralysed, the minutes ticked by as my brain filtered through what reasons there could be. Another twenty minutes passed before I felt it was safe to investigate, sauntering back through to check each room, our kitchen untouched since we left for work that morning, the back door securely locked.

Perplexed, sitting down on the dusty old dining chairs I hated so much, another thought occurred to me. I don't know why, but I went over to the side board and pulled open the kitchen cupboards and drawers.

"Are you kidding me?" I screamed, struggling to catch my breath.

The cutlery was gone, along with utensils given to us as wedding gifts from friends – not mine. This wasn't a robbery. Not by a stranger anyway. Wandering back into our bedroom I noticed the remaining cupboard. Like the dining suite it belonged to this old house when we had purchased it a year ago. Opening the door, it revealed an empty space next to where my clothes remained.

Numb, my eyes followed the fading light back into the lounge where I collapsed. Thoughts sporadically filtered through as recent events leading up to this day were scanned. Conversations we had were relatively normal, and yes Mitch had been acting a little strange but… my heart raced even faster. I felt violently ill. Could he have really packed up and disappeared in one day? After all that we'd been through, why would he do this to me?

That girl and those secret phone calls down the hall; his contemplative moods after our argument when had I found perfume hidden on Christmas Eve that I didn't receive the next day.

My hand reached over to the phone. Lifting it I dialled, calling his boss.

"Hi, Alan speaking."

"Yes, hi Alan, how are you? It's Taryn," I spoke carefully, feeling the panic rising again.

"Oh, hi! How's it going'?" he asked, seemingly relaxed.

"Not bad thanks. Is Mitch still there by any chance?"

"No he left an hour ago. Isn't he home yet?"

Was I just being overly dramatic?

"It's just that I'm a little worried because he hasn't pulled in the drive as yet, and he said that it would only take him a few minutes to drop off some stuff."

I began shaking, struggling with the little white lie I was forced to tell, hoping Alan wold provide a clue. Nervously fumbling for a cigarette, something else was sitting there in the back of my mind. Who was that girl he had once talked about?

"Ok, yes he's probably gone over to Jasmine's house. What's her number again? Sorry I'm just a little rattled and can't remember it?" I said, sucking in some air.

The air was still, I caught my breath.

"Yeah I think Jasmine was with him, so she would know what's up. Maybe she's home now. Hang on I'll get it for you," he said casually, putting down the receiver for a moment.

I nearly choked, struggling with hyperventilation. Something was gnawing away at my insides, engulfing me with dread.

"Are you there?" Alan asked.

"Yes I am." I managed to respond.

"No worries, love. Here it is…" He announced each number as I wrote slowly with shaking fingers.

"Great. Thanks Alan," I said, dropping the receiver quickly.

My hands began sweating, still stuck to the phone as I picked up again and dialled. What was I going to say?

"Hello?"

It was an older woman's voice; must be Jasmine's Mother.

"Yes hello, my name is Taryn. Can I speak to my husband please?"

Without question, the phone was being passed to someone else.

"What are you doing!?"

It was Mitch. His tone was a deep rumble.

Rage filled the space in me where fear and confusion had loomed for hours.

"What? What am I doing? What are *you* doing?" I screamed.

"I'm with Jasmine, don't fuck with me. I have left you."

His words were terse, threatening even. How could he justify this move? And for that matter, why would I fuck with him? I couldn't speak.

"Don't call here again!" Acrimonious, he then hung up.

Was this a joke? Sitting there, the beep taunting me, I couldn't believe it. I'm his wife whom he swore in front of everyone that day in a Catholic Church to love honour and protect. What made him think it was okay to abandon me – and take up with a girl? The painful realisation tore at my heart. My stomach retched, sending bile spilling everywhere as I struggled to get back onto my feet.

It was the coldness of Mitch's departure that shocked me the most. All those years I tried to get away from him and he disappeared in one day. It was over for him, but only the beginning for me.

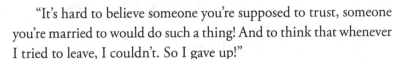

"It's hard to believe someone you're supposed to trust, someone you're married to would do such a thing! And to think that whenever I tried to leave, I couldn't. So I gave up!"

"Gave up, what do you mean?" Simon asked.

I didn't want to be with him but he had no-one else so what was I to do? I gave up believing in my dreams. Drinking helped me to recover from the shock after he left."

I was angry for all the years I had lost, putting up with the drama and his threats. Simon looked over at the clock on the small side table.

"Okay let's talk about this binge drinking? We have time." He leaned back, crossing his gangly legs. "Is drinking still a problem?"

I nearly laughed. "No not at all. I can hardly manage a glass of wine these days."

Casting my mind back, something stirred. A memory made me sit up in surprise.

"Taryn, are you okay?"

Regaining my composure, I chose another train of thought to share.

"Truth is, it was a real problem back then but nobody took me seriously. No-one could help. I had to get sick all these years later, giving up everything I'd ever worked for!"

I looked at Simon as I prepared to share something that no-one else knew.

"No one took you seriously?" he repeated.

"No." I thought about it some more. "Just after Mitch disappeared, I called Alcoholics Anonymous. I needed help, and you know what the operator told me?"

I was agitated, the room felt warm and as if on cue Simon stood up to open the window.

"What did they tell you?"

"Well, the lady on the phone told me I was only a binge drinker and not to worry." I shrugged my shoulders. "Ok, yeah thanks. That's great news, I told her. But I was not happy. I could drink between twelve to sixteen vodkas a night." I looked at Simon. He showed no disgust, but I still felt ashamed. "I wasn't bragging for God's sake. I was left wondering what on Earth constituted a serious problem then?"

Simon scratched his goatee with long fingers, his mouth opened slightly, about to speak but he waited.

"You've come a long way. Such a destructive cycle of working long hours and drinking on top of so much grief was difficult yes? And sadly it sounds like you spoke with someone - one person - who wasn't on the ball. AA is a great organisation supporting millions worldwide."

I looked up, nodding gingerly, no longer heavily burdened by feelings of shame as the relief of sharing took its place.

"Yeah, yeah I know. I've learned a lot over the years since then that we can't taint everyone because of one bad experience, but it hurt!"

"Yes it hurt. And the drinking, it all took a toll on your body, but it's not your fault, you do realise this."

Regaining focus on his face, he had my attention.

"What do you mean?"

"Well, you grew up with anger and alcoholism in the home, and then once out on your own, you tried to take care of your husband, all the while never abandoning him. You didn't leave, Taryn. Mitch did. And when you reached out for help you felt rejected, so the only way you could manage these feelings was to repress them by drinking. Does this sound right?"

Oh boy, it sure did. The gravity of all that rejection and abandonment was overwhelming. My eyes began to mist. Simon leaned forward with the box of tissues I had become reliant on.

"Thanks," I sniffled gratefully.

"Sadly we have a culture that drives heavy drinking behaviour and it sounds to me like no-one stepped up when you reached out for help. But by being here and talking now you're confronting all this. You've been able to help yourself."

Tears were forming, I sniffed as one sneaked out, landing on my flushed cheek.

"Does this make sense of the feeling you have in your body right now?"

"Yes," I answered, the lump in my throat almost crippling me I wanted to howl like a child, but still couldn't.

"You are surrounded by friends here. Remember that. I'm here to help you learn how to let go. You need to forgive yourself. You did what you had to in order to survive."

Simon sat quietly while I struggled with the grief, overwhelmed by realisations repressed for decades as they resurfaced in such little time.

"Okay I think we've had a good session today. What do you think?"

I laughed through the final few tears, grateful for not having escaped.

"Yes, this is quite enough for today!"

He smiled, standing up to open the door for me.

"It's time to go home. Go have a massage and drink some herbal tea. But, most importantly, be kind to yourself, okay? Remember, our childhood is a very impressionable time and you did the best you could. Your capacity to care for others meant you learned to over cope in later life, looking after the needs of these men before your own."

"Thanks Simon," I said, surprised I finally meant it.

After I left his clinic, I drove over to Balmoral Beach and sat in my favourite spot overlooking the marina. Boats were anchored, swaying in the breeze. Kids were playing with the waves that were creeping in to wet their toes. Sitting cross legged on the lawn, I cried for that little girl who still couldn't talk openly for fear of being judged. How could I ever tell Simon about Jewel? Why did I always feel so ashamed? Watching the kids, something anchored deep beneath the surface was hankering for attention.

Simon hadn't probed, so I didn't share what happened when I was eight years old. Sitting there it was time for me to face it, and finally let it go.

It was a Sunday, our family day when we would visit my favourite cousins.

"They're here!" Oscar's shrill five year old voice rallied everyone else outside.

Dad pulled up in the carport under the shade where we all rolled out of the overheating van just as Aunty Rena and Uncle John walked over to help mum with her bags.

"How's our apple pie?" Aunty Rena cooed in my ear, hugging me so tight between her huge breasts.

"I'm good!" I answered happily, breaking away to be with my cousins.

After the fanfare had subsided, my uncle and Dad walked around the garden discussing the next landscaping idea as we kids loitered around our mothers for a while.

"Oh Rena, what smells so nice?" Mum asked. I was also curious; a decadent aroma having wafted past my nose.

"Hmm, we have a goulash tonight," she shared, a spark of excitement in her voice. I loved the way she spoke so passionately about food.

"What's goulash?" Mum asked.

"Oh, meat, and vegetables from our garden," she answered, gradually heading back to the house. We all followed inside, keen to get near the food platters over on the bench top. "Ah, and we also have fresh apples for a pie!"

Teasing us kids, Aunty Rena opened the oven door to give us a glimpse of the rising dough.

"Here, come in. Come in!"

She gestured to my mother whilst trying to stuff a piece of bread laden with cheese and bratwurst into her mouth. "Eat! Try these olives from Maria next door. They're delicious with this bread."

I watched as Mum tried to dodge and weave the morsel of food hovering near her mouth.

"Oh no. That's ok. I had a piece of toast with vegemite a few hours ago, Rena. I'm fine. I can wait 'till dinner, and so can you!"

My mother's growl had me retreat in fear of being slapped. Her limbs were thin compared to the ham bones on my aunty, reflecting one of the many differences between these women.

Tina's fingers locked into mine, pulling me back outside. "C'mon, let's go see where Oscar is!"

Running down around the corner of the house we saw him there stopping on the kerb, waving at two boys across the road before looking behind to make sure we were coming.

"Hi Franko, hi Hans," he yelled.

"Who are they?" I asked Tina. We stood next to Oscar, each holding an outstretched hand to walk him across the road.

"Franko and Hans have just moved in," she said, nodding toward a red brick home on the corner. "Come, let's say hi!"

I couldn't help but notice how big they were compared to the tiny stature of my cousins, even towering over me.

"Hi, who are you?" The larger one asked, looking at me in a funny way. He was almost 5ft tall with shoulders about 60cm in width, overshadowing Oscar who was vying for attention at his knees.

"This is our cousin!" Oscar proudly stated, pleased to get some attention again.

I smiled at him, a recent missing tooth adding to his cuteness.

"Hi I'm Hans. This is my little brother Franko," he said, flicking his hand across his brother's head.

Franko flinched, staring sideways at me. He was not quite as tall, but still broad with a fixed square jaw like his brothers. Small eyes peered through heavy brows, their faces ruby red from sunburn.

"Why do you sound funny? Are you from another country?" I asked curiously.

"What do you mean?! We live here!" Hans pointed his finger into my forehead, easily intimidating me before Tina jumped in between us.

"C'mon, let's go into the back yard. They have a huge swing set!"

These boys were eyeing me in a way that made me feel uncomfortable, but I didn't know why.

"We only let pretty girls come over, so let's go," whispered Hans in an arrogant tone.

"Oh that's nice," I responded, still feeling a little uneasy. "How old are you two anyway?"

"Here. Come inside." Hans insisted. "I'm thirteen next week and Franko is eleven and a half."

Hans smiled as everyone came bounding in behind us, helping me to relax a little as we admired the toys sprawled everywhere along the hallway. Tina and Oscar were thrilled to find Mr Potato Head which kept them distracted as I looked around.

"Where's your Mum and Dad?" I asked, peering around corners into the adjacent rooms.

"Don't worry 'bout them, they're at work," answered Franko, grabbing my hand firm before dragging me through the house.

"Come. Come in here, have a look at my Lego," Franko insisted.

"It's ok, I can follow," I said, trying not to sound scared, but I was. Something did not feel right. I looked around to see Hans kneeling with Tina and Oscar in the hallway.

"Where are we going?"

"Just in there," Franko said, shoving me into a bedroom.

"Where are they going?" Hans mimicked, wandering in after us. Franko laughed but I wasn't amused at all.

"I think I'll go back out with them," I said, watching Tina's head poke back in the doorway.

Franko ushered her out, then chased Oscar back down the hall, making them believe it was a game as they raced toward the back door believing we were all about to follow. But we weren't. Franko came back into the room, making eye contact with Hans who was standing, blocking my way.

"Don't muck around. You said we were going outside! Let's go into the backyard," I said, hearing Tina and Oscar laughing.

"Oh c'mon. We're just having fun!" Franko giggled stupidly, side stepping his brother, banging into him just as Tina and Oscar came rushing in again, squeezing past Hans' legs to grab my hand.

"C'mon, let's go outside," Oscar screamed, giggling again as Franko chased him back out.

I was about to follow when Hans grabbed me hard, hurting my arm.

"Let go of me!" I cried.

Franko, Tina and Oscar were outside again, when Hans pushed me back into the room. He closed the door behind us.

"Hey, it's dark. Open the door?" I asked, trying not to plead. After all, this was only a game I reminded myself; and a stupid one at that. But his eyes looked mean, and my heart pounded as claustrophobia set in. I needed air, and wanted to see the light but there were only shards jostling through holes in the curtains.

"It's not too dark," Hans mocked me, opening the door a little for Franko to push his way in again. "Come here!"

"I'm tired of this game. Let me out." I said sternly, aware Franko had moved in the way, leaning forward into my face, trying to kiss me on the lips.

"What are you doing?"

Trying not to panic, I realised Hans was leaning up against the door, towering over me with Franko moving in behind, wrapping his arms around my body, shuffling me toward Hans. I didn't want to believe this was happening. They had me trapped in between.

"Get off me! Get off," I screamed, kicking and lashing out however I could. "Tina! Oscar! Go get mum. Pleaaase!" I yelled, hoping they may hear my screams through the bedroom window.

Franko leered at me, pinned up against his brother.

"You love it, don't you? Let's have some fun, then?" He licked my lips with his disgusting, smelly tongue.

My head began to spin; their hot bodies suffocating me. The room smelled musky and dank as hands began moving over my body, but what they were doing was beyond my comprehension.

I just knew it was wrong. It was getting hard to breathe with my mouth pressed up against Hans making it difficult to turn my face sideways. His towelling shirt felt damp against my cheek as Franko held my hands tightly behind my back, hurting my wrists.

It was all hurting. I didn't want to die.

"Let me out!" The sound of my cousins laughing filtered through, helping me to detach. Dizzy, barely breathing from the effort, suddenly I was soaring overhead, free to play outside.

The door finally opened, giving me an opportunity to run without looking back, panting as I ducked past my parents and crashed into my aunty.

"What's this?" Aunty Rena screamed over the stereo. "Pete, turn that down, will you!? Are you ok my beautiful apple blossom?"

Looking concerned, she spoke soothingly, scanning deeply into my eyes. Could she what I had just endured?

"I'm not beautiful," I cried, tears rolling down my face.

Aunty Rena squeezed me more as the other kids ran in to throw their arms around me.

"Of course you are," she said, trying to ease my stress.

"I don't want to be," I answered.

"Sorry we ran out," apologized Tina. She was oblivious to the real dilemma.

Aunty Rena swivelled around to tell them off.

"Oh you rotten little monsters! Did they tease you and run away?"

"No. I just got scared when I couldn't see them!"

"Oh don't be so bloody dramatic. Go play with your cousins nicely!" Mum yelled out from across the dining room.

I stared, stunned at her rage. No longer sure of what to say, I made the decision to push the whole episode to the back of my mind.

Mum hollered again, "Now go outside. Dinner will be ready soon."

Why was she so angry, I wondered? Then I saw the reason - a half empty Vodka bottle standing on the table in front of Dad.

"Hi love!" he said, smiling as he waved.

"Off you go then and play like a good girl. She is beautiful isn't she?" he bragged to my uncle, bringing the glass up to his lips.

The numbness wasn't new, but disappointment was. Food consoled me, disarming pain in my attempt to block everything out.

Chapter 6

The Soul Emerges

Barely awake, my hand reached out toward the vibrating device.

"Hello?"

"Hey Jewel, where are you?"

My faculties were slow, trying hard to register where I knew the voice from when it hit me. I was late for work, thanks to the deaf old woman living upstairs above my apartment. She had put her TV volume up so loud only to fall asleep, meaning for me, having conked out shortly after eight pm, my sleep was interrupted. Once my adrenals were aroused, sending a surge through my body that would not dissipate, I had to stay awake! The effect was like having four shots of short black coffees. I would be operating in a foggy haze for the rest of the day.

"Shit, oh sorry Jana! I'm on my way!"

Quickly I jumped out of bed, fumbling around on the floor for my leggings and a t-shirt, running down the hall with Jana still on the phone.

"Who's there waiting?" I asked, forcing a foot through the stretchy fabric of my leggings, which of course weren't co-operating. My toe got stuck.

"No-one yet, but Tim's called a few times. We missed you yesterday. Is everything ok?"

My studies had seeded a process of unfolding that needed my full attention. In order to grasp meanings I was sporadically taking days off, calling to cancel on the morning I was rostered. I was one of the most reliable girls, so I knew they would be curious about what was distracting me.

"Yes I'm fine thanks, sorry! I know it's hard for you." Finally, my last few toes poked through, giving me a foot to balance on as I began pulling on the other leg.

"If Tim calls again this morning can I tell him yes he can see you?"

A triathlete from New Zealand, Tim was tall, lean and quite fit which was great for a girl like me who loved the physical aspect of this work. With a shaved head showing blonde fibres with no grey, I guessed him to be in his mid 30's.

"Yes, yes I'm on my way. If he calls, can we make it eleven then? I'm just leaving now." Grabbing my handbag by the door it was already 10.38am but I knew I could get there and shower in under twenty minutes. Jana knew I could too.

"Oh perfect! Ok, see you soon, and, and drive carefully!"

She hung up.

A fit and compliant client became my favourite after all the months of seeing less than great physical specimens. Tim and other fit men became a specialty of sorts, given there was no deeper meaning beyond challenging the body's capacity for endurance. With these younger testosterone fuelled men it was all about the sex and as such it conveniently tapped into my desire to relieve sexual energy. The more competitive they acted, the more I utilised my own power of control spurned by contempt for men. I realised that as a young woman growing up it was deemed inappropriate to be so highly sexed and free, and I hated that. Why was I expected to repress that part of me? I could explore the depths of my pleasure seeking fantasies here.

Racing in, Jana greeted me with news that Tim was on his way. Ten minutes later I took him up to our favourite room in the second adjoining terrace facing the harbour - but we weren't in there for the view. The more often I saw him, the more competitive he got, which was beginning to challenge me mentally. Often getting into the lunge position, a great workout for the butt, my routine became quite exhausting so there was no room for mental fatigue.

As was his usual style, he threw me face down onto the bed. Sweat began seeping down from the hairline on his firm belly where it then dripped, tickling my lower back. I wasn't happy. Having a stranger's body fluids anywhere near wasn't ideal. Luckily my head was facing the pillow after a rather amorous attempt at doggy so he wouldn't see me grimace. He came quickly, grunting with force as his hands gripped my hair. Only six minutes had passed.

"You're lovely, Jewel," he whispered in my ear, the ebb of passion subsiding as we fell alongside each other.

Turning toward him, I smiled.

"Thanks," I said, cautious of that look in his eyes. I'd seen it many times before with men.

Tim was getting way too close. I needed to resurface, figuring his last few words were just a lapse in rationale that most men usually experience after orgasm, which tends to lower their inhibitions. Grabbing his head I looked into his eyes.

"Tim, you're a great fuck, baby!" The air was dense from the heat as we lay there still recovering.

"Really though, I've not ever felt so comfortable with any one; never thought I would," he said, turning his head to look away.

"That's lovely, me too." I lied, wishing I hadn't. Sometimes it was appropriate to pacify them in here.

"My wife, she left me a few years ago and I was devastated. Had my own business and lost everything. Thought I had it all."

Quietly I listened. My heart was heavier than usual. Hearing such words merely mirrored my own experience.

"Yes, Tim. Sometimes it's like that. But you're here now, and you've built your empire back up, remember?"

He didn't say anything for a while before turning to me again.

"You've been there too, haven't you?" he asked, his eyes wide, insisting that I be as frank as he had bravely been.

What to do, I thought? Should I just relax and be honest? I was a bit frazzled; tired of having to mask my feelings, plus thanks to Simon's unflappable support and guidance I was more comfortable speaking up.

"Yes but I don't wish to talk about it, ok? That was years ago and I've moved on. You will too, Tim."

It was time for me to shift the mood. Moving onto my side, stroking his shaft I shot him a sinister, naughty smile. His smile reappeared, yet I couldn't help but feel lousy for using his confession as an opportunity to manipulate the situation a little, but I needed to stay in control.

We survived the rest of the session with an unspoken agreement registering between us - no more getting too close.

"Hey Jewel," Tim started to say as I was showing him to the door.

I stopped and waited for him to finish.

"Yes?"

He looked a little nervous.

"Well, I know you don't always come in on Mondays but sometimes I just call and come in when they say you are on the roster, only to be told that you haven't turned up. Then they suggest other girls but I don't stay."

"Yes, that's been happening a lot, I believe!"

I tried not to show how pissed off I was. Jana was trying to keep our regulars, moving them around and saying we weren't available so as to keep new girls from disappearing so soon. With the onslaught of internet dating sites, more men were seeking free sex on line making the lesser ranked establishments null and void. This forced the more daringly outrageous sex worker to seek out high class places like ours. But they weren't interested in building relationships, only focussed on fast cash. For management this short term high voltage sex was the drawcard to keeping and attracting new clients. It was becoming a competitive more gratuitous game; one I didn't want to play.

People were getting greedy. The clients were more demanding, asking for kissing which meant my regulars were becoming scarce. Knowing protocol was instant dismissal if management found out that my client had direct contact with me, I decided to shake things up and be more self-reliant.

"Maybe if I give you my mobile, you'll just text me on the day to check if I'm here. How does that sound?"

"That's great. Yes I will only text on the morning. Thanks Jewel."

Tim left with a bigger smile than usual, but mine was completely gone.

Was it the right risk to take for the sake of keeping him happy and me earning good money? Up until now I had been strict with my boundaries, but tiredness and familiarity was nurturing complacency. I was taking the easy route, and knew it.

It didn't take long for his text messages to begin, sometimes just to say hi. A week later Tim made me feel a little nervous as he sat me down on the bed. Still dressed, he gradually moved his fingers along my stomach, stretching me out as they walked along my breast bone. Circling a nipple under the tight red lycra dress, his other hand stretched up to move my arm above my head as we swivelled around onto the bed, with the other hand fumbling for his trouser zip. Momentarily, he bent down to kick off his unlaced trainers. I waited, breathing slowly, unsure what to do but knowing he was a man with a purpose today. He wanted to be in control.

Pulling off his t-shirt to reveal that chiselled chest I'd come to know so well, he leaned on top of me, his free arm coming down around my back to lower me into the cushions with his other hand tickling my arm moving down by my side. I felt that glorious surge of heat from his body; desire for me although it was a little more restrained today, mixed with gentleness. Or maybe I felt uneasy because we're in missionary position? One of his knees sat between mine as he gradually lowered himself, barely allowing his rippling stomach to hover above my belly button where I could see the colour of my belly gem pulsing up towards the base of his navy Jockey shorts. This position felt dangerous - too intimate, but I couldn't deny my own desire stirring. The heat was screaming from my body, wanting to feel his hardness press up against me.

This had to stop. I didn't like the change in tempo between us but I wasn't quite sure what to do. Looking into his eyes, the heat from his stare was almost pleading.

"Hey Mister, what's with you? I'm really horny, come here!" I teased, pushing him off. Standing up, dropping my red halter neck dress to the ground to reveal my oiled breasts (another trick I'd learned) I leaned seductively against the wall, my black stilettos and fishnet stockings on show as I flicked the suspender band.

Confusing my pert smile to be agreeable he raced over, slamming his body against mine, pushing my bum harder up against the wall. His hands grabbed my arms back above my head, holding me firm for a moment before whipping my body around, pushing me face down back onto the bed where he rummaged over every curve of my body. Panting with exhaustion and slight bewilderment, I tried to lift myself up to dodge his tongue licking the edges of my ears and down to my neck. His body was heavy and powerful, pressed up too hard on my inner thigh, too close to my vulva. This was not good; I couldn't move. Uncomfortable it hurt, but more than that I was scared that my ribs would break.

I couldn't afford to not work, not now that my studies were under way. How would I manage to pay and juggle everything?

"Get off me!" I yelled when a breath allowed, quickly turning around to face him.

He was shocked, but then sanity re-appeared just as my foot sat on his throbbing penis, moving the stiletto down as he leaned back onto his thighs.

"Sorry Jewel," he spoke gently, looking a little tentative. "You're just way too hot and sexy for me, babe!"

I cringed inside. How often had I always wanted to believe that when I was younger? Now, thanks to therapy at college and the wise men I met in here, to be considered sexy no longer mattered. I finally understood the power of sexual energy, realising it didn't equate to attracting love. Did I love myself at all?

I smiled. Finally, yes I did!

"C'mon sweetie, let's just pace ourselves a little, hey?" I suggested, noting embarrassment in his tone.

He settled back a little, giving me opportunity to once again set the pace.

"Come here Tim," I teased. "Now, where were we?"

We didn't speak much after this, but I knew exactly where we were. Tim was one of many who came here, lost and hurting from a broken marriage with me there willing and available to listen. But never once did they consider that my being here was my own way of finding an escape. I didn't want to know about their pain, so it was time to say goodbye. Of course he was angry, but it wasn't his choice to make.

It was nearly 2am after another double shift by the time I left. Finishing at midnight, I had to strip the bed, bring down sheets, make up a fresh bed, pack the dishwasher, shower and finally get dressed to drive home. Exhausted, Tim's behaviour had really upset me more than usual.

I drove slowly, trying to stay focussed and fighting back tears.

Why did it have to get so personal?

Thinking about my past relationships I knew I would never be swayed by a man's neediness again.

When I first arrived in Sydney my focus was all about work. Networking and building new friendships was also a priority, however with this came an onslaught of suitors pressing for my number. I was in a new city and didn't want to have a relationship at this stage, so I politely turned them down. Then only a few months later after fobbing off calls, I went out one night with my new flatmates to explore the club scene. Ordering a drink I heard a man's voice behind me.

"Hello. How are you?"

Turning around, I noticed a young man staring but was unsure if it was him who spoke. The music wasn't as loud out here but still I hadn't expected company.

"Hi." I said, trying to brush him off.

Not looking at him again I walked toward the tall tables outside, setting my handbag down on a vacant stool.

"Um, I saw you," he said, leaning very close to my ear.

Surprised, I turned around. *Did he just follow me?* My back straightened defensive as my eyes met his; almost innocent if there was such a thing for a man.

"Hi, sorry um, my name is Greg," he mumbled, holding out his hand.

Calculating all the possible ulterior motives for his intrusion, I picked him to be around twenty nine of European descent. With thick black curly hair and olive skin, I watched as a bead of sweat appeared on his brow, his eyes searched mine for guidance.

I softened. What harm could it do to be nice?

"Hi Greg, pleased to meet you," I said, accepting his hand to shake.

Greg took a deep breath, relaxing a little and sitting down on an opposite stool. Maybe he was gay? This was Sydney, after all. We chatted for a while before his friends joined us. A tall red haired bulky bloke gave me a handshake.

"Hi, I'm Steve, his mate," he said, beaming childishly. "We live together here," he continued, making me laugh.

"Nice to meet you," I said, looking around for the girls.

"It's okay, I'm watching out for your friends. I can see everything from up here. They're happy over there.

It was hard to resist the chivalry of these men. It was like having an older brother, which I would've loved. Over the next few hours we all danced, then the girls grew tired and we decided to leave.

"So, Greg, it's nice to meet you but I'm off home now."

"Let us take you," he quickly offered. "We can all share a taxi and I can drop you off on my way."

"Okay then," I said.

The boys had informed me they lived only a block away from us, so it made perfect sense. Dropping Steve off first, Greg wanted to travel around the block with us to ensure we got home safe, in the end paying for our ride. The girls dashed inside as we stood there by the taxi door.

"Thankyou, that was really lovely of you to pay for us."

"You're welcome," he said, a little shy. "I hope we can catch up again soon?"

Despite my usual stance regarding one night stands, purely because I was too choosy and the available men weren't my type, I knew I wanted him. What the Hell, I thought. This was a special night so I would celebrate my new freedom in this big city.

"Would you like to come up?"

He smiled, following me into the building.

It was during my second week at work when the number appearing on my screen didn't ring any bells at all.

"Hello?" I answered

"Hello. How *are* you?"

I was perplexed. Who would call and speak to me with such a tone in their voice?

"It's Greg. Remember?" The voice whispered, sounding embarrassed.

"Hello Greg, how are you?" I responded, thinking back to the amazing night we explored each other's bodies until dawn.

"So, would you like to catch up?"

"No, not really sorry Greg I'm too busy. But thanks anyway," I answered quickly.

He was silent for a moment. "No worries, just been thinking about you that's all."

"Yes, thanks for that," I answered, wondering what had possessed me to give him my number.

"Ok, ok, then we'll probably just catch up when hanging out at the local."

"What's that? Oh yeah that's right". Wracking my brain to recall our conversations that night, remembering he doesn't live far from me and hangs out at the same local pub.

"Sure, sounds ok. I'm busy but let's see what happens, and thanks for calling. Bye."

"Ok bye!" he responded as I was hanging up.

Hoping this was the last I would hear of him, a few days later on the Friday night we bumped into each other at the pub. This became a weekly ritual, and after one drink too many we would sometimes go for dinner, always ending up in bed.

Weeks became months before I realised this rendezvous was too fixed. I was beginning to like him, moving our relationship into complicated territory as he began calling later at night, no longer available for dinner or to catch up on the weekend.

The time passed by so quickly. During our third year of cavorting I took the opportunity one day to discuss my concerns with Greg, but as far as he was concerned I was neurotic - we were fine and he was just busy like I was. I began wondering how we had ended up like this?

Friday nights were always so welcomed after a fast paced week, and I was pleased to be hanging out with Sally and some of her friends for the first time in months. It was hard to believe we used to practically spend every night together after work. I could feel the vibration of my phone, propelling me away from the joviality as I pushed open the doors to step outside, fumbling to answer before it went to voicemail.

"Hello?"

"Hey babe how's it going?"

It was Greg. My knees still melted despite my attempts to feign disinterest. We had just started seeing each other again as was the pattern of casual relationship, and I was pleased to hear from him today.

"Hey, what's happening, are you on your way home?" I asked, aware he had been in Melbourne all day for work.

"Yeah, you know. Boring as usual and I'd rather be there with you!"

I smiled, pleased with his response.

"Guess what, we've won a new account," I told him in earnest. "I can't believe it! This is what I've worked so hard for!"

"That's so good babe, you deserve it", he said, sounding slightly distracted.

"Thank you! Hey, let's have a drink and catch up when you land?"

As soon as I had spoken, I wished I hadn't asked.

"I can't, sorry. I have to work late still."

Moaning inward, my excitement dissipated as the sweet taste of success began to turn sour.

"Yeah, no problem, I understand," I said, a little flat.

Truth was I didn't understand at all. Greg was happy for me to be around when he wanted, but not once was he available to celebrate milestones, of which there had been many.

"Really, I *am* sorry, there's nothing I'd rather do right now than to give you a big hug, buy a nice bottle of champagne and celebrate. Maybe we will on Friday night? Oh, hang on. It's my dad's birthday this weekend. Maybe tomorrow night OK?"

I said nothing as disappointment lodged in my throat.

"Babe, ok?"

I was silent, acknowledging that I wasn't invited to another of his family's events.

"Yeah. Ok, yep. That's great, I can't wait. Miss you."

"Ok goodnight babe, talk to you tomorrow."

Greg spoke quickly, obviously keen to hang up before any further protest. Sliding into the shadows on the pavement, I shed my suit jacket, wanting to release the sudden heat overwhelming my body. I wanted to run away from the noise of patrons having fun, visions of girls holding hands with their blokes sauntering past as they laughed. I wanted to laugh like that. Greg used to make me laugh – he was always pleasant, not angry or volatile like Mitch was.

"Hey love, what's up?"

Surprised by her voice, I turned to find Sally standing there lighting up a ciggie.

"Let me guess. It's Greg, isn't it?"

Her eyes narrowed, her glare confirming it best to keep my lips sealed. Without further interrogation she shook her head in disapproval.

"Men. Like I've always said love, they're dicks with pricks."

"Oh Sally," I said, trying not to laugh.

Sally began giggling, at the same time balancing her chardonnay in one hand whilst bringing the cigarette up to her lips with the other. It wasn't happening, making me laugh even harder until I couldn't breathe.

"Sally, you know what?" I said, pleased to be releasing some tension.

"What love," she responded, squashing up closer to prop her glass on a nearby planter.

"Well, I think I'm ready for something a little more solid and secure in my life."

Her face looked confused.

"Don't get me wrong, it was fun in the early days, but, oh I don't know, maybe I was too busy with work when he was keen. And nowadays he goes off and disappears for weeks!"

"Hmm." Sally kept staring into space and sucking hard on her ciggie, forcing passers' by to duck the cloud of fumes which were also choking me.

"So when we *do* get together he says he's happy with things being just the way they are."

"Hmm."

"Anyway, I mean, let's face it. The hours we put in during a campaign launch are exhausting. He has always understood how important my career is, and his is just as important. Besides," I said, hesitating to take a breath to settle my nerves.

Sally turned toward me, seemingly aware of my thoughts. I felt the sting of tears welling in my eyes.

"Besides what?" she asked, watching me too closely.

"Besides, I know he doesn't love me."

With a shaking wrist I wiped away the dewy drop before it could run down my cheek.

"Well love," Sally said, taking a long drag on her cigarette.

I waited, wanting desperately to hear words of wisdom as she exhaled the grey smoke.

"He got his end in and he's happy. Men are shits I tell you!"

That wasn't what I had expected, but in spite of myself, I laughed some more.

"Sorry love, but it just is the truth! Get with it girl! He's got it too easy."

My mouth quivered, and Sally softened.

"Oh come here and let me give you a hug," she said, grabbing my shoulders as she squeezed me close.

At first I was overwhelmed by her gesture, but then noticing her clothes reeked of smoke I grappled for fresh air.

"Thanks Sally. Let's go, hey?"

"Now c'mon, let's go back in and have another drink."

"Yeah sure," I said, but knew I'd had enough.

Sally wandered inside without looking back, so I scurried for an approaching cab knowing no-one would miss me.

On the way home I thought about Greg some more. What were we really doing together? Staring out over the city lights, the taxi jousted and switched lanes as it occurred to me that Greg was getting on with his life so I needed to get on with mine.

When we caught up next week I would have to call it quits.

Saturday afternoon I was undertaking the toughest regime of the week, laundry and housework, when the phone rang. Cassie and Lucy had gone off to meet Irish mates down at The Rocks and wouldn't be home 'till late, meaning I had the place to myself - meaning I had time to do chores; no excuses whatsoever given I'd managed a three hour hike at dawn. These walks gave me the greatest pleasure, knowing I was on my own amongst nature with only my thoughts for company.

"Hello?" I answered, a little breathless and tired, having worked out at the gym after my hike.

"Hey babe, how's it going?"

I hadn't expected Greg to call on a weekend. What did he want?

"I miss you," he whispered.

Sitting down, I knew I had to be firm. It was as if he suspected the end was near. Sally's words echoed, '*he got his end in, and he's happy. Men are shits I tell you!*'

"Oh for God's sake, Greg, I find that hard to believe."

"Babe, what's up?" he started to say. "It wasn't like that."

There was silence.

"I told you, yes I went out with another girl a few times as a friend. Nothing else happened, I promise."

I remained quiet, silently wishing I could hang up.

"She's gone. It's nothing!" His voice was insistent.

"If Steve hadn't said anything accidentally I would never have known!"

"Listen, listen to me! You *know* she's a friend of Steve's. We just hung out twice. Coffee one afternoon and I think another time we went to a movie. No big deal!"

"So why then didn't you think to mention it and save me the embarrassment in front of your friends?"

"Because there was nothing for you to be embarrassed about!" he screamed. "We weren't going out together, she wasn't my girlfriend and that's it, okay? Now, can you drop it?"

Did I believe him or not? I really wanted to but, for some reason something didn't feel right. Or was I just tired, going through some mid-life crisis? I was tired more than usual lately too. I kept reminding myself of this fact. Was this the reason I was so on edge?

"I want to be with you!" His voice filtered through, soft; soothing.

Greg was being very patient, but too many questions were clouding my capacity to think. I felt confused. Another voice popped up in my head to interject.

Hey, remember he has never invited you to meet his family or work colleagues, so why should you start believing him now!

My rational side stepped up.

"Greg, you're full of shit, do you know that!? Look, the thing is, you never spend time with me. I *get* what it is you want from me and I'm saying that's it, no more!"

I waited, listening as Greg drew a deep breath.

"Sweetie," he whispered. "C'mon, you just need a break, I can tell."

I laughed.

"A break? Greg, you have no idea."

News of my decision to leave Sydney shocked everyone. Resigning at the peak of my career didn't seem rational but I knew I wasn't well. My mixed feelings for Greg were pushing me over the edge. In the weeks prior to my departure we spoke, agreeing we were good at being friends but not so ready for a relationship as we thought.

"I'll really miss you," he said.

"Yeah, I know. We did have fun but it's time for change in my life."

"I know, I know. I'm sorry for all the crap. But keep in touch, hey?"

I had no intentions of keeping in touch, wanting my freedom this time around.

Europe was exquisite. After a month I felt at home meandering at my own pace around the islands of Greece and through the Italian coastline on a grand walking tour. If it weren't for Greg's constant intrusions, checking up on how my travels were going, I wouldn't have given him another thought. Also if it weren't for a few hair raising risky moments I would never have considered returning home. The next time Greg called me, I didn't tell him about the Italian who tried to spike my drink, or the young stunning model I got to pierce my belly button. I only said how much I missed him.

"I miss you too! When are you coming home?"

Home was luring me, and Greg's tone soothed me even more.

"Well, whenever I can get the next available flight, which is probably next week?" I said.

Greg didn't hide his joy and my own spirit soared. Was our relationship about to take off in a romantic way?

Steve's six foot seven frame was not hard to miss as he stood waiting for me at Customs where I lined up with my passport ready. His quirky red hair with a teenager's fringe and big, bold red rimmed glasses made him stand out above the crowd, waving madly in my direction like a clown on acid. Steve had been working in Hong Kong, and he texted me once he heard from Greg to say he would also be en route back to Sydney the same morning.

"How are you?" I mouthed, hoping to appease him so that he would stop it.

He nodded, waving even more!

"Heeeeey! I'm good! How are you?" he yelled out.

Finally I was given the all clear and Steve leaned it to hug me. It was more like a squeeze, but I knew he would stop before my lungs gave out. He always did.

"Hey welcome back weary traveller! What's the goss?"

"No goss Steve, just bloody weary that's all! I'm so messed up on what day it is though. And you were right, it did land that early! I can't believe I'm actually through by 6am."

"Yep, told ya. C'mon let's have a cigarette and get cracking. Greg will be happy to see you!"

"Um, I did speak to him during my stopover and he's got a meeting early so I will just stay here for a while and call Sally," I suggested nervously.

"What? Don't be a crackpot. You're coming home with me," he said, turning to scurry toward the exit.

An uneasy feeling sat in the pit of my stomach. Maybe it was a bad case of jet-lag or worse, my new belly button ring was infected? Once in the back seat, I sat in silence, meditating on my nerves to be calm as I re-acquainting myself with Sydney landmarks during the brief ride. The taxi turned into a familiar tree-lined street, coming to a halt across the Woollahra driveway. Steve's quick intake of breath alerted me.

"What is it?" I asked, looking up to catch his eye in the rear view mirror.

"Ah, nothing! Um, it's just the car," he answered way too jumpy for my liking.

"What car? What's going on, Steve?"

I waited, anxiety building.

"Ah, well you know about Greg seeing that girl Jodi I think her name was. I friggin' hate her by the way!"

Yes, I did know about that girl Greg had remained in touch with and saw during our breaks. But that was over - wasn't it?

"It's nothing, relax!" He was observing me via the side mirror. "I'm just saying he's borrowed her car on occasions. She turns up every so often and he just can't shake her. There's nothing going on. It's over."

I felt lucid; surreal. Erratic thoughts raced through my mind as I pieced together recent conversations with Greg. I knew all this, I reminded myself. Sally had also sent me an email in Italy, telling me she had bumped into them on the Bondi to Bronte walk. I did ask him and he answered that she had become irrational and needy. Part of me did rise up and have a hissy fit, but I reminded myself that he had been calling *me*.

"Yes I did hear they'd caught up, Steve. It's cool!"

It wasn't cool. My stomach churned over. My heart began to beat faster, adrenalin propelling me out of the taxi, racing toward the slightly ajar door.

"Shit! Ok... thanks driver. Here... take the... Hey, wait!" Steve yelled after me.

I could see the lights were on, probably left on all night. Stepping through into the open lounge, my breathing became heavy. The room seemed different, but I had been away for so long. Suddenly I felt stupid, but something still didn't seem quite right.

"C'mon, See? Nothing. Everyone's in bed." Steve's voice screeched nervously behind me.

My senses screamed with anticipation. "Something's wrong," I said, my hands beginning to shake.

"Nothing's wrong. Come, let's go get brekkie!" Steve insisted, watching as I scanned the living room then the stairs. Shoes were strewn everywhere, left like stumbling blocks.

"It looks like the boys have had a little party!" Steve joked, but I wasn't listening. I was too busy watching Greg skipping down the stairs in response to Steve's voice. He stopped near the bottom step, shocked to see me, trying to recover but it was too late. His eyes couldn't meet mine.

"Hey! What's up! How are you?" Greg spoke in Steve's direction, trying hard to sound confident.

The room shrank. I could almost hear Greg's heart pounding. His words were soaked with guilt. Stale cigarette smoke amped our hazy surroundings, creating a dense soupy atmosphere, the anticipation too much for the boys to bear.

Greg turned to me, trying to step into the role of welcoming lover, but it was too late. "Hey sweetie, welcome back!"

Reeling away from his outreached arms I was silent, still weighing up the situation. Every part of me sensed it was bad. My head was spinning, I couldn't move but luckily for all of us Steve finally did, jumping and prancing around like he had definitely taken drugs.

"Hey! We're going off for breakfast. Just got in! Want to come?"

It didn't work. Greg and I were at a stand-off; his eyes heavy with guilt, mine with questions.

"C'mon food! I know the best place down the road!"

Anxiety kicked in. The desire to get out of there was overbearing just as Steve grabbed my arm, hauling me outside into the sweetness of fresh air. I was numb and confused. What just happened? Then Steve did something silly. He stepped back inside just as my anger kicked in, ready to confront Greg. As I entered, a woman came down the stairs. A stocky blonde, she had appeared from nowhere, trying to sneak out sheepishly as she reached for her shoes one by one. Her eyes were on me as she nervously excused herself.

"So this is her!" I said, glaring at Greg.

"No!" Greg retorted, his face hurling back in astonishment.

"No, she's with me!" We all turned around to see George looking scared, balancing halfway down the stairs. "This is my girlfriend Gail."

"Hi," Gail responded, reaching for the last shoe lying by my feet before running out the door.

Greg looked very pasty while Steve tried to diffuse the situation.

"Hey Steve, is that you?" A squeaky female voice came from the direction of Greg's bedroom.

Everyone froze. Looking up at the landing I saw a petite, scantily clad redhead wandering out of his room. Her brashness astounded me. Our eyes met at the same time as I wondered how she felt about this situation. Or maybe she didn't know about me?

Finally I snapped at Greg.

"We need to talk!" I spoke harshly, pointing toward the kitchen.

Greg followed without hesitation, looking like a naughty little boy. Hopping up onto the sink, legs dangling, I realised we were worlds apart in maturity.

"You know how I feel about you, and you knew I would be back today. In fact, you encouraged me to return. You even called me last night all excited!!"

I looked at him through different eyes. Greg looked dazed, lighting up a cigarette. Empty wine bottles were strewn everywhere along the sink; a carton stacked up against the bin. He was lazy as well as thoughtless.

"How could you do this to me?"

There was silence as he continued to sit there looking sheepish. There he was all slimmed down from those extra gym sessions. It was hard to believe it was that same chubby, sweet man who had nervously approached me nearly four years ago. Was this all my fault?

"I don't know what to say. She just came over, I swear!" he answered, looking pathetic.

"And what, Greg; the couch wasn't appropriate?" I responded sarcastically.

Jodi walked into the kitchen. To say it was awkward is an understatement as this petite girl searched both of us for some kind of direction. How was it that I felt sorry for *her*?

"Um, Taryn, this is Jodi," Greg introduced us quietly.

"Hi," Jodi spoke up first.

I tried to smile, knowing it was a fake one. My head was spinning. What was really going on here with us?

"Hello. Can you please give us a moment?" I said, raising my eyebrows like I had authority.

Jodi nodded, walking back out past me quite confidently but not smug. Turning to Greg again, his energy depleted, I spoke calmly.

"This is it, you know. It's time to just let go of me if you don't know what you want. Nice way to greet me, Greg."

He nodded, looking sad.

"Don't pursue me anymore!"

My whole outlook on life had changed completely, and for this I was grateful. It was an epiphany giving me the leverage I needed in order to create a new life for myself - no longer the victim.

"Goodbye, I mean it. Okay?"

He nodded as I left.

I was stronger and more self-assured, although I wasn't sure how Steve was going to cope. He looked like crap standing there waiting eagerly by the car.

It was a year later when I ran into Greg walking toward me in the city. On my way to work at the gym, we almost cut each other off. I stopped there in front of him, grappling with what to say.

"Taryn! How are you?" Greg cooed slightly.

"Greg! How are *you*?" I answered, noting my body's response.

I felt fine. He was a little nervous standing next to me. Smiling awkwardly, I gestured for him to take a seat at a local café.

"Got a moment?" I asked.

He quickly took the seat opposite me.

"Yes, yes. I'm just on my way to a meeting, but it's so lovely to see you. I mean that, you know," he spoke directly to me, hands upright on the table to emphasise openness. This made me smile even more.

"What?" he smirked a boyish smile that once had me captivated.

"Sorry, it's just so strange isn't it? After everything..." I said.

"Taryn, you look amazing by the way," he interjected.

It was a relief not to feel any magnetic pull toward him.

"Thanks! I often wondered if, when and where we would ever run into each other."

Yes it is nice," he answered, again leaning forward. "And you're nice; such a lovely person."

His face was solemn.

"I was a real mess for months," he continued, "and I couldn't deal with the hurt I'd caused you. I lost my friends. I lost everything. I was an idiot."

He lifted his shoulders, cocking his head to the side.

"Yep," I answered. "Maybe just immature."

He shook his head as we both began to laugh.

"You were always such fun. I do hope you're so much happier?" He took my hands in his.

"Yes, Greg, I am happy," I responded honestly, not asking him the same question. I didn't want to know. This was my moment.

He stood up.

"I'm so sorry I have to go; this bloody meeting." His eyes darted around nervously. "But you have my number if you ever need me. Promise you'll call?"

I caught a glimpse of the chivalrous boy I knew all those years ago.

"Ok, thanks Greg. It's nice to see you too. The past is the past, hey? We were always great friends. And besides, you were the one who always told me to be true to myself – so from now on, I will be!"

He laughed as I waved goodbye, and then he was gone.

Grateful for closure, I had no intentions of calling him in the future.

I met Paul on an Escort booking one evening which was timely, helping me come to terms with the choices I had made regarding men. Wandering into the hotel lobby, looking out for him, I heard my name.

"Hello, you must be Jewel."

Paul's voice was smooth. His eyes hovered over my dress; a long, silvery blue jersey Roberto Cavalli matched with silver Gary Castles shoes.

I smiled, pleased he liked what he saw and loving the power this gave me.

"You look lovely."

"Thank you. Paul." Reaching out my hand, he took it, squeezing briefly.

"Let's make our way shall we? We have a 7pm if that's ok with you?"

"Yes that's fine," I answered, anticipating the marvellous food.

Sherri had informed me that Paul was a man in his 50's, a busy international pilot who stopped over in Sydney once a month. Lucky for me, the girl he usually saw was away. We fell into a nice pace walking side by side making small talk.

Once seated and perusing the menu, he suggested I choose the drinks.

"I see you have a good palate for wines," he said, acknowledging my lingering on the expensive list handed to me separately.

"Hmm, yes I do love a good wine, although I don't drink much these days, but if I do, it has to be worth it."

I was so pleased this was the truth. It felt so rewarding being able to dine out and stay focussed on conversation and food rather than pre-empting an uncontrollable thirst. Deciding on the scallops for entree, I chose the crisp Chablis as accompaniment.

"So Paul, tell me. What's it like being a pilot travelling the world, dining in the best restaurants?"

I could see he wasn't the partying type.

"Hmm, yes busy. Way too busy in fact. I travel too much. Spend too little time with people that matter." He looked down at the menu again, calling over the Sommelier. "So, what shall we choose to drink with our main?"

After ordering our mains and the wine, gazing out through the large window in front of us, the Harbour Bridge lights were dazzling. Watching him carefully, I asked him to elaborate on his earlier comment.

"You were saying that you travel too much." I started cautiously, observing his eyes for a reaction. He seemed relaxed so I continued. "Do you have family somewhere?"

There. It was out. I had asked a more personal question. The timing seemed right. Usually I didn't go anywhere near such a topic – especially on the first 'date'.

He leaned back more pensive this time and suddenly I wasn't so sure my personal approach was a good idea. My studies were making me curious, wondering more about why we humans were here on Earth and what the point to life was. I had stopped caring about my life until now. There seemed to be an undercurrent of energy at play, like a cord connecting me with these people who were asking the same questions.

Staring, waiting for Paul to speak, I pondered the human condition caustically. What was it that drove our need to pursue orderly, egocentric goals in order to feel like we have achieved something in this world? Why did these men choose such a lifestyle, to pay for company when I would think it much more pleasurable to enjoy the freedom of being alone, away from the chaos of their lives? Then again, I was fast becoming aware that my own desire for reclusiveness reflected a dire need for introspection and personal growth. Not everyone was so deep, nor did many of these men seek to evolve via the musings of an Escort. They craved basic comforts like sex and food, that's all, and maybe this was enough. Could it be?

"I do have children yes. Two. Back in New Zealand," he told me, clasping his hands on the table.

His look was still rather pensive, which didn't seem right given that most people happily boast about their kids.

"Oh that's lovely, Paul. Children are beautiful," I spoke earnestly, sensing that he was more open to maternal repertoire, knowing children were a topic closely aligned with the dull ache I pushed down deep.

"Yes they are indeed. But I don't get to see them as much as I would like to at the moment."

It was a subdued man before me so, taking another sip of my wine, I asked another potent question.

"What about your wife, she must miss you too; or, unless you're divorced?"

"She died," he stated, looking at me pleasantly with no flicker of emotion. It was difficult for me not to flinch, but I was adept at being neutral.

"Oh sorry." My voice was direct. "That must have been very difficult for you all."

The room seemed to grow colder as I sat there comprehending his words.

"Yes. But my wife's sister is a wonderful woman. She takes care of the kids and they've been managing well for quite a few years now," he continued. It seemed as if he was very much suited to offering such commentary whenever called upon to recollect a story and repeat it over and over again. "My wife was killed when she stepped out of the driver's side of her car. She didn't see the oncoming truck that side swiped her."

He was looking at me. There was no emotion in his eyes. I took a huge gulp of my wine and breathed out very slowly, trying not to look shocked, but of course deep down I was. How could anyone not be? This was a horrendous tragedy, and a stark reminder that my life was so good. When tragedy struck some people I noted there were those who could soar to greater heights, summoning up courage most of us would never possess in this lifetime. Life offered up twists and turns, the challenge being to keep one's heart open without blaming others or recoiling into victim mentality.

I stared blankly across his shoulder, listening as he expressed feelings for his deceased wife. Words sank deep into my psyche as he spoke; 'the love of my life; no-one would ever be able to take her place.'

Not speaking, not nodding, I could only think more abstractly about all the different reasons we seek out company.

"But I still love women," he added, allowing a smile to appear. "For conversation, companionship and sex - I need it."

His last words brought me back to reality. I'm a professional date which met my needs too. The rest of our evening passed by pleasantly and soon we sauntered off back to the hotel, my mind dashing away in another direction. I'd hit a junction and was unable to continue the act, desperately keen to get home onto my safe, comfy couch.

"Thank you so much for a lovely evening, Paul. Goodnight." Leaning up, I kissed him on the cheek. He stood there for a moment before placing his hand to the top pocket, wads of one hundred dollar bills peeking out. Our booked time had ended a while ago.

"Would you like to come up with me?" he asked, aware of my hesitation.

I couldn't do it. I didn't want to be there. *What's going on?*

"Oh, Paul do you mind if I go home now? I'm quite exhausted if that's ok? I can call Sherri to organise someone else, or...?"

This was awkward. He looked rejected, making me more determined to leave. To retract now would speak volumes about my motivation – and it wasn't money.

"No. That's fine. Thanks Jewel. Good night," he answered flatly. Aloof, we both smiled politely, strangers going our separate ways.

Seated in the back of a taxi, I called Sherri.

"Hi Sherri, I'm on my way back. Be there in fifteen minutes or so," I said, inflecting some cheerfulness.

"Ok Jewel. See you soon then!"

"Oh, actually Sherri do you mind if I go straight home? Paul is lovely but I'm exhausted."

"You ok?" She was picking up that something's wrong.

There was no point hiding anything from her.

"Yes." I hesitated. "He is such a lonely man isn't he? And so sad."

She sighed. "Yes Jewel, he is. Many of them are my dear. Okay yes, you go home and have a good sleep. Nothing much else is happening here anyway."

"Thanks Sherri, I'll just go now while I'm in the taxi then. Goodnight."

"Goodnight dear." Her sweet voice blanketed me, confirming I'd made the right choice.

Soon I was turning the lights on at home, aware of the emptiness as my keys echoed on the kitchen bench. I had an amazing life, so why was I feeling so miserable? The evening had gone well, although meeting Paul had stirred something else. His loneliness, the pain of losing someone he loved so much and in such a tragic way.

"Oh for goodness sake, no!"

It was a revelation to acknowledge that what had really upset me the most was realising I had never been in love. This was not good news for a woman about to turn forty. How on Earth could I have missed out on something so valuable and rare? Was it rare? And anyway, what *is* love, I wondered? This made me think. Did I need to see so many men anymore?

It was time to revisit my priorities and adjust accordingly, sensing my spiritual integrity was at stake. Although it was hard to admit it to myself, I knew I had become addicted to earning so much cash. That's when I made the decision to no longer accept such bookings, which helped to reinforce that I did still have self-respect and focus on long term goals. I'd heard many stories from the girls that often the desire to continue earning so much over-rode the initial decision to focus on a goal and then get out.

It was tempting for sure.

Chapter 7

Seasoned Sex Goddess Gives Good Heads Up

Classes were becoming more intense. Submerged in subject matter such as Emotional Health and Healing, we were encouraged to tackle personal experiences of blocked aggression and subsequent pain. This topic highlighted for me how, as individuals, we expand in a way that will fulfil our need for safety and security, yet whenever this is challenged or threatened by adversity, we have the capacity to summon up empathy - letting go of material gain in order to survive as a whole. These themes broadened my scope of relating to the greater world, bolstering my drive to re-enter it as a counsellor and coach.

There was no longer a great divide between Taryn and Jewel; sex worker and woman. My classes and the therapy I derived from Simon had allowed my true self to feel safe enough to be revealed in front of fellow students. The more memories I confronted, the more amazed I was to learn how I had managed to disassociate, disengaging from life for so long. As my real feelings began to emerge, unravelling cords that tied me to the hurt gave way for happiness to take its place. I was ready to lighten up!

This was when I met Emilee on a quiet Saturday afternoon at Scarlett's. Many of the girls had departed for much swankier new parlours in the city as the industry benchmark shifted, the demand for mistress liaisons becoming obscure – replaced with the more available party girl types.

A blonde, petite woman meandered past, interrupting my thoughts. "Hello!" she said, continuing her shuffle through the girl's lounge.

"Hello," I said, staring at this confident woman. The other girls ignored her as competition was not so readily welcomed on a quiet day. "I'm Jewel, what's your name?"

"I'm Emilee. Started today," she added. "So tell me, is it getting any busier in here?"

I smiled, leaning back into the sofa as I propped a foot up onto the coffee table.

"Emilee, to tell you the truth it's been a rollercoaster the past few months, actually," I explained. "When I came here a couple of years ago, it was always busy. But now…"

She threw her handbag down, rummaging through it before looking up to interrupt me. "Yes, it's like that everywhere I hear. But that's alright. If you're smart, you will be busy."

"What do you mean, if you're smart?" I asked, quite intrigued.

She turned around, a red lipstick now in her hand. "Well," she started, pushing up the lipstick. "You've got to rely solely on your sexual radar, researching what works and what doesn't, analysing ways in which to capitalise on the big players who want more bang for their buck."

Her eyes held mine as she stood up, turning toward her reflection of the mirror. Puckering up as she observed our last colleague sashay past uninterested, she grinned at me. A red line coursed her lower lip as she smooched to herself and put the stick away. "Always have a strategy."

I continued to pay attention.

"Generally speaking," she said, turning to face me. "Being an establishment working lady means we get standard rates for in-calls and out-calls with the usual split. But when I worked private I got to keep it all."

My ears pricked up. "What do you mean 'private'?"

She looked at me with new interest.

"Well, I mean the girl can operate from home if she likes. These days they're found listed on a website or in local papers, and they also tend to visit five star hotels like we do."

"Ok, like when we do an escort from here, it's $300 for the hour, right?"

"Yes, but for a private worker you can keep it all. Or charge more! Some girls I know, they often have a normal day job or they're a group of smart students who only do dinner dates, booking a nearby room as required."

"That sounds really cool!" I said, my eyes turning upward as the brain got a workout calculating all the money I could keep. This sounded like it could be my next move.

Although earning around two thousand dollars a week, it would be nice to keep the full amount to pay for studies then set myself up comfortably. An exit strategy was in order given that I was overwhelmed with assignments and my body needed a rest from probing males. Already the benefit of seeing a select few clients was becoming attractive.

Maybe I could work this way until graduation and buy a house with the deposit I'd save?

"And then there's the real upmarket escorts, usually out of work models," she quipped with slight sarcasm. "They have a five star policy, but charge huge rates and are more likely to have a professional website citing preference for long bookings or overnight stays. And you've probably heard of girls being Courtesans?" She glanced at me, looking cynical. "Well, they would be with an agency. Sometimes it's a global one. I've worked for one once, and earned shit-loads. But there wasn't enough happening for me."

"Fascinating!"

It had never been on my radar to research this. My plan was to be done with this industry altogether once I graduated.

"Yes! Then there's the good old street worker, but you know what?" Emilee made sure I was paying attention. "They can be seen in specific streets all over the country, not just Kings Cross. Often a car will do a drive by and the customer will negotiate through an open window. A high risk venture I would think."

"Yes, yes it would be," I offered sympathetically.

"So, then there's us - the Sex Worker as they call us these days which is much better than *prostitute!*" Emilee spat out the word, making me squirm. It sounded so crass, especially when spoken like that. We all thought of prostitutes as being drug addicts and women who married rich men or hated working, often in low paid jobs.

"Well, there you go. There's so much I didn't realise."

"Private is better, you know," she continued. "Clients like to experience real intimacy, which of course means more money for us."

"Yes. But I don't think I could do that." I started shaking my head.

"Course you could!" she interjected with authority. "You're smart, attractive and very easy to talk to. You have emotional intelligence and sexual power. What's your name again?"

"Jewel."

Listening, I was cautious; wondering what made her think that she could ascertain my virtues within a few minutes.

"Ok, Jewel. Let's talk about it again a bit later shall we? I have a client waiting in the lounge."

"Oh, ok. Sure," I answered, watching her swagger toward the door, wondering if she was just an arrogant smart arse.

Her name wasn't even on the board yet.

Later that day Emilee raced down to find me still resting on the couch.

"Ok Jewel, here you go. I've got us a double together with this guy. Are you ready?"

"What? Oh, ok," I answered, wasting no time in following her up to the room.

Once there together, I watched in awe as she switched from Goddess to whore, between lesbian to man lover, she was full on in the 'full service' department that's for sure! Emilee held the man captive with eye contact and constant pashing. Her tongue probing at every opportunity, taking him more by surprise than me! 'Get on your back and get ready' was my motto thrown at men, nothing like this show. A few hours later when we were back downstairs, she confronted me.

"Ok I can see you haven't had much training," she said, looking business like. "Don't you give blow jobs?"

I was a little stunned at being pulled up this late in the game, but listened, not giving anything away. Truth was I didn't see the need to act. I loved sex, so it was easy to get off with the basic pleasures of genital play. But kissing? Well, that was way too intimate and disgusting for me, and although I never had training I knew it wasn't a requirement to keep the job. For those girls who did and weren't concerned about their health, they just got busier with the blokes that didn't give a rat's about passing on germs to their wives. My client list was minimal, with selective men delighted that they too would be safe from disease with me.

"No? Okay, how about you come and meet a couple of my clients one night?"

"What do you mean?" I didn't want to be pimped, and I certainly wouldn't do natural French (oral sex without a condom) or kiss.

"Well, I know a few men who would love you, so we can have a bit of fun while you watch and learn. And you get to keep all of the money," she added, watching my expression change.

"Ok. Let's do it. Where and when?" I asked, feeling a new flourish of excitement.

For the rest of the afternoon Emilee told me that unlike working girls before us who spent their lives in hedonistic grandeur, (probably starting at an early age and often not qualified in any other profession), this was a short term operative for us. She explained that because we were already in our forties, this was an opportunity to utilise not only our sexual expertise but also showcase our capacity for intellectual company.

"We can set ourselves up for the future by working hard and fast! So there you go. And the moral of the story Jewel is don't get involved with these guys. Use your head. It's a good one. They are all about throwing around the money, and so are we!"

"Okay!" I answered, although deep down I thought she had hardened too much along the way. What about having some fun?

I knew she was right of course, having discovered early on that success was not about having big boobs or being a young bimbo (although there's a niche market for that too). These men we were fortunate to be introduced to in here liked their women to be of equal intelligence, but they also liked us to be adept at sex and showing initiative as leaders in the bedroom. In the end it was all about power - ours.

"There's no laying on one's back if you want them to keep you front of mind," she informed me, barely cracking a smile.

Over the next few weeks I watched as she showed me how to lick and suck – and I'm not talking Tequila. Emilee also taught me where to touch a woman, introducing me into a whole new world of seduction and sexual mastery which amped up our lesbian doubles. Popularity and bookings soared.

Then the situation changed when Emilee decided to bail.

"Bloody Hell!" Jana screamed, storming into the girl's room. "Emilee isn't coming back, and now I'm a girl short. What am I going to do?"

During her rant, my mobile buzzed. It was Em.

Txt: 'Are you busy tomorrow?'

Ignoring Jana's voice, I replied to the text.

Me: 'No. Why?'

Txt: 'Have a client from Melbourne. Back few days here Syd. 2hrs at Casino Apartments. 3pm. Can u do?'

Me: 'Yes. Meet u where?'

Txt: 'Will let u know tmrw. Be ready.'

"What's up?" Jana asked, aware I was distracted.

"Nothing!"

I tried not to smile. The thought of not having to come in and sit through another quiet spell was quite satisfying.

"Well, you look kinda happy for nothing!"

Emilee and I met around 3pm the next afternoon where she ran through the preliminaries; our earnings and my split, before we made our way to this client's room.

"Ok, so here's the plan. When we go up there I will introduce you. His name's Scott."

"Sure," I answered, following Emilee to the lift, her hips swaying provocatively in a Leona Edmiston frock. Fabric clung to every curve, capturing the gaze of every man passing by.

She was sexy. I felt sexy, and knowing I was going to get a fatter pay was also sexy if that was at all possible. My pleasure was obvious when we waltzed into the room.

"Hi Scott, this is Jewel," Emilee spoke demurely, her eyes sparkling with mischief.

"Hello Jewel, nice to meet you. Come in ladies." Scott gestured for us to walk through to the lounge area where he offered us drinks.

Sizing him up, Scott was probably around mid 30's of average height and average weight with nice warm brown eyes and thick blonde hair. Most importantly he had a kind face and was a little nervous, just an average man.

"Yes, thanks," I answered, taking the glass of champagne he poured, then putting it down, thinking it wiser to go for a quick refreshing shower as I watched him hand an envelope discreetly to Emilee.

"I'll be out in a moment," I yelled.

A few minutes later when I reappeared, they were already naked and rolling around. Gesturing to me, I raced over to join them.

"Ouch!" I whispered with shock, my head crashing with Emilee's. She smiled, her eyes suggesting it would be a better option for me to move behind her, so I did. I began playing with her clitoris. Scott loved this little show, propping himself up to get a better view as I licked my way back up to her belly. He no longer concentrated on Emilee who was wildly sucking his penis. It went limp, prompting Emilee to move up along his chest to his lips where she shoved her tongue into his mouth.

Turning away, I began fondling her breasts as she moaned. It was ages before Emilee finally pulled out the condom, placing it on his erection before mounting up.

"Oh oh, yes! Yes!" He screamed awfully loud.

Strange thoughts pervaded as he revelled in his pleasure. I hoped the walls were thick? There's not much joy involved in such a long and arduous session, but at least it was finally over. Emilee jumped off, dragging me into the bathroom.

"Hey, how was that?" she asked. "Did you want to do more of the sucking next round?"

"I'll just go with the groove," I answered, keen not to be so stringently placed. "He may not want that much anyway."

She looked at me strangely. "Listen Jewel, they all want that much."

"Right," I answered, thinking about what I'd just observed, although I still had no intentions of complying. It just wasn't my thing!

When we came back out, our client was sitting up with the bottle of champagne in his hands.

"Thanks so much, ladies. I'm really enjoying this! I'm still excited so I will have to go and do a bit of gambling before dinner tonight to relax!"

"Oh that sounds like fun," I answered, grinning with satisfaction.

"Yes, but would be more fun with company. Do you like a flutter?" he asked, looking closer at me.

I thought about it. Although not a gambler with money I was keen to enjoy the venue and afternoon with company.

"Yes I don't mind a little play," I teased. "But of course we're busy girls so I don't know…" I looked at Emilee, trying to gauge if she could see where I was going with this. She watched as I played my hand.

"What do you think Emilee, if he wanted us to stay another couple of hours?"

"Yes, I will pay for both of you to stay," he offered, getting the hang of how we rolled.

Emilee smiled. "Yes I can cancel our other arrangements. We would much rather stay here with you Scott. Thank you!"

Scott began counting out more notes, no longer bothering to be discreet given we were sitting around naked, not to mention the recent romp.

"Here. It's done then. Let's go play!"

Handing us another $1000 each, we smiled graciously and tucked it away. Then I quickly got showered and dressed before Emilee did the same.

"You are so generous," I said, as he gestured to the door.

Emilee touched my elbow, pulling me close.

"This is not a party. It's work," she whispered into my ear.

"Yes. Ok I've got it. Let's have a little fun!"

We did have some fun, especially after a few bottles of Veuve Cliquet which helped to pass the time.

"Hungry?" Scott asked, eager for us to remain in his company.

Em and I looked at each other and slowly nodded before she spoke.

"Yes! But our time's almost up, we should be going, I'm sorry to say."

Scott didn't look too happy with this idea at all.

"Oh? Come and have dinner with me, unless you have another booking - somewhere else to be?"

Understanding the protocol, Emilee took the lead.

"No, not at all! What do you think, how much longer would you like us to stay, say another couple of hours?"

"Perfect! But I'll have to eat you both for dessert!"

Scott's confidence had clearly peaked, and then too soon it was time to head back up to the room so he could organise our final payment for the extra time.

"Ok folks. Excuse me while I take a little... er, pee!" I giggled, staggering toward the bathroom.

I wasn't gone long, but when I came out Emilee was naked on the bed with Scott. She had taken his request for dessert seriously. Approaching them, I was already having flashbacks of alcohol fuelled clients. I would have to turn on my sex goddess charm in the hope of making a polite exit.

"Oh, no room for me then? How sad!" I joked, trying to focus on Emilee. "Good thing Em wants me to leave you alone, hey?"

"Sure. Here!" Scott pointed toward his trousers still hanging precariously off the corner of the bed.

"Why thankyou lovely man," Emilee responded, grabbing the cash as he counted it out. She did the same, taking an extra from the split as fee before handing me my share.

"Thank you *both* for a magical evening. And now I have to go."

Blowing air kisses I waved goodbye as I head toward the door. Emilee was right. Tonight had been a good reminder that we were paid really well for the hard work involved, but just how far was I really prepared to go? With this in mind I prepared myself to step up and take the lead. I would reconsider my repertoire; doing more oral and faking my pleasure more than ever.

Six months down the track, Emilee was confident enough to introduce me to some of the most affluent businessmen around town, building up rapport and regular bookings until one day she made an announcement at my place where we were relaxing, enjoying the salmon salad I'd prepared.

"Hey, listen up. I'm done," she said flatly as I continued to eat. "And I'm very pleased with how you've been received so I would like to recommend you to my private clients. Are you ok with this?"

Emilee spoke in her usual cool manner. Could she really be that detached?

I nodded yes, trying not to spit a caper across the balcony as I contemplated what she had just said. At the same time I was playing with scenarios, what impact would her departure have on my income?

"My private client list is elite and it has taken me a few years to build it up, so I need to know if you're in or not."

How could I go on seeing these guys without her? She was pivotal in screening their needs and securing locations for rendezvous. Meeting strangers made me nervous although this may sound funny given that there were more strangers coming in to Scarlett's. But the girls usually knew them, giving me a heads up on their personalities. The men Emilee knew would never be seen dead in an establishment. This was an on demand kind of man that she had mustered – one who expected that we attend a function, turn up at a party and be at a designated residence by a certain time whenever they called. It was too laden with uncertainty for me. I had my boundaries and I liked to be the one calling the shots.

Being high rollers around town, it was highly unlikely I would have ever met them during my PR days, but still it didn't feel right. What if I met a future husband's brother, or a lover from years ago?

"You have seen what happens. It's easy," she continued. "I can give them your phone number and when they call, just remember to ask 'where shall we meet, for how long?' They will always have an envelope ready when you arrive. The rest is up to you, just be alert and work hard." Emilee's voice quivered with a slight jovial inference I rarely heard. I knew she was referring to our dalliance with Scott.

"Ok. Deal!" I answered firmly.

146

"Okay I will give you a list which you will enter into your phone immediately. Oh, and I will take a fee for the handover of each client you intend seeing."

I laughed. Emilee was back to her efficient self within seconds.

"Sure. This is fine," I responded just as efficiently, understanding the kudos plus potential earnings.

"Good, Jewel, I knew you were the one. Here's my account details for the deposit upon each booking you take. I trust you will always let me know?"

Within weeks I received calls from at least five men whom I already knew. It seemed Emilee had secretly poached these guys from Scarlett's which was a bonus, having met a couple of them many times making it less daunting after all. Emilee would've known this, in which case she was able to pocket a very nice commission.

Soon I became much more business-like, my ambition a good thing. Once I'd made the commitment I had my eye on the prize, that being a house deposit and enough cash to set up my therapeutic business. My vision was becoming real!

However, dealing with these men's ego's and flashy playboy lifestyles took more than sexual efficiency. One of the challenges was how to equal that which Emilee provided as a service. It wasn't as easy as I had thought given my skill was to manipulate men into submission. These ones were hard work, phoning when I was in the middle of a delicious dinner at home, expecting that I would drop everything to meet up within an hour. To be available at any time they called did not sit well with me at all.

Firstly there was my health. I liked to be in bed by nine. And secondly, study commitments meant catching up was not always possible if I had a class early the next morning. I would suggest they make a booking the following day, or if they required my company for dinner they should give me warning so I didn't eat already! Within months I lost half of these high end (high maintenance) blokes. They did not take kindly to my time management spiel, not negotiating at all, implying it was all about them - which it was to some degree, I know.

Luckily the Goddess of good fortune was blessing me as the private sector began to boom and I was ready to go out on my own, which meant I no longer needed to work at Scarlett's. More efficient, with a head for business not really honed before, I asked Mr Gem and a couple of other regulars to visit privately, meaning my overheads would be paid until I could recruit new men to replace Emilee's fickle few.

Lilly, the lovely motherly type I had met at Scarlett's years earlier had gone private the year before and became a confidante. I got her number from a client, and during my transition she allowed me to work from her premises while I set up my own apartment near the city. We worked well together, completely in flow as she occupied the apartment from Tuesday to Thursday then Friday to Monday it was mine.

Advertising in the Adult Services section of the local papers showed me that by changing my name I had waved a red flag as many old faces appeared along with a few new ones who were about to test my resilience yet again. Private work meant I had to personally deal with all the crass callers, which was when I missed Sherri terribly. Her innate ability to gauge within seconds whether a man was genuine or a prankster was indeed a rare skill and one I had to learn very fast.

Intuition was imperative. While listening to my caller, gut instinct was monitored before making the final decision, meaning there were very few who managed to get as far as my front door. The array of questions included the following;

Do you do natural French?

Do you like mutual oral?

Can I go down on you?

Do we have to use a condom?

It didn't take long before I knew who these hard core dicks were. Surprisingly most often the corporate family man with a great deal of baggage, ego and no scruples, they didn't seem to care about tomorrow, only what they could get for their money today. I felt so sorry for their girlfriends and wives. Who could live with a man like that; or worse, how wouldn't they know?

I didn't know. The thought was quickly eradicated.

There were those who tried to bluff their way into getting me to agree to a natural service by saying the following; "I'm looking to make you my regular", to which I would answer, "Oh that's lovely, so what's wrong with your current regular then?"

This was all much to my own amusement of course, because no doubt they believed that a girl like me must be pretty stupid to be working in an industry like this. Then there were my general responses such as, "Well let's see if we click and if you decide to come back, who knows?" But the truth was that a) he may turn up only to be bitterly disappointed that he couldn't trick me or b) men rarely let on that they're disappointed, they just didn't come back.

During these first few years I discovered that a lot of men were not naturally good lovers at all, which went a long way in explaining why many of them couldn't get their wives or girlfriends to have sex more frequently. Some became a little too familiar, expecting to spend more time with me, or at the very least trying to haggle the price, not wanting to pay me as much, like they're offended they have to at all. I became aware that there were a few things I could tolerate in the private game. Firstly, I owed none of these men anything other than to have sex during their session, and secondly, I could not stand hearing a man beg or barter with me, which would turn me off completely, making it difficult to act keen to have sex with them.

But I did.

It's at this point in my sex work career that I figured out the answer to every bad relationship. What would happen if women were to charge their partners a fee every time men asked for sex? What if they sat down together and asked each other what really turned them on? I got asked this all the time and it was wasted; ours a shallow physical exchange at best. Only my long term regulars who bothered to build rapport were given ample scope and shared sincerity.

Maybe men would work harder at being more attentive, given they would have to pay for their women's time. Or did it just come down to biology? It's just sex – a physical exercise in order to procreate.

Sex and desire had nothing to do with love and intimacy at all, I would learn.

Chapter 8

Unmasked

It was during one of my classes that I thought I was finally going to lose my mind. Understanding Loss and Grief proved to be the most confronting subjects to date. Our lecturer talked in depth about the variable experiences of grief we can have during our lives, discussing events such as divorce, relationship breakdowns, infertility, life changes and death. Each week I could feel myself shutting down. I didn't want to continue with this subject because it was pressing on some old wounds.

We had to write about our own experience of personal loss for the final paper which meant I had to consider my topic. One Saturday afternoon during the final weeks, I sat quietly at my dining room table, looking out over the ocean through the window.

"Just start typing," I told myself in the hope that some story would take shape.

Writing a few words about Mitch, I pressed the backspace key. Looking at my notes, I knew the essence of grief wasn't quite there. Complex grief; when had I ever felt that? Thinking back over the years, there was one death in particular that had a significant impact on my life. Six months after Mitch left was when my grandma had died. Staring at the key board I began typing a few sentences, remembering how she would come over to sit with me, offering comfort and support as I tried to make sense of Mitch's actions.

I recalled how she would always stroke and pat my back when I was a child. Unwavering no matter how tired her arm would be, she would continue until I was nearly asleep. I had always relied on her to be there for me. During my teenage years we would go shopping and have lunch at least once a fortnight. We talked openly, me confiding my discomfort in having to experience a monthly period and how bloated it made me feel.

"Yes, it can be a time when your body bloats, but always make sure you eat really healthy," she said.

My grandma loved ordering the roast lunch with loads of green vegies finished off with a cup of tea. My eyes began to mist over as I wrote. It hadn't occurred to me before that our day out was a ritual sorely missed. I hadn't stopped to consider this or anything about our relationship before now. The tears came. It was another twenty minutes later before I could continue with the assignment.

Thinking back to when I got the news that she had died, feelings of shock, not being able to breathe all came up again. Pushing my notepad away I stood up, moving into the kitchen, for some reason thinking that this would alleviate the overwhelming need to cry but it didn't work. The next few hours were spent huddled on my kitchen floor, allowing the tears to flow. It was horrendous, but later that day once the assignment was filed away I knew I had given myself a gift.

It was hard for me to believe that I had held on to that much pain for so long, but in revisiting this period in my life it became evident that the impact of her passing was too difficult for me to process on top of what was already going on. I had to block out my relationship crisis so that I could cope with this bigger event.

As I sat there feeling her loss, the loneliness crept in and I remembered my last client at Scarlett's.

"Hello 'Scarlett's House, how can I help you?" Sherri answered.

It was 11pm and we were sitting there at reception, chatting to pass the time on an otherwise quiet night.

"Oh! Hello there Jason, and how are you?" Her eyes lit up, momentarily meeting mine. She was excited, given that most clients had gone off to new 24 hour establishments in the city.

"I'm really well, thank you. Yes. Yes. We have Ashley and there's a new girl you haven't met." Sherri looked at me, grinning. "Yes, she is lovely. I know you'll like her very, very much."

My ears honed in, not keen on taking a booking at this time of the night.

"Ok Jason I'll have Ashley come there tonight, followed by Jewel. Just up the road still, at that penthouse?"

My pulse quickened. I didn't want to go out to someone's home. I didn't do that and besides, I thought our establishment had a strict policy on this? Sherri ignored my hand waving in her face.

"Ah, well ok let's see," Sherri spoke with rehearsed precision. "Stephanie still hasn't come back to us, sorry. I only have the new girl also available at the moment and the other three beautiful ladies have been booked out on a dinner escort."

It was always amusing to observe Sherri's manipulation of the truth. There was only me and Ashley on tonight.

"Jason, I think you will really love this new girl. However, I'd recommend that you come meet her first as she hasn't been out before, only on dinner dates. I wouldn't want to spoil your evening by sending you a mouse."

It seemed Sherri knew Jason fairly well, but I was way too nervous for this kind of meeting. Shaking my head, none of this felt right.

"Ok see you soon!"

Looking quite pleased, Sherri was ready for my onslaught.

"What do you mean *new* girl? You *know* I'm not going to his home!"

"It's ok! Really Jewel, he is a lovely guy! He hasn't been in for over a year. Just meet him, see what you think, and if it doesn't feel right, that's fine!" Sherri fired back with a little spirit.

I was reminded again that it wasn't an ideal time to be so choosy. Following her down to the girl's room whilst contemplating how I would handle this predicament, she prepped Ashley laying on the lounge in her denim shorts and t-shirt, watching Sex and the City re-runs on Foxtel.

"Ashley, get ready. Jason will be here in ten minutes."

"Oh excellent! It won't be a dead night after all!" she squealed sitting upright and pushing away the remaining piece of chocolate she had been nibbling on all night. Ashley and her husband were about to buy their first house after this month and she hoped to retire to try for a baby. I really liked her and didn't want to see her go.

"Yes. He's just popping down to meet Jewel and then you two will go back up to his apartment," Sherri continued to explain while Ashley scuttled around to get condoms and lube. She wasn't subtle, which is what I adored about her the most - no 'airs and graces'.

"What's up?" Ashley asked, aware I was not looking so pleased.

"She's nervous about going to his home," Sherri explained, looking intently at Ashley for support.

Ashley turned to me. "He is such a nice guy, Jewel. You don't have to do anything you don't want to".

"I don't want to go!" I rebelled.

The doorbell rang and my stomach lurched. There was no way I would be going anywhere with a stranger. Deep within, my body recalled how dangerous a predicament this can be. The eight year old hadn't forgotten Hans and Franko.

I barely heard the words as Sherri greeted him at the door. "Hi Jason, just take a seat. How've you been?"

"All is well, no problem here, thanks. How about you?"

His thundering voice unnerved me.

"Oh bloody hell."

He sounded like a huge bikie or murderer. Then I realised, how would I know what a huge bikie or murderer would sound like? Ashley was so casual, laid back as usual, checking her lipstick before sashaying out.

"Your turn, sweetie," she said, coming back to sit on the couch next to me.

"I can't. Ashley I don't want to."

Placing a hand on my shoulder, she soothed me. "Love, he's really nice. I promise!" Her big blue eyes did make her look like Meg Ryan after all.

"Thanks Ash," I said, squeezing her hand.

We hugged before I stood up, taking in a deep breath before meeting our guest.

Stepping into the room, my eyes took in this man, gasping internally at the size of his shoulders; one of his legs was the size of my whole body. His hair, a thick, dark mass, sat into the nape of his neck. Dark, moody eyes met mine, holding my gaze with such softness it was perplexing. He was handsome in a rugged, exotic sort of way. This unnerved me, but why? I wanted to run. But where?

"Hey, Jewel is it? How's it going?" He spoke in a way that danced, his voice no longer such a threat given it matched the depth I could see in his eyes. "Love your red nail polish."

Watching as he pointed at my toes I relaxed for a moment. It was a strangely observant comment for a big man, I thought.

"Yes, thank you," I answered, surprised by how silly I felt. Then I backed out of the room, trying not to meet his eyes again.

Sherri appeared at the girl's room doorway.

"OK girls, he wants you both."

"No way!" I yelled.

Was he serious?

"Look, its ok honey, I will go first. It'll be fine, and I can even stay with you once you get there." Ashley reached out to touch my arm as she sauntered over to pick up her bag, ready to go.

Sherri was deep in thought.

"Ok then Jewel. I will go tell him Ashley first then he's to call when he's ready for you."

An hour later, Jason greeted me at his door wearing undone jeans and a t-shirt which looked like it had shrunk.

"Hey gorgeous, come in," he said, smiling too pleasantly.

Ashley raced past me at the door. "Ok kids, bye! Have fun!"

"What?" I said, dumbfounded as I watched her jump into the lift.

"Come in, quick! I don't want my neighbours catching me dancing around in this bloody t-shirt!" Jason joked, making me laugh.

He did look ridiculous, I thought, as I wandered in behind, walking past the bedroom where cushions lay scattered around the room.

"We've been chatting and bouncing around, nothing else happened really," he stated, seemingly aware of my discomfort. I liked that he seemed observant and caring.

"I'm not really one to go to a man's apartment."

Did I just say that to a man who has paid?

"What are you smiling at?"

Jason caught himself, quickly turning toward another small room, pointing to a chair in front of a computer.

"Come on, sit. I would just like some company, ok? So don't give me shit young lady. Sit down."

Sitting beside me, he powered up the screen.

"Ok, now of course I'm aware that you are so fucking sexy but hey, there's nothing like red nail polish to get me going but its fine. Tease me if you must but in the meantime, humour me and look at my holiday photos."

Remaining on high alert, I prepared to see porn.

"Ok, this is me and my best mate in Monte Carlo…"

He was showing me his holiday photos! After a few screen changes I completely relaxed, this man becoming hard to resist.

"Is that a Ferrari? What are you up to?" I asked.

"Yep! You wouldn't believe it? We got to Rome and hired a car, right? Then we took off and decided that we would drive to Cannes. Well, we were almost there when we were stopped for speeding!"

Jason's excitement was infectious.

"Oh I love Rome. I've been down to Cannes too!" I shared. "Then I went to Naples, Paris. Europe is so exciting and beautiful, isn't it?"

"Yes it's amazing," he continued. "The winding roads, just travelling between all those little villages, it's like another world. We had so much fun, Louis and me." He pointed to his mate who I had already witnessed as his passenger in most of the photos.

The hours rolled by before we heard Jason's phone ringing.

"Oh shit, who's that?" he asked me.

Laughing, I shook my head from side to side. "How should I know? It's your phone! Oh, actually. Oh my God!"

"What?" he asked, looking for his Nokia.

"I forgot to call Sherri! I was meant to check in two hours ago!"

He answered his phone as I searched for mine.

"Hello? Oh, sorry Sherri. Yes, she's still here. Yes everything's fine!" he said, shrugging his shoulders as he grinned at me. "I, you know, we've just forgotten the time. I'll pay you for the extra, I promise," he said before hanging up.

"I should probably get going." Feeling uncomfortable again, I couldn't look at him, instead picking up my bag ready to leave.

"Please, stay for a little while. It's ok. In fact, stay the night, no sex!" he added, watching me recoil. "Just keep me company and I will pay you double in cash. Sherri doesn't need to know?"

His shoulders slumped. This wasn't good. It wasn't about the money because I was already earning loads, but what was it I saw in his eyes? He was lonely, just like me.

Liking him wasn't what I had expected. More silence fell between us. I could smell his cologne; Armani. His expression changed, looking embarrassed almost afraid as he spoke.

"Are you single?" he asked, stepping back a fraction to give me space.

Taking a deep breath, staring past him, I answered.

"Yes, Jason I am. So if I'm to stay, you had better pour me a drink."

Jason's name flashed up on my mobile as I rehearsed my response before answering, knowing what was in store.

"Hey there mister, how are you?"

"Hey babe, I'd be much better if you were here. Coming over?"

It had been three months since I met Jason, and already I was annoyed at myself for giving him my number. We hadn't done anything else that first night, but since then he called at unusual hours, and never for just a chat.

Now remember what you've rehearsed? Be strong. Don't become his free bonking buddy!

"Seriously, I'm pooped and staying home, you hear me?" I responded clearly, not wanting to be manipulated by this charming man. I should never have stayed over that night, but loneliness had got the better of me.

"Hey gorgeous, c'mon please! I will send a car around for you. Anything you want. Come. Please," Jason pleaded.

I laughed, loving every minute of it. "No! Take me out for lunch during the week or something," I suggested, partly wondering why he hadn't before now.

"I need you, Taryn. I've had a crap day at my families. You know what my parents are like," he moaned yet again.

Yes I did know, but I didn't like the inference that I should be sympathetic when I hadn't even met his parents, so how could I really know what they were like? Was he trying to start something with me, or simply taking advantage of my empathy and free time?

"I want you to stay and just hold me tonight."

"No, I should go. Jason, it sounds like you've been drinking so don't try the 'drink and dial' thing on me." I laughed. He was so demanding and cheeky which dispelled the discomfort I was feeling.

"Ok bye," he answered, disappointment filtering through.

I hung up, relieved, until ten minutes later he called again.

"Hello, Jason. Now what?"

"Please. Just for one hour. Just for a hug." His voice was pleading. I should have turned off my phone.

His silence stirred compassion within me. "Oh alright then, but only for an hour okay?"

"Ok of course gorgeous one. See you soon!"

Fifteen minutes later, having thrown on jeans and a jumper I walked to his penthouse close by on the lower north shore. Buzzing on the intercom, a concierge allowed me entry and I took the lift to the top floor where he was waiting at the door.

"Well hello," he whispered into my ear as I sauntered past. I snatched the cigarette dangling from the corner of his mouth. "Finally I can relax in the arms of my Goddess."

Shrugging my shoulders I knew he was laying it on really thick tonight.

The stereo was playing; bass way too high reverberating in the sparsely decorated space.

"You ok?" I asked.

"Oh fucking hell. I just hate it. I still don't seem to be able to make my family happy, you know."

I nodded, following him into the kitchen, searching for a saucer to use as an ashtray.

"I'm sure you do," I responded, noting how sullen he looked. His big, black eyes were hollow, miserable almost.

"Hmm, yeah well. My brother and his wife christened their little girl today. My younger brother," he continued.

I looked away so he couldn't see the hurt. Why didn't he ask me along? He kept talking about catching up during the days since we met, but maybe he thought I wasn't an appropriate woman to introduce to his family? I pushed this from my mind, convincing myself that I was being paranoid because of what I always heard people say. Clients dismissed the idea that a man would love me if he knew what I did for a living. Their words rang in my ears, wounding me deeply; *No-one ever falls in love with a prostitute – no offence!*

"You okay?" he asked, noticing my distance.

"Yes, yes I'm fine. Go on," I said, pushing all my doubts back down.

"So there I am, and my parents, everyone was looking at me and saying, 'When are you going to be next, Jason? When are you going to settle down, have a family?' he mimicked.

Wandering into the lounge I stood still, facing the floor to ceiling glass which gave a majestic view over the city. The glass was trembling with fierce winds - this wasn't a place I could live in. I was an earthly type of woman, a garden being what I desired.

"Want a drink?" he asked, handing me a beer.

"Sure, why not."

Turning toward him I felt edgy, wanting a hug but not comfortable to ask. I didn't want to seem needy. Isn't that what always stuffed things up for Sally and my single forty something friends?

"I'm so tired of it all," Jason said, flopping onto the couch.

Observing this man, I saw a big boy. He needed an audience, a shoulder.

"Come here?" Holding his arms open, reluctantly I joined him, sitting at the other end so as to create an open space. I wanted him to see me, to sit up and talk.

His head rested between my breasts.

"Jason, what are you doing?"

Was this man so insecure? He began talking more again about his family until finally I was beginning to yawn.

"Ok that's enough. Time for me to go," I shouted, pushing him off.

"Noooo. Please don't leave me now. I'm ready for bed too. You come up with me, please?" He beckoned towards the mezzanine bedroom. I had no intentions of falling into bed with him in his state.

"Go on, go have a shower then."

Delighted, he leapt up the stairs two at a time then disappeared. "Ok. See you in a minute!"

Hearing the water running, I quietly let myself out and was nearly home when the phone rang.

"Hello," I answered, expecting a simple 'goodnight'.

"Taryn! Do you know how panicked I was just now? I've come out to find that you've gone! It's late, you shouldn't be out there at this time of night it's dangerous!"

His concern shocked me, making me feel guilty for judging him. "Ok, sorry Jason I just thought you'd understand and just fall into bed. It's one o'clock!"

"No, I'm not happy that you're out there. Please, come back. I will get you home safely in the morning."

My body resonated in response, pleased with his words. Maybe he really did care about me?

"Oh look ok, but I want to sleep. Deal?"

"Deal young lady. See you in a few minutes then. I mean it."

I smiled. Five minutes later pressing the intercom buzzer he let me in, greeting me with the warmest hug I could have ever wished for. We didn't sleep, but we didn't exactly make passionate love either. It was an awkward encounter, already filling me with regret.

"C'mon join me in the shower? I've got to get moving! Bloody Hell! It's already seven o'clock and Adam's meant to be picking me up in twenty minutes!"

It wasn't the warm embrace I had hoped for, worse than being with any client I felt empty and used. Easing myself out of the bed, I drank from the water bottle he had placed there the night before then wandered into the bathroom down the hall.

"Where are you now?" he yelled out.

"I'm just down the hall having a quick wash." I didn't want to give away any more of myself, so I dressed quietly before stepping out onto the balcony to wait. *How do I nurture a relationship with a man who is so self-absorbed?*

"Ok, there you are? Got everything? Let's go!"

His body language reflected distance between us, confusing me even more. Deflecting that something just wasn't feeling quite right, I followed him out to the lift. Standing there waiting side by side, he finally spoke.

"I love what you're wearing, by the way. You always look so good!"

"Oh. Thanks. Yes, funny enough would you believe I had these on last night?" I responded, trying to make light of the situation.

"Very funny. You're a lovely girl. Oh, here we are."

Jason gestured for me to enter first, standing quietly for the few minutes before we arrived on street level. Following me out into the street, he looked around.

"Ok, well then, thank you again. That was fun, hey? You take care."

Hugging me quickly before jogging over to the car, he didn't turn around.

Entering Simon's tiny consulting room, I knew this was where I needed to be.

"How are you? Come, sit down and get comfortable. Let's make sure you have room to move."

I took a deep breath, ready for the perilous journey he always took me on.

"Hi yes, good thanks!" I answered a little strained.

"What would like to talk about? You seem to have something on your mind?"

"Yes," I answered nervously, aware this was not going to be any fun.

"Good. We'll begin first by taking a few minutes to breath. Deep breathe in, and relax. And out. Close your eyes."

Looking back, it occurred to me that my sober life hadn't been much fun at all. Happiness was relatively false in order to convince everyone my life was great.

"Okay what would you like to talk about today?"

I was ready.

"I never felt attracted to Mitch or Greg." This sounded bizarre, even to me. What had hooked me in? "And recently I met someone who I wanted to be with but he didn't want to be with me. Well, not in a relationship anyway is what I mean."

Was it Jewel he was attracted to? Should I reveal that part of me to Simon? My eyes opened to gaze at fingers tightly entwined. Was she the reason I lacked real intimacy in my life?

"I was seeing him professionally - at first, that is."

Prepared to meet Simon's judgement, he didn't flinch.

"By professionally, what do you mean?"

Squirming, I was challenging myself. Did I really need to reveal this much?

"At work."

"At work," he repeated, not prying further.

Relieved, I closed my eyes again. "Well, I met him and knew it was not wise to get involved, I guess."

"It wasn't wise to get involved?"

I became agitated.

"What's happening for you?"

"Yes it wasn't wise. He was a client."

Pointing to my throat where there was a lump building, my mind re-ran events; specifically that last morning when Jason had left me standing there. It had been a month ago and I hadn't heard from him since.

"I see you are feeling uncomfortable. Are you ok to ask more questions of yourself, and maybe express those feelings that make you feel uneasy?"

I was tired of asking questions. I wanted the answers. Fidgeting, I fought the urge to open my eyes, choosing to follow Simon's voice.

"Let your feelings guide you; try not to think. Ask your throat area what it feels? What can't be said? Give it permission to speak."

Aware of the soft music in the background and the aroma of incense, I began feeling lighter; my shoulders dropped, thoughts evaporated, allowing a portal for direct communication to flow. A big sigh, then words came.

"From the moment I met Jason I was attracted to him." My shoulders slumped forward, remembering the overwhelming struggle to resist any feelings for him.

"You were attracted to him?" Simon repeated.

"Yes. Strange isn't it? I was never attracted to the others, really. They pursued me which became part of the attraction for me."

"Nothing is strange, Taryn. It is what you felt. Trust it."

Sitting with this, I smiled.

"Okay well it gets more interesting. As you know I've had a couple of disastrous relationships, but with Jason, I actually felt him."

"You *felt* him?"

"Yes. I never felt anything before, like a connection, wanting to feel his touch if that makes sense." I faltered, feeling a little too exposed.

Did this make sense? I often wondered how to explain this to people, but then realised I never had to. I never talked to anyone about my life outside of Scarlett's. I wanted to look at Simon to make sure he understood, but realised there was no point. I had to unravel this one for myself.

"I knew that with him, well, it felt really soothing for me to have my body respond in some way."

I sighed, feeling embarrassed.

"It's okay, there's no judgement here. It felt really soothing for you."

Another deep breath, I continued.

"Once this happened, I felt more like I could be myself. Maybe it was desire that made the sensations so real. That's what I mean when

I say I *felt* him, like actually registering that the physical connection was quite beautiful."

I sighed, the magnitude of this claim making me sit up and open my eyes.

"That was big for you then?" Simon responded, matching me.

"Yes, it sure was. I guess it makes a little more sense now. On top of this it then felt wonderful to be needed."

"To be needed?"

Simon was responding rapidly, stirring unfamiliar responses from my body.

"To have his attention, I mean, and to feel something I think. Um, I don't know really – to be honest it was physical, not emotional."

"That's okay. You don't have to know anything more right now. Let's see if your body knows more shall we?"

Unlocking my fingers, flicking the cane fibres on the arm of my chair I notice how harsh, yet fluttery they felt. My eyes closed again.

"I felt something for him because his life mirrored mine, I guess. There he was, handsome, successful and yet so lonely just like me. But he also had good family values; he cared, he really did!"

I opened my eyes to look at Simon, still sitting there quietly, observing my body language.

"I can see that you've moved your hand here." Simon mirrored my pose; arm across chest, palm across heart. "What is it you're feeling right now?"

Looking down, I saw what he meant, but what was it I felt?

"I don't know, um. I think it's that I wasn't so much in love with him but loved being with him. I loved that he wanted to be with me but I don't think he was really present. Does that make sense?" I asked again.

Gosh this was hard, pushing out words in the hope that sentences would form.

"Does it make sense to you?"

I nodded, looking up to the ceiling for some insight.

"You know, I didn't want to drink when we met up but he was always so exciting to be with; so dynamic, I suppose. And we would have a little fun. He really did like me, he loved my body!"

Simon leaned back. "You had a little fun, and he loved your body. Do you love your body, Taryn?"

I recoiled at his words, my eyes opened wide. I loved that I was attractive to men; that they would pay to be with me. I felt confused, struggling as I thought hard about what was coming up. Then something happened.

"I can't believe it!" My eyes widened as I sat up straight. "He just wanted someone to listen to him and I guess I wanted the same."

But, I realised. I had wanted more.

"I was just a distraction; someone to play with, and why not?" I answered defensively, releasing the whore that my mother said I was.

"I can see you're getting angry. What just came up? Do you really think you were just someone to play with?"

I sat with that for a moment, then realising the truth.

"I just thought about my mum, but really it's about my dad."

"It's about your dad?"

Little pieces of memory pervaded my process as it became clear.

"Yes," I said. "It's about these men I've known. They've needed someone to take care of them."

I closed my eyes, remembering how my mother would berate my father, only to dress us up in Sunday best and encourage us to act like a happy family. We would go out and pretend everything was well, but Dad was sick.

"What's happening in your body as you remember this?"

I nearly choked on the sobs, the realisation too big to ignore any longer.

"I can see it now, my pattern that is. I can't believe it! I'm attracting men who've been wounded as children and need someone to look after them. I can't abandon them. I'm trapped. I stay until they abandon me!"

166

Leaning back, my body suddenly felt sore. Hadn't I got that message before? My spine ached, like it had been supporting my shoulders for too long. I felt tired. Exhausted to the point where it became justifiable at an unconscious level not to bother with feeling anything.

"What's happening now?"

"I'm exhausted, actually," I said.

My eyes wandered around the room as everything became clear; old patterns easy to see. I was astounded.

"I don't want to continue that pattern, Simon. Please, help me to understand how I get to that place?"

"Yes there do seem to be patterns. What patterns do you see?"

Pondering this, it was hard for me to speak but I knew it was time.

"I can see how that passive aggressive thing plays out," I said, squirming with anticipation for more pieces to fall into place. "My mum, she stuck by my dad as he healed. Then with Mitch I was trumped from departing but with Greg the pattern threw me a bit. He suffered with low self-esteem, becoming narcissistic, always needing reassurance. The men in my life have all been emotionally unavailable because of their issues."

I laughed, leaning back to hug myself.

"That was a lot, Taryn. How do you feel?"

For a moment I felt wonderful, and then it happened - I cried.

"I feel hurt, but at least I've faced the truth at last. When I've needed reassurance that I was safe, no man gave me this."

The sobbing subsided.

"These men think I'm tough and hard to reach but the truth is I'm only strong because I've had to be. I feel overly sensitive and vulnerable when I'm involved more intimately."

"More vulnerable when involved intimately," Simon repeated. "What does being more vulnerable mean to you?"

I sighed. The word had such impact.

"Vulnerable." He repeated the word.

Taking a moment to form meaningful interpretations, I answered.

"Vulnerable because I've never felt safe in this world. I don't know what it's like to be protected. You know, I don't recall much about being joyful in my own way unless it was controlled by my parents on their good day. And same with the men I seem to attract. The idea of being feminine means being vulnerable, which is why I act more from my masculine energy, which is what you highlighted to me."

Simon looked at his palms, then at the clock by his side.

"I know this session is coming to a close, but I'd like to give you more time to really process these patterns you're becoming aware of. These emotionally unavailable men in your life, how do you feel about all this?"

"I see I went for the nice guys but they were wounded like me, often with low self-esteem. How could they have ever stepped up to take care of me when they couldn't even face their own fears and insecurity?"

I sighed, a sense of relief flooding my system – euphoric release becoming abundantly obvious as my body regained composure.

"Once I got sucked into that vortex of being needed and accepted, there was no escape. I settled, becoming dependent and giving up on having my own needs met because nobody asked what my needs were. I didn't even know before now."

My shoulders hung heavy.

"I gave away my power but I'm ready to take it back!"

Chapter 9

The Shadow Wants a Life

The weight of juggling two lives became tedious.

My well of optimism was running dry as I pushed ahead, crawling towards graduation day. No longer was I achieving the same lucrative financial targets which had become increasingly difficult to reach given the competition flooding into the private sector. On top of this, I was managing micro relationships that no-one knew about, further challenging my multi-tasking skills as my body struggled to rid itself of the memory of energy depletion.

Energy – I needed to understand this more.

Gazing over the crowd at an outdoor eatery across from my apartment, I observed a restaurateur as he negotiated where to seat diners keen for a harbour bridge view. Platters laden with succulent seafood and fruits were placed on tables. Fabulous food always soothed me. I ate much more these days, and as the quality of my diet improved, so did my health. My body was amazingly agile and healthy once again. Regular visits with the naturopath helped rebalance my body's metabolic rate and with the increase of proteins in my diet I no longer fell into adrenal exhaustion or hypothyroidism.

A healthy hormone system meant my glands were functioning normal again with the production of regular levels of cortisol, and my blood sugar levels were normal - I felt great! I thought about my presentation on eating disorders. I was keen to show that it's such an insidious affliction not given the same kudos as alcohol for the destructive impact it has on people's lives. Often hidden for many years, maybe since early childhood as was the case with me, I'm well aware of how an eating disorder may manifest into erosion of self-worth. I could see how this had fuelled my obsessive, self-destructive behaviour that probably led to my health complications in adulthood.

Highlighting such behaviours as modern day dis-eases may help health practitioners to tackle the issues with their patients. If it is better understood publicly, then we will be able to give people reason to seek help without them fearing ridicule. Pondering this further, I knew my purpose was becoming clear. I smiled, pleased that my throat chakra (Sanskrit word for energy wheel within the body's energy system) had finally become unblocked, making it easier to speak up.

I had found my voice.

This made me think about my mum as I realised the courage it must've taken for my parents to take responsibility for their lives. In recent years they had begun taking better care of their health by giving up cigarettes and alcohol. I really missed my family. My mother had loved to cook for us on Sunday's, allowing us to bring our washing around so we didn't have to rush home afterward. She would throw everything into the dryer then fold my nephew's clothes up, leaving my sister and her husband playing outside with the kids while I talked openly for hours with dad about my work in men's health. Consequently my dad then spoke to an uncle who was experiencing blood in the urine, encouraging him to get a check-up which confirmed prostate cancer - immediate treatment began with excellent results!

In recent months when calling my mother, no longer were there difficult pauses often overturned by talking about my nephews or the weather. I could thank my training for giving me the capacity to stay centred when we spoke. I had come to understand that her intention was never to hurt me even when she projected anger which was hers to own. I could hold the space between us with more dignity and compassion, understanding my parents for the way they had tried to deal with their past. To identify these traits not as flaws but instead as survival mechanisms helped me to forgive them without expecting anything more. I wrote down my feelings as they arose throughout class. I could see the way forward;

'To know is to identify, to understand what it is that supports me, what triggers the old pattern is a feeling of being vulnerable, to apply that I can accept humility and the not knowing I can open to feelings of love and recognise my life's purpose.'

My parents and I accepted each other at last, prepared to meet in that centre where unconditional parental love resides. Not only did my family relationships benefit from my healing, so did my sex work. Clients who were becoming familiar were easier to manage as I kept them on the periphery, acknowledging them as men with needs within the premise of a paying client. Boundaries were redefined and drawn. However, the more evolved I became, the more aware I was of the energetic connection between us. This was a cue that I was ready to begin a relationship outside of sex work. My body was beginning to feel the impact of non-intimate sex, craving intimacy where more meaningful love making was desired.

Through coaching practice and clinic, I learned my archetypal energy was The Warrior. Energetic Healing studies validated the vibrational sensitivity I had experienced, further investigation concluding there were blocks within my base chakra which helped me identify my strong need for security and trust. Sexual energy was my source of power but I needed to worship my body more. Part of me was still battling with two other archetypes. I was The Caregiver, with subsequent reference to discomfort in my sacral area (near the bellybutton, associated with safety, nourishment) and The Seeker, manifesting near the solar plexus (under the ribs, honouring one's identity, transcending self-limiting beliefs).

Moving through these blocks was challenging but this wasn't to say I was totally cleared. The fact that I denied the truth to myself about engagement in sex work meant I experienced the occasional heart palpitation in the middle of the night. My body would go cold as I lay there wondering if this lifestyle had caught up with me. I realised it was symbolic of death – or an ending at the very least. I was aware that some of my clients felt a certain degree of love for me, but it wasn't reciprocated by me. I was resonating energetically with the lie. It was time to be more congruent on every level. My body knew this. My emotional and spiritual essence knew this too.

During the final stages of integrating study with practice, I adored the spiritual messages I received when reading text such as Victor Frankl – 'Man's Search for Meaning' - his story of survival in a concentration camp impacting upon me immensely. He talked about the human condition and why some of us may overcome anything given the strength of our spirit, which spurred feelings of contentment, recognising that unintentionally I had transformed and become whole.

Notes written in 2005 during coaching supervision sessions reflect this;

'I choose not to be alone and to find the joy in sharing my life with others; thus sharing love and acknowledging the beauty of being alive is part of my greater purpose.'

After three months of clinical practice seeing clients, our lecturers provided us with feedback during supervision and debrief. Soon I was competent, aware of the value in listening and being patient as people began opening up. Each individual was unique, every outcome dependent on what they found most problematic as I held an ethical space for them to vent anger, then determine the path they needed to take in order to find resolution and peace.

The time was flying by, and then it was time for graduation. My parents flew in to Sydney for the weekend, and much to my surprise I was overwhelmed with emotion, hugging my mother as we cried and reconciled the hurt unspoken for too long. We spent the mornings walking along Balmoral Beach, my mother holding the space for us to talk openly and heal the past.

I missed them when they left.

Once everything settled down again, I realised that setting up a holistic counselling business with paying clients wasn't going to be that easy. I gave a few friends free sessions to keep up my skills as the weeks after graduation flew by. Sex work was still my reality. It was good money, but not where I wanted to be, especially as it meant I had to continue managing my high maintenance regular clients who were becoming more demanding, wanting to see me on short notice, making myself available even when Mother Nature had clocked on. Fortunately I never had any issues having sex during my periods; I hardly ever bled anyway, but as the years passed by, a new evil lurked.

PMT.

This was when the reality of sex as work began to grate on my nerves. PMT is a struggle for most women, but there's the luxury of making out you're reading something whilst staring blankly at the computer and stuffing in another morsel of chocolate. Not in this gig you can't; not when one was expected to look great naked and ready to pounce!

Achy breasts and bad moods were never sexy to a man who paid good money for an hour of perfectly happy, hot feminine charm. It was just luck that in the first few years my symptoms were rare. Also, having regulars in weekly time slots (usually) I was aware which clients I could see at what times of the month without committing a murder. However, I had to ensure absolute control over my mood swings whilst asserting my body to groping all the while oozing seduction and desire.

Over the years I knew a lot of women who could use a sponge or some other diversions but I found it all way too invasive, therefore leaving me one other choice. I had to start taking a day or so off every month, working harder the week before. Juggling periods and personalities had been easy once, but there's no beating the odds, with my feminine side emerging the victor as my biological clock started clanging once again. My womanhood forced a revision of resources as the truth screamed at me; *how much longer can you keep this up?*

I had reached my limit. The ache in my belly needed attention as I pondered this, the wet feeling between my thighs indicating my cycle had begun.

"Oh for God's sake," I muttered, racing into the bathroom for sanitary pads. I couldn't use tampons. That just never seemed hygienic, plus there had been stories of toxic shock. Chemicals had become my biggest enemy. Having been socially withdrawn for some time, no longer commuting within polluted zones, my immune system had become much stronger but at a cost; sensitivity to the environment, cleaning agents and toxic fumes.

Looking into the bathroom cabinet mirror, I poked out my tongue at the image. "You really need to get your butt out there and get a life!"

Get a boyfriend, I thought. But where was I to start?

Thoughts were interrupted by my work phone ringing over on the bathroom vanity. It came everywhere with me because typically a client would ring at the most inconvenient moment. Glancing at the screen, it was Bill. I had met him on one of my first nights at Scarlett's House and he had happily followed me into private practice. A colloquial type in his late 50's, with leathery skin and a 'larrikin' attitude, we often had a laugh. God knows as a banker, Bill certainly needed to let off steam.

"Hello there, sexy man," I answered. "So, what can I do for *you* today?"

"Hello Jewel, oh I don't know?" he answered. "That depends. What are you up to?"

It was Tuesday. Bill was always a Friday 'beer o'clock' booking, although I had managed to get him to visit me *before* hitting the pub.

"Um, well." I began. "I'm just making my way to the car and heading back to the office. And you?" I asked, propping myself up on the bath, PJ's hanging around my knees whilst jostling to get a pad into my knickers. I hoped he couldn't hear the echo and guess my real location.

"Well, I'm heading off overseas again Friday, so I'm hoping you can see me today. What do you think? Say five pm?"

Nooo. A month! That's a thousand dollars gone!

"Jewel?"

I contemplated two very important aspects. One; he was an extremely valued client and two; I badly needed a Brazilian.

"Jewel, are you there?"

I made the judgement call.

"Yes, yes. Perfect. I can't wait to see you!" I lied yet again. This was getting too difficult. I really didn't want to act anymore. "What time did you say?"

"Me neither," he answered. "Five o'clock, is that okay?"

"Can we make it six?" I answered too quickly, buying as much preparation time as possible.

"Six pm is fine. Okay see you then," he said, all chirpy before hanging up.

By six pm my period had eased. It was the wax job that had me close to being completely debilitated down there. But I would manage somehow - I always did.

The buzzing of my intercom perpetuated further resourcefulness.

Fake it like you used to; imagine that you feel nothing. Believe it to be true and it will be.

This little voice heckled me, just like old times when I'd first started out.

I let Bill in.

"Hello lovely lady," he swooned, kissing my cheek before heading off to the lounge room. This was his usual procedure. We had one, I realised. It was a well-worn and rehearsed sequence week in and week out. For years we had indulged in this ritual.

"And good afternoon to you!"

I smiled. I was usually more genuine but not today. He took of his clothes, watching me place everything neatly on a recliner as he grabbed a towel.

"How was your day?" he asked from the bathroom. I heard the water running, and responded in a louder voice.

"Oh, I've had better ones. And you?"

"Oh what's up? What's happened?"

In the bedroom ready for his entrance, he came strolling in and lay down immediately onto his back, waiting for me to make my usual moves.

"So, what were you saying?" he asked, his erection too hard to ignore.

This was where I would normally hop on top and we would continue the general conversation. I began with the small talk again.

"Oh nothing. It was good," I answered, allowing my silk red negligee to fall off my shoulders.

This was when I recognised the lack of authenticity. Mine. I wanted to facilitate healing and not do this false action anymore. Bill would be my last client.

Good thing I had enough savings to pay all my expenses - for six months at least!

My first lazy morning after retiring from sex work was spent lounging around allowing wonderful ideas to come flooding in. I couldn't wait to get started on researching clinics to approach, but firstly I would book myself into an energetic healing session.

At sacral level, the facilitator hovered over what she described as a barren space; a hole that had me feeling weak and unstable for so many years. Gradually she managed to close the hole, my new perspective filling the gap that once contained emptiness.

I felt so much more grounded and whole, even though the concept of this auric and energetic world was still a bit beyond my understanding. Nevertheless, my body embraced it and I felt amazingly clear. Dressed in my running gear I drove to the Avalon beachfront where my favourite cafe was. Along the way I grabbed the local Times newspaper where both my sex work and therapy ads appeared.

"Hmmm. Morning Jack!" I said waving to the barista I had befriended over the years.

Jack, born to a Hawaiian mother and Hong Kong Chinese father, was tall and robust. Always jovial, his big blackish eyes opened up under the heavy bushy dark fringe. I had never seen such thick hair on a man, making this forty nine year old look like a boy of twenty five.

"Hey, gee you startled me! Boy, you're a little 'up' today. What's happening?" His mouth opened into that gigantic familiar smile, making it difficult to ignore the magnificent row of huge white teeth. His warmth was so adorable, my coffee ritual defined by the familiarity nurtured here where I belonged. Every morning his enquiry about my day was the most personal conversation I would have before transforming into Jewel.

"I've recently graduated, I'm a counsellor now!"

"Well done! That's great!" He took money from another customer as she left, turning back to brew my soy latte.

"So, tell me. What's next then?"

I sighed deeply.

"Well, I have to find somewhere to practice,' I said, glancing at the row of pastries that I never ordered, nicely laid out in the display cabinet, icing sugar shimmering; plump apricot Danish looking rather more tempting than usual.

An idea formed quickly in my head, spilling out of its own accord.

"Jack, you know how we've talked about energetic and shamanic work. What do you think about me offering this within my therapeutic space?"

Jack turned to nod at me. We had talked at length about his Hawaiian upbringing and the many healing rituals and beliefs of his mother's ancestors; all natural healers. For him, this had been a way of life and I sensed it was fast becoming mine. Maintaining energy during sex work had become a core focus during these years of study, which in turn had been of great benefit, teaching me how to keep enough energy in reserve so that I could function after work, no longer collapsing at home on the couch.

Turning to face me, Jack nodded to the nearby seat as he set up the frothy glass onto a saucer.

"Well, I think that's a great idea!"

"Really? I responded, taking my coffee.

There was no one else coming in so Jack walked around the counter to come sit down with me.

"I'm pleased you said that, Jack. Because after chatting to my healer I signed up to do further study. Did you know that masseurs and therapists' who touch bodies all day, are more prone to absorbing negative energies as well as losing their own positive and or negative flow to the client?"

"Yes, that's true!" He nodded.

"So healers need to balance their energy in order to stay efficient. Let's hope I can get some work in a clinic soon, then. I can't wait to practice!"

I knew I had made the right choice to stop sex work in order to balance my own energy. Jack looked at me momentarily before reaching for a nearby alternative lifestyle magazine.

"Here, maybe have a look in this. There's a listing for health practitioners and clinics in the back." Flicking through the thick pages, he pointed. "Look under New South Wales – Therapies. Oh, I gotta go."

Tapping me lightly on the arm, he stood up to greet another customer, leaving me to stare at the page open in front of me.

Wellness and Tantric Massage Centre; Leading Master and Tantric Goddess requires practitioner to share facilities Inner West. Please call Bhakti Sophia Macarena (Guru).

Looking around to see there was no-one standing nearby, I called the number.

"Hello?"

"Hello, is this Sophia?" I asked.

"Hello yes, this is Sophia. Who are you?!" she said, surprising me with her aggressiveness.

"Oh, I'm Taryn," I continued, a little put off. "I saw that you have rooms to share. I'm a counsellor, um, primarily interested in health and nutritional issues."

I don't know why I felt the need to explain this, but I did.

"Oh yes! Please, come and meet me and see the rooms."

Her demeanour changed completely, which made me a little wary.

"Oh okay, thanks. I will. I just wanted to ask a few questions first, if that's okay?" It didn't sound like it was, given the deep sigh I heard, but I continued. "Where are you exactly?"

"Inner West. You know Five Dock? Balmain?"

"Yes, I know where Balmain is. Okay let me take down the address and I'll come in tomorrow. Is that ok? In the meantime…"

"You come today," she abruptly interrupted.

I was stunned, my silence prompting a different response from her.

"Ok tomorrow is good. What time?"

Noting her accent, I chose to accept that maybe her manner was due to a cultural difference therefore not taking offence to the tone.

"Say nine am?"

"Yes, yes this is good!" She responded much more pleasantly this time, making me feel excited once more.

I had to trust my instincts, and my gut told me it was vital to take another risk. It had paid off when entering the sex industry so I could trust it again, couldn't I?

Chapter 10

Temper Tantra

Walking into an open space, a reception desk took up most of the right hand side and a large room decked out with wooden floors was covered in colourful yoga mats.

"Hello, anyone there?"

My eyes drank in the vast space which seemed twice as large due to a mirrored wall at the end. Shelves packed with rolled up posters and books by New Age authors filled the massive book cases that ran along the street side wall. Posters depicting yoga salutations and Indian Gods and Goddesses were tacked onto the spare wall. I could smell incense, sticks mounted on the massive elephant headed God Ganesh statue taking pride of place over in the far right hand corner. It was situated near a slightly raised stage surrounded by flowers and other rich pieces of tapestry.

She was right. I did love this room. It was huge, probably twenty five by eighteen feet wide. I couldn't wait to see the potential counselling space which was not obvious. There were no other doors, just a hessian curtain hanging behind the reception area. Was this it? I wasn't so certain this would be the right look for me. It seemed a little too esoteric for what I had in mind.

"Hello I'm Sophia. Welcome!" A voice greeted me from behind.

I turned around to see this colourful, thin woman standing there.

"I was resting at the back and thought I heard something. I had a meditation class this morning. Six thirty; very early," she said, rolling her tired eyes, dark circles clearly showing.

"Hello nice to meet you! Oh wow. So you're really busy then?"

"Yes Yes. Always very busy. Come in."

"Have you been advertising long?" I asked.

"Please. Sit and let's talk," she said, sounding too eager, dropping down onto the floor, folding her petite body into crossed legs. Sophia was wearing black tights and a green leotard ballerina style covered with an opaque sarong.

"Where are you from?" I enquired cautiously, in case she thought this rude.

"I'm a dancer originally," she shared, her big brown eyes brimming with pride. "From Spain."

"Oh. Lovely," I responded, noting her enthusiasm.

Her hair was bountiful; thick and dark, flowing half way down her back in bouncing waves, her skin an olive tint.

"Sophia, can I ask you something?"

She nodded, white teeth moving into a fixed wide smile.

"What do you mean when you say you're a Goddess and 'guru'?"

"I danced all over the world," she shared with an exaggerated pride. "Then, when one of our tours was over, friends asked me to go to India where I fell in love with the culture and the spirituality. The Divine Master then took me under his wing for many years, training me in the art of Tantra and other religious rituals."

I listened with interest, trying not to baulk at her idealism. I didn't believe in Divine Masters. From what I'd heard, these types generally led masses of naive people into belief systems that weren't really founded. That was just my view of course, and I hadn't really had any experience otherwise, so felt I owed it to myself – and Sophia, to be a little more open minded.

"That's amazing," I responded kindly, trying not to look confused. "What does that mean?"

Sophia leaned back, becoming more animated yet seemingly delighted that I had asked. Sadly I was sorry I had. When would I learn not to be so inquisitive? The hours passed as we sat together, me listening as she shared everything about her life; her spiritual journey, how this led her to the tantric teachings bringing with it the opportunity to become ordained as a guru and therefore more recently a master.

"I will also include tantric teacher training when you join my business, and you can share in my meditations each day. Of course once you are more comfortable you can also run classes with me," she suggested, watching carefully as I sat upright.

"Sounds interesting, yes I'm comfortable with some of that," I said, noting she had already come to the conclusion that we would be joining forces. "I've worked with a lady once who was a tantric teacher but I don't really know all that much. But I am an avid meditator!"

"Yes, yes meditation. Ok you know Tantra is about mastering the subtle kundalini energies and breath? It's the life force, the Shiva and Shakti aspect of connecting heavens with the earth. Okay?"

I smiled, not sure at all what Shiva and Shakti was.

"You will love it, and I will explain more as I teach you!"

"Oh, okay," I answered, quietly considering whether I should continue with energetic healing studies or take up her offer of tantric training. "Tantra sounds great. I'd love to be trained and assist at times. When I'm quiet, that is!"

Tantric practice made so much sense. During energetic healing class we were taken through chakra healing, and I was even more blown away with breath work. I already understood sex to be a divine and sacred act, so to learn and practice Tantra seemed the natural next step. In my research I considered how it would benefit my clients in relation to shame and self-esteem issues.

"And what about your qualifications, do you have certificates handy?"

She was staring at me a little strangely, which was becoming the norm. Digesting my question before hopping up to run toward the hessian covered doorway, I waited for her return.

"Yes, yes I do have many qualifications but everything is with my family. I will organise to get them emailed to me. You can see them tomorrow?" She returned with some documents in her hand.

"What are these?" I asked.

"Here's a contract for us. Okay?"

"Oh? Not just yet. Can we talk about me setting up my business; you know, as a counsellor? And where's the room? How many clients come through here each day? Then I'll have a read of this."

She made me feel a little too rushed, well aware that I didn't have all the facts as yet.

"Yes have a read first. So are you able to make a deposit for the room? Then you can come back in the morning and you meet with clients."

I had barely flicked over a page to read the fine print. Stopping to look at her, I couldn't believe she was serious.

"Oh, already? Why are you in such a hurry? And I haven't seen the room yet!"

She shrugged defensively. "No hurry! Okay yes come with me."

She hopped up, wandering back out toward the reception area. Quickly I followed, observing as she ducked behind a partition. Once I caught up, I noticed that there were two more doorways; one was marked 'toilet' and the other was a room.

"Here," she said, pointing into the space.

Glancing in, I noticed it was poky, barely large enough for a massage table and maybe a book case and a chair. But it was enough. It would work once I added my own posters.

"Oh, okay that looks fine. So let's talk about how much, shall we?"

"Yes," she said, skipping back out toward the large space we had just occupied.

"You can put down five thousand dollars deposit."

"What?!"

I stared at her, shocked that she thought for a minute that this seemed reasonable.

She took a moment to register my horror.

"Oh, for the month, that is. For Tantra teacher training and one month's rent."

"Why so much? I mean, how much is Tantra teacher training?"

I thought about what I would pay for room rental, and calculated that one hundred to two hundred a week was reasonable, given that's what I'd paid to share with Lilly so long ago.

"This means you're looking to charge me say approximately twelve hundred a week. Can you tell me what for?"

She gestured for me to sit back down on the pink coloured yoga mat.

"I will have an updated contract ready for you in the morning which will break it all down. Then we can continue talking yes?"

Hesitating for a moment, this did make sense so I agreed. I would compare the cost with the energetic healing diploma and then make a decision about that component.

"Yes okay that's perfect. How much were you outlining here?"

I flicked through the thick document, quickly scouring the dot points.

"You can put down one hundred dollars. And with the contract we will say five thousand – I will add in the additional clinic partnership offer in tomorrow's version for you."

"Five thousand. Right."

Who was she kidding? Surely the diploma would be much more worthwhile, and it ran over eighteen months. How could I possibly learn so much in one month?

"I have to read through this contract completely first, you understand."

Sophia looked at me like I was an idiot, but then retracted, aware I was about to walk away.

"Okay yes, sure. Let's look at this one now if you have time?"

"Yes I have time now. That's a good idea, so you can explain everything to me," I said, staring at her more sternly.

This was a business discussion therefore I needed to stand my ground. Sophia nodded, hopping up to get out a folder from behind the reception desk, opening it up to reveal wads of paper work.

"Okay, here. Let's look at a plan and schedule shall we?"

I nodded yes.

"If say you can come in three days for the next month from 9am to 9pm I will provide training. Let's break it down like this." She pointed to the paragraph outlining daily rates she wanted to charge me, as I calculated hourly rates for the training she would be providing. It didn't add up just yet.

"Maybe for the first two weeks I will, say Tuesday, Wednesday and Thursday - then I will come in five days a week?" I offered, keeping Friday, Saturday and Monday for insurance purposes. I might have to consider seeing regulars again until my new therapeutic business was up and running.

"Okay give me five thousand dollars. We can make that the monthly figure plus bond."

I froze. This woman was unreal.

"Sorry? Five thousand all up, but that's one hundred now, then tomorrow I give you the remaining four thousand and nine hundred if I'm happy with the final contract."

There was silence. Our eyes locked, neither of us wavering.

"Yes of course," she answered, eyeing me with annoyance.

I quickly worked out the figures in my head again. Looking at the hours I would be putting in, it looked rather good. Diploma subjects were approximately 2 hours a week per term so I could look at this as a fast track exercise while working here, meeting potential clients.

"Ok. So, can you give me a list of what you will teach me? I can review it tonight and bring cash back in the morning, when you will have a revised contract ready."

Her big black eyes lit up.

"Yes of course! I have that all listed here in this Tantra Teachers Manual," she said, grabbing another wad of notes to hand me. "See you at nine am tomorrow, right?"

Again her forthright manner unsettled me, but I chose not to let it override what I considered to be a great opportunity presenting itself. Quickly flicking through the copious amount of paperwork in what seemed to be a legitimate teaching manual, I felt much better. It was probably just her nature to be blunt; no people skills at all. I needed to trust more.

"Right. See you tomorrow then. At nine am."

She gave me a big hug, seemingly much more appeased as I opened my wallet, handing her a crisp, green one hundred dollar bill.

"Here." Sophia spun around to the wall, grabbing books off the shelf then dropping them into my open arms. "Take these books. We will do a practice and I will ask you more questions on chakras and what they relate to."

Once I was home I looked up the diploma criteria as I calculated the hours and cost. It looked comparable. After dinner I had sat down and carefully reviewed all the modalities she offered within this Tantra Training, much of the theory concentrated on aims of Tantra, the human body as a mandala, levels of spiritual awakenings (lokas), Tantra Sadhana (practice and yoga moves), Mantras, Yantras and Ayurveda aspects of medicine.

I knew it was the idea of making a commitment that I feared the most, which is why I reminded myself it was important to take the risk. A potential partnership was on offer, and I reminded myself that it had worked out well with Lilly when we stretched our rental agreement to include sharing of clients. It was time to let go of my fears.

Besides, what could be better than to start out with a spiritual woman as my guide?

Eager to begin a new chapter of my life, I arrived early, knocking on the front door. Trying the handle, it creaked open.

"Sophia?" I called out, enjoying the echo in my potential new workplace.

"Oh you're here! You have the money?" Sophia asked as she approached me.

"Here," I responded, again trying not to be overly cautious, showing her the crisp green notes in an envelope.

She leaned forward and gasped. "Oh wonderful! Here," she said, offering me the revised contract.

"Let's sit and do some breath work then move into yoga. Do you do yoga?"

"Yes, yes of course and what about Tantra practice?" I asked.

"Be patient and we will train once you've read more of the manual. By the end of the month you will be running classes with me! Then when I go away, you can run your own Tantra workshops."

I sat upright, not ready to consider this. And what did she mean about going away?

"Don't worry about that yet," she interjected. "Let's start! I have lots of people coming through so we should get you ready."

Taking a careful final look at the contract, it seemed okay. The contract was clearly outlined, stating what she would be teaching me, plus outlining my possible partnership upon agreement at the end of this contract term.

"And the rent for the room?"

"Yes, yes here. See? On this last page."

I checked again and was happy.

"Done!"

"Okay this is good!" Sophie laughed, clasping her hands together. "Here's a pen, and you sign. Then we can start!"

Sophia showed immediate commitment to teaching, making me much more relaxed about the investment I had made.

"Once you get comfortable with this, we can move onto understanding better the three aims of tantric sex. That is, Pleasure (Sukha), Progeny (Janma) and Liberation (Jivanmukti)."

I blinked, wondering if I was ever going to get the hang of this new language.

"Ok?"

"Oh. Yes, okay." I smiled nervously.

"Now put your hands like this." Sophia guided me to place my hands on my knees. "Good! Watch me and follow." We were doing the Sun Salutations, key yoga practice.

After a couple of hours we stopped for a break.

"Hey, let's chat yes? I'm tired too." Sophia said, observing my weariness. Extremely relaxed, like we were old friends, it felt a bit too soon given I wasn't one to get too close to new people. Her manner made me uncomfortable and wary once again.

"What else do you do eh?" she asked boldly.

I stared at her, unsure of what she meant.

"To make money," she reiterated, waiting.

"Oh, right." Turning around I saw her grab some more books off the shelf before walking out to the reception area.

"Someone is picking these up at lunchtime," she informed me.

"Oh. Okay," I responded, following her to another small room I hadn't noticed before.

"Come. Have a look. I do other things too!"

I didn't want to be distracted from our course.

"Sophia, how about we talk about personal stuff at the end of the day? I've got lots to do myself, so let's get back into it hey?"

She looked at me in disbelief.

"Sure okay," she answered despondently, moving back outside onto the yoga mats where we continued practicing some more tantric style positions. Soon she was showing me how to master fire breath through the nostrils. Then we moved into ocean breaths and other key pranic work. Finally we switched from this to discussing theory, all of which was a little overwhelming but fascinating, keeping me intrigued.

The day finally came to an end and I promptly began to pack up.

"You happy with today?" Sophia asked.

My body ached a little and I was tired, but otherwise the day had met all my expectations.

"Yes thanks Sophia. I can hardly wait to get started and meet your clients!"

"Soon, soon," she said, helping me pick up some books. "Read these tonight. Learn more about Shiva and Shakti, the story of the serpent, kundalini and the energies. It's all very important. Okay?"

"Okay," I said, copying her as she placed her palms together.

"Namaste."

"What?" I asked.

"This is a salutation. An honouring of the spirit and a greeting in India."

This was a brave new world for me, and as such I had to chill out. Everything was going to be fine. It was just a new language and new lifestyle that's all!

A few weeks later when I arrived, we moved onto the mats to begin practice as usual. After hours of movement, breathwork and homework revision I was exhausted, finally taking a break late afternoon.

"Okay come and have a look at my other work?" Sophia asked, taking me by surprise.

We had agreed upon a rigorous schedule, eight hours a day with two hours split into half hour food and rest breaks, with little interruptions for her to indulge in storytelling which was becoming tiresome. She skipped through the hessian curtains, gesturing for me to follow into what I discover was her bedroom with filing cabinets along the far wall.

Sophia stopped at the desk, turning to face me. "Internet dating. It is very popular; a good business," she said, watching as I absorbed everything around me.

"People want love. Men want sex. They need help hooking up. I do that."

"How?" I asked, more curious as to why men would so easily part with money on the internet in order to meet a woman.

"Easy. I have ads in the paper and men then go onto the website where I have the girls listed. Then when they see someone they like, they call and give me the code and I ask them to make a deposit so that I can arrange the date!"

Sophia was quite blasé about the whole thing, but I knew this wasn't my idea of an appropriate arrangement. How could it be authentic to set up lonely men with internet images; women they haven't met let alone spoken to? Calming down, I knew it wasn't my business to question other people's motives given my own choices.

"Great! And what about your tantric workshops? When is your next one to be held?"

"Oh not now it's getting slow, nearly the end of the year so I won't do another one until the end of January," Sophia casually told me while pulling out a chair and pointing for me to sit, "which is why it is very important to have another business. You can maybe help with this."

I leaned away, the wariness creeping back in. Had she just deflected my query?

"Oh. No thanks Sophia. I'm quite busy right now," I started to explain. "And then when it gets busy here, I will let that go. I'm good."

She didn't move, but I could see her mind trying to work out what it was that I did.

"So tell me, what else do you do?"

Looking into her face, knowing our arrangement, I decided to tell my potential partner the truth.

"Well." I hesitated.

Sophia sat still, staring at me looking innocent.

"I do sex work."

Her gaze never changed.

"Pro," I muttered, not wanting to elaborate, thinking this word would be a Universal language she may better understand.

Our eyes held for a few moments before she finally spoke. Her response far from what I had expected.

"Ah that pays well. You can work here if you need to. Then you can pay for next month. I will work out our new contract, and maybe you can pay me three months in advance. There's a shower at the back."

I watched her point out toward the toilets, un-phased by my announcement. If anything, the entrepreneur in her was delighted to see another opportunity filter through.

"Oh hang on. I don't make that much," I shared, trying to reel in this overzealous woman. "I will see how we go this week before making such a commitment after this month. We've agreed on a month, remember? That's all."

She stopped pulling together the paperwork and looked at me.

"But sex work pays really well. You can do both. That's ok, I don't mind."

I laughed. Sex work didn't pay so well when you no longer wanted to do it.

"Well thanks. I appreciate that," I answered, realising I really did. It was worrying me that there may be a clash in my values given it was a physical act versus this spiritual, energetic sex which Tantra was all about, but it seemed I needn't be too concerned.

"But seriously, no I'm not interested."

"Oh, okay then," she said. "Well, what about this business?"

I blinked back the disbelief.

"No thanks Sophia, can we get on with our training?"

Not another word was mentioned about my sex work or her dabbling in internet dating. In fact if anything, the final week went without any talk of personal endeavours as we became busier with creative dance, watching Indian documentaries on ritual and continuing with daily meditation practice. I had never felt so alive. Tantra helped to anchor me, contributing to a greater energy flow which boosted my capacity to continue seeing regular clients for a while.

Entering through the door on the last day I found myself once again subjected to Sophia's overzealous desire for further commitment.

"So it's been a month! Can you now pay for another two? You see what we can do next year, yes?"

I was stunned.

"Sophia, I've just walked in! And besides, not until we see clients and not if you're planning to take off overseas!" I retaliated, maintaining a direct tone which didn't go down too well at all.

"You MUST pay!" she screamed at me, no longer hiding her anger.

I almost fell back with shock.

"What? Are you kidding me?"

Disingenuous, this guru had clearly misrepresented herself. On that note, I was still waiting to see her credentials.

"You've learned about Tantra now. You could easily go off and use this for your clients and I've taught you everything!" she screamed at me. "Haven't you seen 'The Secret'? You do NOT believe! How do you expect to receive gifts from the Universe if you do not give back?"

Words were vehemently tossed at me. Where's her inner Goddess now, I wondered? My skin crawled, but I knew this was a test I had to pass. This was the real world and it was harsh.

"That's it, Sophia. I don't think we can work together if you're capable of firing up like this. What's wrong with you? I've barely completed this first month!"

"Yes it's quiet; I did not expect it to be quiet so yes I've booked to go home for Christmas. What is wrong with that?"

Everything was wrong with that. This was the first time she had told me that her trip was confirmed, in the meantime there still weren't any customers coming through her door. What was I supposed to do?

"Sophia, I don't feel comfortable with this. I'm going for a coffee, and we can talk about it when I get back."

Making my way toward the exit, I heard a bellowing, shrill voice.

"You will not leave! I will go on YouTube and tell everyone you are a whore! I know your name and so too will everyone else!"

Of course this got my attention, emptying my reserves of patience. I turned around to face her.

"What? That's such an awful thing to suggest! Let's just part company with some dignity and…"

"You show me no dignity! You've taken everything from me, from my business, my friendship. I tried to help you grow and you won't keep going. You're lazy. You are so ungrateful!"

My stomach tightened as beads of sweat lined my palms. Feeling cold, recalling a similar reaction in my body years earlier when experiencing my first panic attack. Fortunately I was a lot wiser, knowing logically that this feeling would eventually pass. These were only words, I reminded myself, blinking to see her face, confirming that this raging scene was in fact taking place.

I continued walking out the door, ignoring every nasty word she threw at me like daggers. Once inside my car, I breathed in deeply before checking my beeping phone. Sophia had already left a few messages but I wouldn't listen to them until later.

The messages were vehement and threatening.

"You need to come back. We have work to finish. You signed a contract!"

That cold feeling crept up my spine again. What was she talking about? My fingers began to tremble as they dialled her number.

"Hello." A stern voice bellowed, again reminding me that she probably didn't anticipate any other callers today.

"Hey Sophia, how are you?" I asked politely, determined not to stoke the fires of her contempt. God knows what else this crazy woman was capable of.

"I'm fine. You need to come back," she demanded.

Fuck, I thought. This had been a stressful and challenging venture, but why?

"I don't think so. If you look closely at the contract you haven't met the terms," I responded directly with no malice. "It included advertising as you know, and there haven't been any clients – your place was empty the whole time I was there!"

"If you don't come back, I'm getting a solicitor. I will…"

I hung up.

A solicitor?

This was more than I could handle as I imagined my neighbours' horror if they ever found out about my line of work. Or what if it leaked out further in the news, reaching my friends and family?

"What am I going to do?" I cried, sinking into the soft leather of my couch.

If I was forced to go to court, could I keep my secret life hidden? I felt nauseous; panicked more than I'd ever felt before. Here I was being emotionally blackmailed. It felt way too familiar, like when I was younger being stalked by a lover then my ex-husband who wouldn't take no for an answer. For the rest of the day I lay around on the couch rationalising my position, imagining the possible outcomes, determined not to be a victim anymore.

Surely Sophia couldn't be that serious? Was she willing to go that far with getting a Solicitor just to get more money from me? Sadly, yes she was. After tolerating another week of her nasty calls, along with a tirade of threatening emails, I reached a junction. Do I relent or retaliate? Holding my breath, counting to three I closed my eyes, listening to meditation music playing in the background.

It soothed me, giving my mind clarity. Why should I be the one to feel threatened when she had more to lose?

"Right, bitch. Bring it on!" I screamed, searching for a phone book. My plan was crystal clear.

Contacting a Solicitor to review the contract, he confirmed that Sophia had no legal matter to carry forward, agreeing with me that I had clearly met my part of the arrangement therefore I could move on. I made it perfectly clear to her then that if she threatened me again I would have no choice but to let the authorities know about her little on-line dating scam.

Grateful to survive this learning curve, I realised I needed to trust myself more. No more guru or self-declared expert input was necessary. From now on I would grow my business my own way, with integrity and self-belief.

Chapter 11

The Naked Truth

My experience with Sophia made me think more about where I belonged, stirring up an urge – a sudden desire to be near my sister and two nephews living on the Gold Coast. Throughout the years I had proudly watched her make a good home for her two boys who, at ages eleven and eight, were growing up so fast. When I talked over the idea with her, she was thrilled that I would consider moving up.

I believed this to be the best way to distance myself from sex work in order gain the lifestyle I had been longing for.

In the few weeks that followed my decision to leave Sydney, it wasn't my family or friends I thought about - it was my clients. These men with whom I had been so intimate for five years were about to be cloistered into the deep vault of my mind and I would be free! During my last days I thought about the diversity of all these relationships; ones that were organic with my sister and friends, the one I had resurrected with my parents and those that I was in denial about although they had supported me the most. Some men had become more than clients, they were friends.

Was moving to Queensland wise, or was I running away? The whole 'woman meets man, falls in love with man and lives happily ever after' scenario had never happened but through my friendship with Jay I learned the importance of valuing companionship. We loved each other dearly but there was no sexual chemistry at all.

Having survived years of study in psychology I had learned that this time around I wanted to attract the right man; someone who would respect me, plus match me in equality, integrity and independence just like we would expect from any of our friends. Leaving this city to start somewhere fresh seemed like the right thing to do.

Being single in my forties meant my dream of having a family was quickly becoming obscure. Whilst many women were now able to source options such as sperm donors or one night stands, this wasn't a choice for me. Given my own family history, the father needed to be someone who was prepared to step up and be known to my child. They wouldn't have to financially commit; only be emotionally and intellectually available whenever the child needed to connect. It was a personal thing, and something I could never compromise on, therefore I would just have to wait and see – I hadn't given up.

With one last act of defiance I relinquished Jewel, freeing her with a simple toss of the sim card containing all my client's details, although I did write down a few key contact numbers, just in case. Packing the car with my quilt and toiletries plus a suitcase full of my clothes, I drove up North with this new vision firmly in my mind, not too concerned at all that I didn't have any work.

Slowly we settled into life, and within a few days I got a job with a local charity. In the meantime my sister met a man and was slowly settling into a new relationship when we began to clash on ideals. Had I surreptitiously taken on a role of co-parenting, of which she had every right to be annoyed? I couldn't help it. I was used to being the big sister, the carer and in control. Also, the job wasn't quite as rewarding as I had expected it to be. My role wasn't senior enough, and I struggled with not being able to have input; not being an instigator of change. I was a pawn and didn't like it. This place, my life was all wrong!

Within the first few months I knew I had made a mistake, and by the end of that year was already planning to go back to Sydney. As much as I loved my sister she was so busy with the kids. Sports on Saturdays and a new romance meant I hardly saw her anymore as it became clear to everyone that I was the unhappiest I had ever been. Soon depression set in, my mother calling to offer advice.

"Love, you need to get on with your own life. I'm worried about you!"

How could this have happened? Wasn't this what I had done? Weekend drives to Byron Bay, a place I discovered by accident, kept me sane. It was magical; like a sanctuary for the soul, soothing me as I walked around the coastal forest up to the lighthouse where I could bask in the ocean breeze that cleansed my mind of erratic thoughts. Visiting a local psychic helped confirm my decision to leave.

"Your body cannot stand the toxicity. Go back to Sydney because this is where your work needs to be done."

I looked at her, perplexed.

"Isn't Sydney more toxic?"

She pointed out toward the sky.

"The Gold Coast is man-made. It has been plundered by property developers with greed on their mind. The land is crying," she said.

"What kind of work?" I asked, trying not to sound selfish.

She continued to stare at me.

"Yes, I know. I'm sure it is!" I quickly added.

At this point I was no longer sure about anything.

"You will know. You needed to leave Sydney to realise your own true potential. Be courageous, and be open. You just need to be a little more patient," she said.

Patient? I think I've been really good at that given my age!

"What about a relationship then? Am I ever going to settle down?"

The reader smiled, drawing a man and woman on the notes she was making as we talked during a tarot card reading. I knew tarot quite well, having attended workshops years earlier, continuing my revision whenever I had the time – which was a lot!

"Yes through your work back in Sydney. You need to embrace your vulnerability and then this dark handsome man, your soul mate, will be drawn to you."

I leaned back, more appeased yet sceptical. Isn't that what we all want to hear? Well, if that's the case I figured returning to Sydney wasn't such a bad idea after all, but as for being vulnerable I wasn't quite sure if this was relevant for me anymore. Hadn't I dealt with all my fears?

"You will learn a great deal from one another."

I looked at her carefully, trying to pick up further meaning.

"I don't understand?"

"You will know when you meet him. Just trust and be patient. There will be much growth, much change and a great deal of success coming your way!"

The following day when I told my sister about my decision to leave, she understood, at the same time showing me a scan. She was pregnant; a happy accident indicative of a new beginning for us all.

Part Two

Disrobing
An Illusion

At the end of my third month back in Sydney, working in the sex industry with no other viable option on the horizon, the world plunged into turmoil once again. The global financial crisis forced corporations to shut down, meaning those on high end salaries lost their jobs.

Although the news kept screaming loudly that the financial sector was headed for dark and interesting times, I just didn't think it would affect me. How arrogant was I? Within days of some big organisations going bust, more clients got a little nervous and, as such, I was quickly retrenched. Christmas was looking grim. Sure the GFC was a huge surprise to most of us, but having spent all those years building a business closely aligning myself with the male crème de la crème of the corporate world, I had deluded myself just as they had; believing there was an endless supply of money to provide me with income whenever I needed.

They were wealthy and bored once, but not anymore. Most could no longer afford me! Even worse for some who not only lost their retirement they could no longer manage an erection. Adamant I would never return to sex work, self-analysis forced me to review what I had learned. In the past my clients had consisted of a couple of stockbrokers, a CEO, a few entrepreneurs, accountants and last but certainly not least, a high flyer from the once booming Sydney construction industry.

Things were looking grim, with my dear, wise old client Mr Gem commenting, "Well Jewel, time to get back out there and get a real job, hey?"

"Hmm well yeah, that's what I'm trying to do, isn't it?"

I tried not to look unimpressed. Thanks to my own internal battle with the long held beliefs that sex work wasn't sustainable, I convinced myself I wasn't trying hard enough out there. Didn't I have an amazing CV? Hadn't I ridden the wave of success, knocking back head hunters year after year in preference for fewer hours and greater pay? Well, no-one was knocking anymore.

After a long and laborious search of my inner resources, I was quite unsure of how to go about pitching myself back into mainstream work in Sydney, given the landscape had changed so much. Considering all options carefully and researching all the criteria suiting my experience, with cautious optimism I sent off my resume to clinics, communications recruiters and non-profit organisations, but came up empty every time.

It was clear I couldn't get a job doing anything. Well, almost anything. I did manage to score a stint in a local 'mature ladies' gym, but I nearly froze to death - most of them were having hot flushes so the air conditioning was turned up to the max. It was hard to justify the travel time for an hourly rate which equated to two hours for $20! A nice, relaxed day at home could earn me $300 for one hour. Who would seriously make an effort?

Well, for the record – *me*!

This was humiliating. With a glowing career portfolio I could no longer cut it. I was now up against more recently experienced people out of work and vying for the same roles. Added to this, no-one called me back any more. And temp work, which was once such a great fall-back, was impossible to secure. Resumes were to be sent on line, face to face meetings not required. When did *that* change, I wondered? How were they going to get to know me and observe my personality?

"C'mon Universe, give me a break!" I pleaded.

My meditation hour was extended to morning blocks in an attempt to combat all the defeating thoughts crawling their way into the corners of my very rattled mind. What could I do? What were some other skills I had? There was no way I would ask anyone for help. A few weeks turned into months when my life was about to take another major turn. Reminding myself yet again unconvincingly that at least I was resilient and had resources to draw on, I had no intentions of contacting some of those needy clients whom I had conveniently let go years earlier, choosing instead to justify that it was time for some new faces. Accepting this to be my next course of action, I advertised in the local North Shore Times.

Jewel. A smouldering and seductive thirty something. Lower North Shore, no private numbers will be answered. Available 10am-5pm (except Wednesdays)

It was only wise to get my butt back out there given these harrowing times, but whichever way I spun it the tension never eased, along with the underlying feeling that my preference to see new clients was another attempt at side stepping the truth - I didn't want to go back. I knew my old regulars would be asking questions about why I was coming out of retirement and wasn't in the frame of mind to deflect with ease. It was hard enough to find the answers myself.

Meeting with a new client conveyed another realisation; I would have to act all over again. This sombre thought played havoc with me for weeks. Who was Jewel again? My past regulars were well and truly warmed up, even knowing me by my real name, but now there would be strangers to become familiar with. Again I told myself that it would be a quick fix and they would be easy to forget once my real career finally took off.

Nervously I waited for the ad to appear in the Tuesday edition of the paper. Once the calls started coming in I could pick the old players instantly, but there were many new callers; young men who were much more sophisticated in their dialogue. I hadn't expected to hear polite voices asking very specific and well researched questions, soon finding that there had been a quantum shift in the kind of man who now visited a professional for sex. Yes of course many of the players had changed, but so had the game!

I knew it wasn't going to be easy to secure such a high level of clients this time around. Not only did I want to keep my re-surfacing persona low key, I could tell the newer blokes no longer had the same kind of money to splash around. Not like they used to, that's for sure. Finally after a few rigorous meetings and greetings, an array of interesting usuals and some stand-outs popped up until a few were selected. With this task now complete, another few months' rent reprieve was greatly appreciated.

During my re-entry into the industry four men became regular clients, although I heard through colleagues that one of these four was also seeing another girl. This little lie was futile! Men, not only in my professional life but in personal relations as well, who feel that they may upset me by being honest, didn't understand that this was the very reason many relationships fail. I couldn't be myself around them as much anymore. It was not their right to think for me, or protect me from the truth when they were lying to themselves about the depth of our liaison. The energy resonating between us became toxic; the anxiety and unease sitting unconsciously in a place waiting to seep through.

Two of my clients had erection issues hence proceeded to bonk me with a flaccid penis, equal to being rolled and tackled like a rugby player. The intention wasn't to hurt me but it did. Tolerating softies was one of the hazards of this work, challenging me to maintain decorum during the unfettered throes of passion whilst guarding against a fumbled and desperate attempt to gain entry when half-mast. When one regular I'd seen for many years became too excited, thrilled to see me back, he lunged onto the bed with his shoulders pinning me down as he tried to have sex without a condom on. I was dazed, taking a few moments to register the experience tearing through on an emotional level. Demanding that he hop off, the look of surprise on his face said it all. He was shocked to catch a glimpse of the person before him; a woman angry and hurt. Although we had a respected relationship as client and sex worker, in that moment I felt violated and the session had to end.

"You cannot do that!" I screamed.

Within seconds my professional face returned to uphold the safety as I deliriously began raving in a ditzy manner until he was dressed. Why I did this, I did not know at the time until a later counselling session at a sexual health clinic confirmed I was in shock. Even through his meagre apologies and concern I knew he hadn't got the full impact of what he'd done in those few minutes. It was an episode which heralded a lot more inner work for us both. My physical and mental plane had been displaced, within my body it resonated as rape, taking days to shake off. These feelings were to be acknowledged, requiring a lot more spiritual reckoning to accept his intention was never to be violent or hurt me.

Actions have consequences no matter the situation or profession. I had no fear in speaking up when my boundaries were crossed, knowing that if anyone outside of the industry found out about this episode they would most probably judge the situation like this; as a sex worker shouldn't I expect this to happen? Didn't I ask for it? After all, I get paid for this kind of behaviour, don't I?

Wrong!

As with every sexual liaison it was about respect and consent. Speaking to a counsellor helped me work through certain confused feelings around this episode. Fortunately this helped me to transcend the shame. As for my client, he did call to see me again, apologising profusely in the hope of rebuilding the relationship, informing me his marriage had become a casualty. It was important for me to stand firm, suggesting he see someone else - or at least consider counselling. He needed it more than me!

Such a bad experience was unusual and he was a long standing client! I didn't have too much trouble with the new men I met. They respected that with my higher prices came exclusivity and strict health practices, otherwise they would not get through my front door. The younger men I had the pleasure to see were far smarter and more able to understand the big picture in terms of acknowledging our meeting as a business transaction. With plans for a future or maybe even having a girlfriend in another town, they never questioned nor did they put their health at risk for one hour of pleasure. It's not fun to have to worry about whether we've been given a bout of chlamydia or something worse. Also it was important for these young blokes to feel happy, safe and relaxed therefore more inclined to share more time with me.

Discovering that most men were gleaning their knowledge of the sex industry through the increase of internet sites, which also offer chat rooms and feedback, I became fascinated with their use of acronyms and direct dialogue when they called. These men had greater expectations. They read about what other sex workers were offering and at what rate, so their bargaining increased. Once exposed to the new online world of sex industry sites and social media I became more educated on the language being used, although one acronym had escaped me until someone phoned asking for a GFE.

"Hey Jewel, I saw your ad in the local paper today, can you tell me a bit more about yourself?"

"Yes, hello. What exactly would you like to know?"

"Um, well, can you please tell me a little bit about your services?"

"Ok, yes. Would you mind giving me your name please?"

"Oh! Sure, it's John."

"Ok John, I offer a full passionate service in a very private and discreet apartment centrally located. I'm extremely health conscious so please don't ask for anything 'extra'. If you have something in mind that you're looking for, please let me know now."

"Do you offer a GFE?"

There was an awkward silence. My mind was swinging in all directions but I couldn't dismiss the fact that I didn't know what he was talking about.

"What's GFE John?"

"Um, well, I'm looking for someone who's really passionate, like a girlfriend I guess."

Silence again. Was he serious?

"As I mentioned, John, I can be quite passionate in the room but I don't kiss. I'm experienced so I can guarantee you won't be disappointed," I said more encouragingly.

"So, am I allowed to go down on you and kiss you? I'm hoping to connect so we can see each other every week."

Trying not to lose patience, I could already tell he sounded like a high maintenance kind of guy.

"I love mutual oral, and am sure you'll want to come back, John. Let's make a booking shall we? And then, of course if by some chance you're not happy, it's completely up to you to move on."

"So, can we cuddle and even shower together? I'm thinking that I'd really like the girlfriend experience."

I tried not to sigh aloud, acknowledging that as it had been a while since I had to win clients.

"I see, John. You want me to be like a girlfriend as in, you want to walk in and hear me say "Where the fuck have you been!?" And then, of course, I'm supposed to be all romantic and ready to roll over?"

Thinking I was funny I tried even harder not to spit the words at him. "Well, if I'm to act like a girlfriend, chances are I'm *not* about to put out for you easily then, am I!?"

The phone went dead.

From this time onward, if anyone asked for a girlfriend experience I recommended they get onto RSVP, or if it was a case of only wanting the sex, there were plenty of forums starting up that were promoting the availability of horny married people looking for hook-ups and fun for free!

Some of my more worldly clients with whom I spoke to about this growing trend informed me that newer escorts were charging a very high rate for extremely personal, porn services, and I feared it allowed a manipulation of boundaries. What had created such a high yield of expectation in this profession when there were fewer men and women building lasting relationships in the real world?

In the meantime I discovered the web based industry has bred another form of client, the Punter. Punting meant seeing a SW (sex worker) then racing back to their desktops to share the experience for all to read on a website board. One man who saw me in the first few weeks of my advert going to print was no sooner walking through my door when he began to ask strange questions. I knew something was not right.

Punter: "Hi, how are you? Thanks for seeing me." (Noting already that this guy looked familiar, he had seen me years earlier but couldn't remember me - obviously.)

Me: "That's fine, come in and let's get you comfortable."

Punter: "Yes, I saw your ad and thought it would be great to see someone. Hopefully we can connect and I can make you my regular." (Noting his use of the word 'regular' meant he had been around.)

Me: "Well, let's just get you showered and comfy and see what happens, hey? Have you been seeing someone else up until now?"

Punter: "No. You're the first!"

Punter: (He returns showered and on the bed) "So, how long have you been here? Do you do natural French? I don't like using condoms..."

My radar was going off. What did this dude want? Why did I have the distinct feeling he was checking me out? Has he not yet registered I've seen him before? I don't forget a client; we never forget the weird / bad / strange ones.

Me: "As I stated, I prefer safe sex and also we've just met! Let's just relax, hey?"

Punter: "Oh, okay. Yes sorry."

This guy talked nonstop, hardly even raising the bar so to speak. It was obvious he wasn't really horny, just curious about me, giving me the impression that he wouldn't be back for another visit soon so I cut to the chase.

"What are you really looking for?" I asked, rolling alongside, not bothering to do anything more.

He looked at me a little astonished.

"Um, I don't really know! Just heard about you, thought it would be nice to meet you," he said, looking a little dodgy.

He crawled out after the interrogation, only to be replaced a week or so later by another new guy. The situation was almost identical except I had not met him before and, by this stage having already encountered some new promising 'regular' prospects, wasn't prepared to play too many games with this one. I got straight to the point, asking why he was so curious about so many details of my service.

"Wouldn't it be way more sexy and enjoyable to find out?" I asked.

He blinked, drawing my attention to the hair also protruding from his ears. A middle aged geek bachelor with too much time on his hands, it didn't take long before he cracked, leaking details of this whole new world of The Punter and a website that he had helped to create. At this point I was partly amused but mostly pissed off. Who on earth would want to kiss and tell? Wasn't the whole idea of such a personal and intimate encounter one of privacy?

Once this session concluded I couldn't help but log onto the internet, signing up to take a look around. There I was, written up with phone number and area listed. My privacy and personal service was always one of discretion, and over the years that it had taken me to preserve this, not only for myself but for my respectable clients, it was disappointing to be exploited in such a way. This was a sign to me of how tacky the industry was becoming, with a lot of the newer punters more potent in their reviews, blunt to the point of being slutty and demeaning in their description of service.

Most of these guys seemed to be in rotation to put the proverbial notch on their belt. From what I was able to extract, their exploitation of women in the industry came about because they felt emasculated in their personal lives.

Some of the forum punters seemed to get a kick out of talking up their experience, many of which sound highly incredible, even flagging where one could get value for money when seeing a particular girl. Although I do support an open and fair playing field, it's my view that this kind of ranting has become extremely detrimental to the profile of sex work.

How can a 'value' be placed upon a personal interaction between two consenting adult human beings? Ok even three or more depending on the scene, but the bottom line is this; some of the women were being put under a lot of scrutiny by these guys. In some cases I could tell that if they were in dire need of the money yet talked up as being a dud, they became more daring to win back these jerks. Where was the fairness and value in that? Decent women were trying to make a living in an industry that can be challenging enough at times. Sex workers just want to work safely, without fear of being bagged by smutty men who have nothing more important to talk about or do with their empty lives.

Chapter 12

Sex: Why Are We Whispering?

My return to sex work was teaching me so much about my inner strengths, in the meantime giving me ample space to master new skills. Intermittent discussions with younger men inspired me to take a closer look at technology. I often sat in a local café typing ads on my savvy new mobile smart phone when not writing notes about the industry.

Our liaisons were nurturing a capacity for self-love. Once rapport was established there was no sense of having undermined myself at all, even if it was true that I hadn't wanted to go back into the industry. I found myself wondering why society deemed sex work – or non-monogamous sex for that matter, to be wrong, so I decided it would be rather more fruitful in between bonking and job interviews to capture my thoughts in essay form. I had no idea why at first, other than there was an element of cathartic release, and it kept my mind off the ulcers I was beginning to suffer from.

This initial writing process sparked deeper contemplation as clients encouraged me to share what I knew about this industry. At first it felt weird expressing my feelings so openly, reminiscing about antics which had in the past not only seen me well kept but sometimes had me in hysterics. Usually sharing this kind of flashback with a client was denied and rarely did I get caught off guard with friends when the conversation peaked in relation to lack of good available men. I was seeing some delicious ones who were intentionally avoiding commitment until their financial situation improved, or more often they declared to be waiting for the right girl.

My two personas were still worlds apart, and in the past that's how everyone liked it. It was safer that way. I wondered why, and could only answer for myself. I would never have acknowledged Jewel as being part of me. I had judged her as dirty, naughty and wrong – a lot of men also thinking the same because of the belief we were all brought up with. Where did that belief come from? Our parents and society, that's where! Shame had kept us all prisoners.

These younger men seemed to harbour little shame but there was a great deal more low self-esteem, making it easy to share my real story rather than make it up any more. This in turn made me aware of just how much my secret existence had manifested into isolation. Chatting openly gave me a perspective I would never have viewed before.

Triggered by my jaded view of men due to painful, destructive relationships, sex work had provided me with more good times than the personal bad, so why should such work be kept hidden? Notes piled up, and so too did the number of books being published by sex workers, although I felt there wasn't enough focus on the psychological drivers behind man's need for connection and physical touch. My sessions often resulted in ongoing relationships occasionally without sex, so I began to flip the situation around to identify more closely with what I had truly felt – *not* with what I thought others might think or feel about me. This gave me compelling insight on the positive, nurturing power of sex and how beneficial it had been in restoring trust.

When thinking back over my life, I asked myself what I had hoped for in an intimate relationship and the answer came in waves of emotion, washing over me. I wanted to be loved, to belong and to feel normal – a word which made me laugh. What does normal mean? And as for love, it was clear that the attachment we place on romantic notions undermines our potential to attract real soulful love. My regulars cared about me. We belonged in a union that was honest and sustainable, and although I was aware it didn't equate to romantic love, given the circumstances for some of us it was a start!

Why hadn't love come along as yet? Was it a consequence of my choices therefore love wasn't attracted to me? What about sex as a portal for spiritual growth as well as pleasure? Had I begun that part of the journey yet? Stepping back further, it was upsetting to recognise that my desire for control was still sitting at the base of my spine. I wanted to start my own family but wouldn't get pregnant without the commitment of a man, mindful of not having the means to care for a child when working long hours to build a career. From what I experienced growing up, later observing with colleagues and my sister, the cost of juggling work with kids as a single mum was a huge sacrifice to make. Happiness seemed a privilege to these exhausted women.

Were women really that evolved then? I thought about this, and the views held in society at large. The women I had met were often alone, sometimes single mothers dedicated to providing for their children with sex work offering the chance to get ahead.

I had learned that the key to happiness for men and women was our own responsibility.

Seeing my sex work industry counsellor with whom I shared my views, she filled me in on changes the industry and we chatted about how hard it was to get life insurance or other health benefits. The industry was already stigmatised as being an unhealthy, unregulated practice which was why those operating at a higher risk level weren't doing any favours for championing the cause. There were no workplace safety guidelines or income protection insurance for sex workers, which prompted me to work harder on establishing my health coaching business, registering myself as a therapist and freelance PR consultant.

Industry groups such as Scarlett Alliance and SWOP were working on making the industry a safer place, offering advice and support but generally the responsibility was our own, with expectations that we will operate with duty of care for our clients i.e. we were safe and clean. Without the pretence of seduction and big money, given that many considered this work to be glamorous, the truth is that sex work professionals are real women and men who just want to pay their bills and or university fees, often sitting for hours on end in the waiting room or creating website businesses of their own. As an unregulated service industry we have to constantly evolve and co-exist.

Being more honest with myself was the precursor for sourcing feedback from my new clients, doing further research in sexual behaviour. Staying open minded, flexible and willing to learn, I opened up the authentic part of myself, becoming somewhat more vulnerable when balancing precariously between meeting my needs and those of my clients. Communication flows in this kind of environment between sex worker and client. Often we shared similar values - like attracts like, building mutual respect and understanding of each other's views and life experiences. We revealed more of ourselves once the shield was down, me listening intently as they contemplated why they paid for sex, articulating their reasons which were varied.

Although I loved sex I was aware that I desired none of these men. There were a few fleeting attractions, but nothing earth shattering as the realisation that having chemistry with someone was what my body craved. This made me wonder who all these men really were, and why did they visit me?

The Old Timer

These men, aged roughly between 65-85 years, had similar stories. Often an unhappy husband they declared to me that they would never cheat. This man loved his wife and had no intentions of leaving or having an affair. Seeing a sex worker was not considered a betrayal of marriage vows.

I was always happy with such a description, understanding from my own experience that it was indeed a physical contract whereupon a man could fulfil a sexual need sorely lacking in his primary relationship. Sadly I heard too often that they weren't conditioned to explore nor were they encouraged by their fathers or friends to discuss their relationships when it came to issues around sex.

This was a very important point for me to contemplate as I observed the generational changes in how men operate. Overall, men are very good at being able to sub-divide relationships in this guise; love, marriage and sex! The old timer had probably been hitting the brothels from an early age in order to release sexual tension. Imagine what it was like for this age group way back when men courted women who fuelled their desire and intrigue when behaving seductively – sexually unavailable. Women curtailed advances with their sense of decorum. Taught that to be alluring and hold on to their virginity was the power they could wield, they would soon be getting hitched.

Marriage and procreation was their aim; seduction was the game, hence men expressed to me that this drove them mad. Babies changed everyone's routine and expectations, these men sharing that they found themselves bound by an arrangement, expected to never have sex with another woman again, which often included his wife. That's what the blueprint of marriage was, and still is of course; a contract confirming two people will stay committed romantically and sexually in order to procreate and raise a family together. It does not include a caveat for sexual freedom. Marriage tends to uphold an idealistic view that this sexual arrangement is tenable, but we know it's not.

For many couples back in the 50's, it was rare to end a marriage. Not getting enough sex was never a reason for divorce, which is why the Italians have mistresses.

There was also an element of dissatisfaction I heard from those men who had married their fantasy woman. In the early 60's, men held a great deal of power over women who were happy to be portrayed as 'sex objects' in the media, showing off their perfect hourglass figure which would later change shape due to childbirth and the natural process that occurs with ageing. Older clients were more obsessed with women's perfect figures. They had not valued emotional needs early in their relationship, and as such had not managed to build an intimate bond with their wives, rejecting them. I believe this was how eating disorders were triggered as women grew dissatisfied with their bodies, passing on the vanity and obsession to their daughters.

"Do you think I'm too fat?" This was the catch-cry many of these men were tired of hearing, but I could understand the confusion given they may have been the ones who created the insecurity. I knew what that was like. A sex worker epitomised the perfect sexual woman they could have.

Men with healthier egos and more realistic perspectives stated that they found it sexier when a woman was confident and comfortable with her body, no matter what size or shape she was in.

The Lonely Married Man

These could be any age. An average bloke from middle to upper class background and generally highly educated, he didn't consider himself unfaithful and often had an affair, his desire for connection far outweighing the moral obligation to his partner.

I asked these men why they didn't think it beneficial to instigate more intimate sexual time at home, and heard 'my wife no longer has any desire for sex' and 'she no longer wants to experiment or have fun in bed!' Some men claimed that with no adventure or opportunity for sexual experimentation, and in some cases serious lack of communication, there was nothing except the children and friends left in common. It was fascinating to discover that many would have preferred an erotic experience with his wife than to keep paying me!

I also met young successful men whom I thought were single. It turned out they were lonely because their equally successful wives were often busy with their careers taking them overseas. Of course I'm the first to step up and say that women have every right to equality but I wondered at what cost? If a marriage contract can be openly discussed with clear understanding of the emotional and biological boundaries, why not review the physical obligations too?

Not one of these men had ever contemplated such an agreement with their spouse, yet they confessed to lying in order to diffuse questions pertaining to how they were feeling and what they were up to. Is this healthy? Does this really build a trusting, sustainable relationship?

Those men who spoke of having no intimacy within their core relationship seemed to need validation. I realised how much men also like to be told that they are attractive and desirable more than how great they are in bed (just). One man told me that if sexual advances were regularly rejected then he sought out alternative companionship in order to compensate. This wasn't to say it's the wife's fault – far from it! These men are unable to communicate clearly with their partners therefore fall into a space whereupon they live very separate lives.

There are also men silently suffering within a bad marriage because it was either an arranged union or due to their partner's illness. Some men were in transition, newly separated from his wife or partner, not ready to contemplate the dating game yet craving the fulfilment that a non-committal, safe sexual experience can provide.

Naughty Married Man

For all the reasons regarding the overall positive benefits of paid sex, it's just as important to note that there were maladaptive players out there. Some men were deluded by the myth that their penis equalled power, this attitude spurning an eagerness to prove self-worth via performance in the bedroom. These men had serious self-esteem issues – often narcissists.

The thrill-seeking narcissist was often a powered up suit from the city; usually mid-forties and often a real 'dick'. I've met many. These men want to be validated at all costs. They paid for the lie so it was completely up to me to deliver.

Others stated that they loved variety, engaging sex workers to fulfil their egocentric fantasy which would never be revealed at home with the wife. 'She would *never* do that!' or, 'It's my escape' said one client who later revealed to having been jilted back in college by a girl he claimed was the only love of his life. He was away on camp when she had packed up and left their flat – never to be seen or heard from again. When I asked if he had opened up to his wife about this trauma, he said he didn't believe it was necessary to share past disappointments. Their marriage was good, his wife was nice.

Abandonment creates a whole range of co-dependent behaviour for these men.

Another client in his late 30's was in a loving partnership with the mother of his young child, telling me that he enjoyed the thrill of being wicked on the side. However, I could see he was in denial about the real reason for his visit. He had an addictive personality, struggling with a cocaine habit his wife knew nothing about.

Pleasure for Leisure

Calling on a few ex clients whom I had not seen in a while, I asked them the question, why did they visit a sex worker when they had such a healthy relationship with their wife? Let's take for example my old regular Bill and his answer to this. Many years earlier after attending a work seminar he met a woman and ended up having an affair. The excitement was addictive, and when the affair was over, he went to an establishment to seek more of that same thrill. He figured that once the seal of fidelity had been broken, there was no reason to bother his wife for sex; pleasure and variety becoming his goal.

I asked Bill if he loved his wife and if they enjoyed a good sexual relationship? His answer was yes. Did I believe this? For him, yes and for her no, having experienced Bill. He believed himself to be amazing in the bedroom, but it was far from true. Many a man may consider himself to be a sensual lover, however some of my clients didn't seem to realise they showed disconnect with their bodies, and no understanding of how pleasure could be derived from gentleness and foreplay. "Why would I touch her there," or "she would never let me go down on her" was a common response, proving to me these men were testosterone fuelled with no desire to explore. They just loved to bonk for ages until they came!

Another interesting thing he told me was that after another dalliance (nearly affair) he believed it was safer to go to an establishment where the girls were reliably discreet. With some coaxing, he was honest enough to say that sometimes a change was as good as a holiday. (I think that's probably why he didn't feign sadness when I retired after our Brazilian episode). He also preferred an establishment central and easier to place in his diary as a 'meeting' if anyone saw him.

Lastly I asked a few ex clients if they had ever worried their wives would know they visited a sex worker. Would they possibly give themselves away when in bed together?

Most believed this would never happen, citing that their marital groove was sporadic but the same. How was she to know what she's missing? Mr Gem was asked the same questions to which he responded that his wife was not always interested in love making. He enjoyed being able to fuck without the pretence of love and the freedom of exploring sex which was not so welcomed at home.

I was beginning to see a pattern. Although many of these men could all initiate a better sex life at home by undertaking Tantric practice, or simply by discussing options openly, they were quite happy to live in blissful ignorance - unless something unforseen occurred such as their wife leaving them or having an affair. We all agreed that affairs bring up worse case scenarios when people mindlessly enter into a situation which could lead to further psychological warfare down the track. None of my regular clients wanted to venture there, which was very good news - having been deeply wounded by my own experience of this!

The Single Man

When a boy becomes a man, it's not always a given that he's going to a) fall in love then b) fall into bed with him/her, confident of his sexual expertise! Some young men may be single for quite a while before an opportunity presents itself for him to engage in sexual activity, therefore it makes sense that we as a society consider what is on offer as an introduction – a rite of passage. Education in this area should be just as important as learning to read or being taught etiquette. Western society chooses to remain ignorant, not wanting to acknowledge that a first sexual encounter can be an important step in a person's mental and emotional development with physical pleasure embraced as a healthy part of life.

It's quite uplifting to acknowledge that I've played a vital role in introducing some boys into the world of sexuality. Engaged in a situation that was neither demeaning nor a drunken one night stand, it was a soothing transition for many. I recall one particular eighteen year old at Scarlett's. Extremely lanky, pimply and quite nervous he was brought in by his supportive uncle; age ID checked. After our introduction I took him into a nice, fairly basic room where we began to chat. To be honest, it was me who did all the talking, openly discussing what we were about to do as he lay there trying to focus on my eyes and not my breasts.

Suggesting he relax more, I encouraged him to move his big hands away from his penis, only to be met with a look of embarrassment. Slowly he removed them, allowing the gangly fingers to rest alongside his body. Gradually I was able to encourage him to lie down sideways so he could view my body as I undressed.

Trying not to become too motherly or ridiculous, I sexed it up a little in the hope he felt respected, and after another half hour we found a happy medium; him asking more personal questions about how it felt when he touched me and where was best. I whispered gently to him that within the vagina there was the clitoris, parting the flesh with my own finger and playing with myself as he watched. After a few minutes I gently took his hand, moving it between my legs. From here he warmed up quickly.

Finally I brought the session to a conclusion by showing him how to put a condom on in a way that wouldn't seem too clumsy or dissipate the mood, then manoeuvred on top just as he experienced an orgasm. It was a privilege to witness his expression shift from surprise to ecstasy. He left the room brimming with self-esteem, smiling as he greeted his uncle who was waiting outside on the porch.

Our first sexual encounter is given a great deal of kudos as the promise of pleasure lures us in, but we don't acknowledge that this may in itself present young men with pressure to perform. Sex plays a huge part in a person's mental and emotional development beginning when most of us are very young.

Speaking with my friends about their first sexual experience, I discovered that most of us agreed it was a traumatic and unsatisfactory event. For those who were lucky enough to be with somebody they really liked, they confessed to having no idea about what to do, feeling awkward and not always experiencing orgasm. Opportunity often outweighed expertise in these instances, which can be part of the fun when there are two consenting adults enjoying the adventure together.

Single men over forty may also lack sexual contact for several reasons; never marrying or not having the confidence to approach women for a date. Bachelors had a distinct air of detachment at first, only to become overly friendly and sometimes a little too dependent for company. These men usually frequent establishments and private girls for most of their lives, often searching for connection whilst requiring certainty in terms of whether one is going to be available on a regular basis.

When asking one of my clients about seeing other girls, although a little embarrassed to admit it, he finally confessed that variety helped guarantee that he wouldn't fall in love with one sex worker, which does happen a lot more than people realise. I remind everyone who baulks at the idea that the strongest relationships are based upon heartfelt love. If we like someone – tell them or ask them out. It doesn't matter how much sex they've had.

Love vs Sex

Biology plays an integral role in defining our sexuality on some level, often leveraged by lust caused when hormonal arousal occurs, sending hard to ignore signals to our brains, but it doesn't mean that men are the only ones who enjoy or desire sex more. Pleasure may become addictive and more highly sought after depending on the individual's drive therefore some people are quite confident in being able to experience non-committal, consensual sex.

Procreation is the actual goal of humanity, and once women have moved into a more defined role of motherhood they may not feel up to having sex as frequently. Quite often men are still as sexually charged as they were when they were teenagers, most enjoying it too much to manage going without during these periods of maternal leave.

Most men I spoke with and have known professionally and personally do believe in the importance that is placed upon monogamy, especially given that our society is subjected to the perils of sexually transmitted diseases. Paid sex is a great option for the responsible highly sexed male who can define this as an activity – not an indiscretion as such. They understand that loving a partner means taking responsibly to ensure that their emotional and physical health is never at risk, therefore by co-creating an intimate sexual relationship at home and with a sex worker they believed their wife benefitted as they often felt more nourished and content. (They weren't so keen to consider that their wives could possibly be doing the same.)

Sexual Repression Needing an Outlet

Usually this client would say his sex life at home with his wife or partner was normal, however he may come into Scarlett's seeking to do things with a sex worker that wouldn't be tolerated at home. Most often this was just oral. However some came in asking to be dominated, often having been severely abused as children, or possibly unloved and even rejected one too many times either by a primary caregiver or a love interest.

When encountering unusual behaviour, I was prepared to inform the police if I suspected they were committing a perpetration within the community. For example, I once saw a man who insisted I act like a twelve year old, talking about my day at school while he pinned me to the bed. I said no, not condoning such behaviour recognising it was inappropriate, suggesting he consider seeing a psychologist. There are fetish houses that cater to those who are not perpetrators but have bizarre sexual fantasies.

The most common signs of repression I saw amongst my clients often stemmed from fear. These men didn't have the courage to ask their partners for sexual exploration, or were timid about how to instigate sex therefore a little insecure.

In extreme cases where clients requested intimidation I felt there was a need for them to visit a psychiatrist. Mr Abbott fell into this category. Sherri told me his story, one of disgusting childhood abuse at the hands of his mother who had tortured him from an early age. When he was ten he was locked up and humiliated, emasculated to the point of cruelty and subjected to taunts about his naked body before apparently being berated further, then made to beg for punishment. This, I heard, was dished out in the form of having objects rammed up into his anus.

I recalled the look on everyone's face when his name went up on the board. Given the opportunity to decide whether or not to see him, I was definitely a no. He liked to be given anal with a vibrator whilst being told off, then losing bodily control covering the bed in excrement. I had so much empathy for him, and wondered how many others were out there constantly re-enacting their trauma.

Later when offering tantric services I began to see men who had suffered sexual and/or emotional abuse, tears flowing when their trauma was released through energy that I had inadvertently tapped into. Proving to offer relief, together we would give this repressed pain space to show up so that it could be shifted and honoured as a serious wound. Exploring deeply held trauma through bodywork became integral as part of their healing journey, giving them courage to confront the shame and acknowledge that it wasn't theirs to carry any more.

Chapter 13

Heart Attachment

It was a month before Christmas when lethargy had taken a huge stronghold over my body. Springing from out of nowhere I couldn't regain energy nor shift the discomfort I felt in my stomach with regular exercise or meditation practice. Rationalising that it was due to the move, given that it was my third in a couple of years, I knew it had taxed me on every level. Fed up with packing and unpacking boxes, returning to Sydney was an expensive exercise.

I tried not to whinge, but it was futile. Why was I overwhelmed once again? Hadn't I dealt with challenges before? Sitting back, I contemplated something else that needed my attention. I was spitting out blood into the hand basin after brushing my teeth each morning. Convinced I was probably just brushing too hard, that fearful little voice was momentarily soothed. However, symptoms got worse, forcing me to surrender to the possibility of something more sinister.

Racing to the local surgery as soon as I could, I waited patiently for a doctor to see me. Finally my name was called and I was ushered into a small cubicle.

"Hello I'm Doctor Haddad, how can I help you today?"

I shuffled into the seat she pointed to.

"Well, I've been getting really bad gut pain, and I have found blood in the basin in the mornings. It feels like I can't swallow, like I can't digest anything. It's quite uncomfortable, I must say."

"Are you under any kind of stress at the moment?" Dr Haddad asked without looking up from her note pad, no doubt a typical diagnosis during this recent GFC.

My health had been excellent for quite a while before this, adrenal fatigue well under control.

"Well, yes. I've been having trouble securing work," I answered a tad too dryly.

And I'm having sex with strangers to keep afloat at the moment. I wanted to add with a daring look her way. But I didn't. My big secret was the only thing familiar to me right now.

"Yes, we're seeing a lot of people feeling a little more stressed than usual. Tough times, hey?" Dr Haddad made the off handed comment before looking at me.

It made me think how crazy we human really were, living in the fast lane and accepting it, as if by calling it 'stress' we're alleviating it without making any change to our lifestyle at all. The irony; if we didn't starve or die from disease like cancers then there was the likelihood we could always die from stress – the very thing that worked against us!

A huge smile covered my face. Laughter spilled from me like it does when we find ourselves caught in the contagion with friends, hysterical for no reason and unable to stop despite the fact that no-one no longer knows what was so funny.

"Are you okay?"

"Ah, I… I'm sorry," I said, although still unable to explain why.

"Are you on any other medication, antidepressants or the pill?" she asked, looking back at her notes.

"No, nothing. And definitely not the pill. I'm hoping to have a baby in the next year or so."

"Oh, don't wait that long!"

I sat back, surprised at her reaction.

"Sorry?"

"Well, I can see you're well into your forties. Don't wait - do it now!"

I leaned forward, gripping the desk hard.

"It's a bit hard when I'm single!"

"Oh you must know someone." She leaned in, conspiring. "You cannot wait to fall in love."

I flinched, but why? What was so wrong with that idea?

She smirked a little. "You are attractive, I'm sure you know someone."

"Um, so like I was saying. No. No other medication. What do you think is wrong with me?"

Her face changed, reverting back to a professional stance. "Sounds like ulcers. I've seen a lot of people coming in with them." She grabbed a prescription pad and scribbled a few words down. "Here, take these and let's see how you go."

Leaving the clinic I felt defeated, desperately trying to brush the doctor's comments out of my mind. Was my time to have a baby really over? Was there a chance that I may never fall in love?

January 20th, 2009 was a huge day in the US with President Obama's inauguration well under way. Seeing such a wave of positive energy emanating from the millions who had flocked to Washington was such a nice reprieve, watching as a whole world waited to herald this auspicious occasion. Glued to the face of this man, I marvelled at such boldness; his purpose, to be President, knowing he would be tested from this moment on. I liked him, sensing he was able to tap deeper into the psyche of communities set apart from the norm. Who cared about what colour he was or where he grew up? What was wrong with people who questioned such things over the more important factors like food and shelter?

Sighing with such deep contemplation I was moved, realising new feelings of despair. Not only was I struggling to get back on my feet, visions of having a healing practice looking grim, but I was also single; alone with no prospect of love in sight. Who would want to be with me with nothing to offer? What if they ever found out about my sex work? Would I tell them? Probably not, I decided. At a deeper level I recognised my real fear; according to society I had reached my 'use by' date, making me hate my life even more.

"Yes we can!" Obama stated firmly from a podium halfway across the world.

These were only words, yet so passionately fuelled they resonated deeply. I smiled. My world seemed a little less daunting after all.

"Yes we bloody well can, baby!" I shouted back at him.

My chest welled, and with each deep breath repeating the words 'yes I can, yes I can', I managed to leverage excitement from this wave of energy. Everything would be ok, I told myself again. And yes I did believe that. I had to.

The buzzer began its warning scream from the front entrance, snapping me back into position with TV remote aimed at the crowd.

"Ok, a nice, deep breath," I whispered, sharing a private moment with myself before wiping away Obama's image with one flick of a switch.

Heading toward the door I casually threw in a CD when passing the player, thoughts still circling in a heady mix of hope for new beginnings. One last deep breath and here we go again I mused, dismissing any awkwardness before my new client arrived for the first time.

Pressing the intercom to allow entry gave me an opportunity to check his face. Would he look menacing? What was he wearing? Make sure he's standing there by himself. Peering at the image squashed up in a hole he looked fine, a little cautious if anything but that's perfect, and now I had to be. Perking up, I reached for the front door at the same time greeted by a tap tapping sound registering his arrival. I opened the door slowly.

"Hello Andrew, how are you? Wow, isn't it extremely warm outside today?" I said, sweetly tainted with seduction.

This was one area of my life where I still had some control. In this moment when the final potential of a client was summed up and my personal life was pocketed away. All my nerves were steeled as senses were called upon to embrace a stranger in a loving and soothing space. In the meantime it didn't escape my attention that this was a rather attractive Latino looking young man.

"Yes, yes I'm well thank you. Yes it is warm."

It was a nervous response. His dark eyes began darting quickly from my chest back up to meet my gaze. This was not unusual. I was standing there half naked in lacy underwear and very high, sexy black stilettos. What was unusual, however, was my response.

"You are a nice tall, dark and handsome one aren't you?"

I smiled even more seductively, my mission being to ignite his inner passion and engage the devilish side. His face was strong, the gradual smile genuine as it appeared, yet those eyes tried to avert mine, a sign of some virtuous battle within. This boy before me was quite endearing for a woman in my position.

"You make me feel a little intimidated," he said, speaking coyly, meeting my glance with a little less reserve once we walked into the lounge room.

"Really! Sorry. Here, let me take your jacket," I proposed more sedately. "What kind of work do you do, if you don't mind me asking?"

Making my way around to his left hand side slowly peeling away the smooth, well-tailored garment, he extended his arms. When standing on tippy toes from behind, I quickly sneaked a glance at his body. Not bad for a man probably in his early 30's, I guessed.

"I work in finance, for a large multinational banking firm." His voice filtered across his right shoulder, giving me a glimpse of those full lips barely visible but so tempting.

231

"Oh right then. A Banker! Not good times, hey? Let's leave your jacket out here in the lounge so it's not in our way. We won't get any creases and you'll look like you've just stepped out for a meeting."

"Ok, I'll throw the rest of my clothes here too?" he asked with more confidence than witnessed only a few minutes earlier.

"Yes for sure, great idea. I'll be waiting for you in here. You might as well head straight for the shower first!" Making my way back towards the bedroom, I waited nervously.

Five minutes later he joined me, carefully leaning on the bed, casually looking at my sleek pose spread out along the white fitted sheet; cool Egyptian cotton, crisp and clean. I could tell that he was pleased, and I'm not referring to the sheets. His gaze was unabatedly drinking in my milky skin barely held in by the rich pink fabric of my lingerie. My full lips pouted their intention and with one eyebrow raised I beckoned for him to lie down beside me. It was all part of an act. His eyes twinkled, but then darkened a little again.

What was it about this man?

"Do you feel more relaxed?" I asked politely, reserving more of the inevitable for another time.

"Hmmm yes. You have beautiful eyes. So dark and mysterious," he said, laughing a little, noting his own attempt at playing the game.

In that moment I wasn't sure what captured me most. Was it his boyish charm or the foreign accent which I still couldn't place? I felt his hand brush a strand of hair from my cheek as I moved to the other side of the bed to make room for him to come closer. I gestured that he ease into the mattress so I could lean across his body, stealthily moving on top, holding up my head to show off breasts bursting the corset. Our eyes finally met to linger, leaving me no choice but to respond.

"Thank you," I whispered gratefully. "You have beautiful eyes too! Where are you from?"

He went timid. "I'm half Egyptian born to an Australian mother. Have you been there?"

"Yes," I said. "Yes it's a gorgeous, exotic place."

I began to slowly kiss my way down to stop at his dark nipple, giving it a teasing tweak with my teeth before moving onto his belly. Looking up to grin at him a little wickedly, he smiled.

"Come back up here?" he asked politely, catching me off guard.

"You're beautiful," he said before looking away nervously again.

His hand moved up to my cheek as I came closer, catching the warmth of his breath on my chin. At the same time I felt a sensation never experienced before as our bodies became parallel. What on Earth was *that*! It was beautiful, I nearly cried, quickly turning away.

It was time to begin a more scandalous exploration, but then he grabbed my upper arms, tenderly easing me onto my back. I was a little surprised and yet grateful for the reprieve, stemming an attraction to this man, for some reason thinking it would be nice to enjoy being seduced for a change. But I wouldn't let that happen.

Staring up at the ceiling past his neckline I couldn't help but wonder what it would be like to be free to surrender; a moment of reckless abandon not allowed in this space. His cheek leaned against mine, like a newborn baby looking for warmth and shelter. I did like this feeling. It was new. Again tears welled but I had to carry on. What was happening to me? Giving his head permission to lean on the pillow beside me, our eyes met again. I couldn't believe myself, my face felt hot. Was I blushing? He pulled me closer and we giggled. My arms found their way around his body and one hand rested on his shoulder while the other one snuck up under the nape of his neck where it tenderly held his head. His eyes soaked me up and he spoke yet again.

"I love your hair. It's so rich and red. And your face; you are beautiful, you know."

He had said that already, but at the same time I noticed he looked sad. His words were like wisps of fairy floss encasing me, so soft and sweet. But they were only words, I reminded myself. I couldn't afford to be foolish enough to care about this man.

"Well, so are you actually."

I barely spoke, trying to gauge what it was we had going on.

We smiled at one another, sedated then by the slow burning heat lingering between our bodies. My next move was to try and get him on his back but to no avail, leaving me feeling rather silly, again stilted in my well versed repertoire. Nothing was working which spelled the end of a well-rehearsed manoeuvre. Geez a lot *had* changed in a year!

Frozen, I didn't dare look up for fear he may see something that I wasn't even sure I understood. My head turned slowly to face his chin, which was now resting just above my cheekbone. I could just see whiskers slowly breaking their way through his fresh, young skin. Allowing myself to breathe him in, accepting my body was doing its own thing, I empowered my senses to gorge greedily, my lips wanting to find his. I parted mine and moved ever so delicately close with him not reciprocating at all.

He wasn't mine.

"Are you married? Girlfriend?" I asked, steeling myself for the truth.

As I pressed my whole body so much closer, his arms stayed by his side as he shook his head in answer.

"No, there's no-one," he said.

My heart soared. It was ridiculous to be so pleased! Sensations not worthy of simple words encompassed my body, and I hoped that he would hang around afterward. Continuing casual banter and exploration, we respectfully kept in low tempo.

"Here, maybe stand up against the wall? I love your back, and your skin it's so sweet!"

I stood up, allowing his hand to touch the base of my spine, his fingers delicately following the curve up to my neck. I shivered. I could hear the music playing from way out in my lounge room, Duffy's voice suggesting my senses should be reasonable but I knew it was too late. What was I thinking?

"Is there anything I can do to please you?" he asked, in that voice I had now become a mistress to.

"You have no idea how satisfied I am, thank you. Now, let me explore your body," I said, in the hope to show the temptress I truly was.

Thankfully this worked. At last I was able to block out all those voices beguiling me. He allowed me to press him back down onto the bed; his thick, black hair resting on the pillow while those huge dark eyes invited me to dive right in. Exciting yes, but I was not so sure I wanted to feel so welcomed. Thoughts swam around in my mind, driving me to distraction, dipping fragments of my heart into despair. Terrified I caught myself thinking there was some distinct connection – but that was absurd!

He couldn't possibly be feeling as much as I am, could he?

All of my senses were on high alert. I could hear Duffy screaming *'You got me begging'* Stinging in my ears, the words slapped me around; my body flinched.

"What was that? Are you ok?" he asked, taking in a whiff of my hair curled between his fingers.

I could barely breathe for fear my heart would burst.

When on earth did my heart enter the room?

Smitten with Jason a few years earlier, I'd never felt anything like *this*! My whole body was drawn to this man; my heart was racing. It knew something I didn't. It was time to regroup. Too many parts of me were seeping through, like beggars surfacing after internment; darkness and starvation readily disposed in the wake of salvation. There was a faint recollection that once I had believed in an experience like this, having long since swept such beliefs aside into a dark place I had disowned.

That place, I now realised, was my heart. I had one after all. Again I found my voice.

"Well, best we get on with it, shall we?" I said, trying to smile.

I reached over for the condom.

"Oh, no do you mind?" He grabbed my arm delicately. "Can we just lay here?"

I was stunned.

"What, sorry?"

"I didn't mean it that way, sorry."

This was *really* awkward. There was work to be done by the Goddess of sex and desire even if it wasn't going to plan.

Jewel simply must step up now – or else!

Introducing a slow Tantric touch as I stretched my arms out from behind his body, he reached orgasm then relaxed, turning around to observe me as I fumbled about with the Moroccan cushions to prop us up with.

"So, as you can see, you no longer intimidate me!" he said, joking around a little more.

"Hmm, well that's good news!"

I plumped up my pillow against the tall maple headboard. Slouched, we stared ahead at the ornate colours of my walls.

"I love purple, this is a lovely space," he said.

Staying on my side of the bed, I desperately hoped he wanted to hug but he didn't pull me close. It was difficult, like a rejection but of course it wasn't.

"Yes, it was my aim was to capture opulence and passion. A Moroccan theme encompasses that vision quite well don't you think?"

We talked about other things, still steering clear of what had transpired, making for an easy conversation about families far away and work that must be done.

Leaning back, analysing the scenario, I turned to see his eyes still staring at me. There was something engaging as he seemed deep in thought. I wondered what sort of questions he wanted to ask.

"You are good. I can imagine that you're very popular," he stated, his eyes no longer so deep.

Frozen, my veil fell back in place. My guess was that such words made sense for this gorgeous man to say. To engage reality was a wise move, one that I should've made. Staring blankly at him, I rolled off the bed.

"C'mon then, let's get you showered and back to work," I quipped, heading toward the corridor.

"Yes, that was great thank you! I must get going."

Once dressed, he told me more about his work. His firm, a global bank, were gearing up for what was going to be a very challenging end of year. We wandered back down the corridor to the front door.

"So I'll have to take more lunch breaks to relax with you!"

I was reluctant to see him go.

"Ok, well I do hope so!"

"Yes for sure, thank you, it's been lovely," he whispered politely up against my ear as I discreetly took the money planted into my palm.

"I'm glad not all clients are so delicious at lunchtime though," I spoke demurely, knowing he would get my meaning.

It was also a relief to feel that I had finally regained my composure, reminding myself that the cash in my hand was confirmation of this union's end. My phone rang over on the kitchen table, reminding me it was time to switch off the sentiment and get down to business as I opened the door to usher him out.

"Ok, have a wonderful day, must go now - running overtime!" I laughed.

I watched him disappear into the lift.

Closing the door I sprinted back down the passage past my phone. Steadying myself, looking into the bathroom mirror, I realised my head was throbbing, battling desperately the tears I had fought so well during our interlude.

"You can't do this much longer." My reflection yelled at me.

Hopefully I would never see him again.

A week later he phoned. I tried to ignore his name flashing up as I contemplated my irrational feelings, deciding it was silly to think anything more of our meeting. After he had left, I had wound up meditating then crying on the lounge room floor for hours afterward. I couldn't work. I could barely breathe for the stirrings in my heart his visit had aroused.

"Hello?"

"Yes, Jewel. It's Andrew here. Is there any chance I can come see you today?"

It was a Wednesday. My designated day off to go job hunting and continue with the notes I was writing from the conversations with clients. I drew a breath.

"Yes absolutely!" I said, secretly berating myself for the betrayal. But at a deeper level I also knew I was testing myself.

An hour later I let him in, having paced the apartment, psyching myself up to be more professional.

"Hey," he said, walking past me.

"Hey!" I reciprocated, mimicking his bounce as he boldly made his way to the bedroom. I caught up before overtaking him at the doorway. "Welcome back! Ready for some fun?"

Turning around, expecting him to respond like all men, he surprised me yet again.

"Um, I really only wanted to come back and check on you. Are you okay?"

I observed the boy again before realising what he had said.

"Sorry?"

We wandered back a little, standing halfway between the lounge, me teetering on stilettoes, him clasping his hands and smiling nervously.

"Well, I felt like you were a little bit, I don't know. I was worried about you. Are you okay?"

I stumbled backward, then stood firm, observing this banker boy wearing a pale white knitted vest over his blue shirt. He was so old fashioned.

"Yes, yes of course! It's just been a mad few months back here in Sydney. You know, the GFC. Can't get work. Don't really want to be doing this anymore..."

And there it was. I'd just told this stranger all about my crazy life. He was paying for time out, not this!

"Why, what kind of work do you do?"

We stood there, staring at each other as my mind raced. Weren't all my young men asking similar questions and sharing personal details these days? Why should this one be any different? For some reason I just knew he was. Did they call this chemistry or was it vulnerability toying with me again? I was definitely getting way too old for this crap.

"Come, sit down in here and relax," I said, leading him into the bedroom once more.

As he walked past me to sit, my arm brushed his shoulder sending a surge of energy flashing through my body. I reminded myself not to be foolish. I was delusional probably from the PPI's I had to take for ulcers that were giving me Hell.

Andrew reached out to touch my arm. "You're lovely. I really enjoyed seeing you last week."

I felt sick. There was more than a physical attraction going on.

"Thanks," I said, knowing that these were words I'd heard many times before.

He was a client. We were just relating well, that's all.

"What else are you doing?" he asked again.

"Well, I've worked in PR and then moved into alternative health as a coach and counsellor but there's no work anywhere! But don't get me wrong," I said, realising I was rambling like a mad woman. "This pays well and I'm having fun, but I'm ready to get my life back."

With those last few words I noticed a heaviness in my body as his eyes averted mine. Had I told him too much?

"Yes, I know what you mean," he said, leaning back onto the bed. "I want to get my life back too. I've just been given the all clear after having been diagnosed with leukaemia a year ago."

A silence fell between us.

"That must've been a frightening time," I said, sitting up in a favourite negligee, picked out and worn especially for him.

"I love this," he said, touching the pink silk fabric.

"Thanks! Yes it's a Peter Alexander piece. Pretty, isn't it?"

I laughed, admiring his good taste, me feeling embarrassed.

"Can I ask you a personal question?"

Breathing in, I thought for a moment. What could he possibly want to know?

"Sure, there are no secrets here!"

"Do you ever want to settle down and have a family?"

And there it was. He disarmed me! My head leaned forward in order to drop the mask back in its place. Moving off the bed he took my cue to rise, preparing to leave the room.

"Yes, very much so. This is why I need to get out." I whispered.

He held my arm gently, the energetic shock sending me stumbling through an adjacent door that led into my bedroom. Just as I tripped, he grabbed me, pulling me back toward him.

"Oh! Oops don't look in! You meant to do that, didn't you?" I said, trying to hide the panic. I didn't want him to know I lived here.

"It's okay, I won't look. I'm sorry," he said, holding me so I could close the door again.

In that moment I teetered on the edge. Should I ask him in or close the door? This was my energy; my very private space where no man had entered.

"I'm nosy," he said, making me laugh.

"Okay, come in for a quick look then," I said, my head spinning.

The night before I had imagined what it would be like to have him in my bed. Had I manifested this? Had he?

"What's this?" He pointed to my Destiny cards on the dresser. I panicked – nearby were notes scribbled out questing for love.

"Oh, nothing! Hey! Stop being nosy now, please!"

He laughed.

"This is a lovely space, and the photos. Who are they?"

"My adorable nephews, and there's another one on the way!"

He laughed again. The hours flew by as we chatted more about his family.

"What's the time?" he asked, sitting up. It was getting darker outside.

"I don't know. Hang on a minute."

Wandering out to the lounge I grabbed my phone; it was 4.46pm.

"Wow, it's getting late!" I yelled, wandering back into my room.

"Oh! I have to go. Sorry if I took up too much time."

I watched as he placed money on my dresser, my belly flipping in distaste. How could he think it was appropriate to pay me in here? Then I reminded myself, how was he supposed to know how I feel?

"Um, no. Please don't pay me. This was us here in this space. I can't take it."

My eyes lowered as his did.

"This feels awkward," he said, following me as I turned around to walk to the front door. "Thank you, you're so lovely to chat with."

I leaned in to give him a hug.

"And thank you. You're lovely too."

Our eyes met then lowered, uncomfortable with the tenderness we were sharing. Breathing in his smell before releasing him to the outside world, afterward I allowed myself to bask in the euphoria, excitement – and fear. Was this what love felt like or was it an addiction to nice men?

No, it was definitely love, my spirit whispered back to me. I just knew! But this wasn't part of the plan at all.

"Why *now?*"

Moving back into the unit I opened the curtains to reveal a magnificent array of pink and red bougainvillea dancing in the sunshine. It was a beautiful day. Looking up into the blue sky it was time to reach out and ask for divine guidance.

"Oh please Universe, how can this be happening?"

Over the next six months I searched for any work I could possibly find. Now more than ever with my feelings growing for Andrew I could barely tolerate my old regulars touching me, recoiling every time. I got snappy with some, pissed off with others and well aware that I was simply in it for the money; for survival and I hated knowing this. My body knew it, rebelling at every opportunity, the ulcers getting worse! I couldn't eat much as my throat constricted with feelings I was trying to swallow.

I wanted to feel Andrew's touch. His visits were few and far between, and although we never had sex there was a sensual energy that seemed to bridge a gulf between us. I knew he was avoiding getting attached to me. This made complete sense. I was a sex worker. How could he allow himself to possibly get involved? Andrew continued to visit sporadically in between travelling overseas and my unavailability after hours. Even though we became such good friends, I wasn't about to skew my boundaries given I had no idea how he felt.

Occasionally after a long absence I wondered if there was someone else. I would ask and he would always say no, only that there was an ex-girlfriend who was travelling overseas and they were still friends. His actions told me he wasn't over her so I needed to be cautious.

At the end of the year I landed an admin role through Eva, a friend I had met through college.

When Andrew visited me one particular Saturday afternoon before my retirement date, I was really nervous. This was either going to be our last time together or the beginning of something big. The idea terrified me but I knew I couldn't waste any more time denying myself the chance. Since that awkward late afternoon rendezvous I had put up stronger boundaries and the professional relationship was back in place, although he did try to push it on occasion to re-enter my bedroom, which I secretly liked. Our time together was something I looked forward to in an otherwise glum year, and still we hadn't had sex which inspired me to get out of the sex industry as soon as I could. I wanted to clear a space for him to step into my life.

Had I begun reading too much into it? Would I be brave enough to take a risk and ask if he wanted to stay in touch? Should I just say goodbye and never tell him this was my last week? There was only one way to find out.

After we talked and played around for a couple of hours, finally he had to leave.

"Andrew," I said, leaning up against the front door.

"Yes?" he responded, looking happy. "You gonna talk my ear off again?"

"Well, no!" I grinned. "Actually, I want to tell you something."

His eyes were searching mine, waiting.

"Well, I've landed a job. This is the last week for me doing this work!"

"That's great!"

"Yes it is. And well, I'll miss you but if you're comfortable, maybe we can catch up for a coffee one day? Although let me make one thing perfectly clear, it's not an invitation to continue in this way. Do you understand?"

He looked sedate. "I understand."

"So on that note would you like my personal number, or not?"

I waited, breath held, heart beating. My life was over. This was wrong. I wished I hadn't asked.

"Yes that would be great. And congratulations by the way!"

What a relief!

Now for stage two, I thought. Would he ever ask me out?

Andrew began texting me on my personal number the following week. Soon we had a daily repertoire comparing our commute to work and commenting on the pleasure of our day's first coffee. Part of me felt elated, like I was in a dream that was becoming real. This was me getting my life back and I couldn't have been happier!

One afternoon a few weeks later, Andrew asked if I'd like him to pick me up after work. He was due to drive through the city around that time, but I said no, wary that we may move too fast. I wanted him to ask me out, not come back to my place where we had become so comfortable and familiar.

A month later he called on a Saturday afternoon to chat, suggesting that he drop by for a cup of tea on his way out that evening. It seemed like an okay plan in order to share some face time but his visit was a little strained. Was the intention behind his visit purely sexual? I suspected as much and made sure that he left without us touching.

His calls became sporadic with no hint of going out until finally he suggested we spend a weekend away, telling me that it would be a chance for both of us to have a break. I wasn't so sure about this, and said as much. Why couldn't he spend a Sunday with me first?

Months passed before he finally asked me out for a Sunday lunch; rescinding on the day citing family commitments. The alarm bells rang again as I made it clear that if he was trying to tee up a sexual liaison rather than spend quality time with me, I wasn't impressed.

"Are you really interested in getting to know me better?" I asked.

"Yes I am. I'm sorry to stuff you around! It's cousins from interstate; they've arrived early to spend a week here before our other cousin's wedding next weekend!"

I was disappointed. Did this sound like an excuse or valid reason? Was he hoping to become a casual lover or build a more intimate friendship?

"Sure. Okay now what? Should I trust you or are you thinking I'm easy because I was an escort?"

"No way! You're far from easy," he said, laughing. "And I certainly don't judge you. I need to get out of the house and have a break from them, so how about we go up the coast? We can stay overnight, no funny business. I can come pick you up later today and we'll wander around then eat dinner?"

I hesitated. We both had work the next day.

"Come on, let's be impulsive! What do you say? I really want to spend time with you, and it's been months since we caught up and I don't want to wait another week! C'mon pack a bag. You *know* me. You can trust me!"

As I heard myself say yes, I knew it was a compromise.

When we arrived at a seaside resort we talked a little more about our childhood and his fears of intimacy. It was getting late so we lay down, and he didn't attempt to seduce me, only touching me clumsily like a teenager, his commentary ambiguous. What was going on with this man? Why weren't we talking as openly as we used to? Afraid to speak up, I simply lay there wondering how I could have ended up being this desperate for love.

The next day we hardly said a word as he drove me back toward the city, dropping me off at the train station so I could make my way into town for work. He waved and drove off, leaving me perplexed, rendering me even more fragile. My intuition informed me he wasn't ready for a relationship, or at least not one with me.

Andrew did call later that day to apologise profusely for his erratic behaviour and I asked him if we could discuss it later face to face, but he said no. He wanted time to process the situation and other events that he hadn't dealt with therefore would get back in touch with me soon.

He called a month later, once again apologising and explaining that he wasn't handling situations at work or in his personal life very well.

"Are you seeing a counsellor, then?" I asked, knowing he bloody well needed one.

"Yes, yes I am. I spoke to a friend and he suggested a psychologist. I've been to a session and mentioned what happened with you; talked about my fear about becoming ill again, about getting involved. I'm so sorry!" he said. "That's just not me! I feel horrible about how I treated you."

"Okay yes it was horrible." I responded, still feeling the sting. "But stay strong and you'll work through it. And thanks for having the courage to get back in touch."

If he felt anything for me, he would say so when he was ready. I needed to trust this.

"Yes I will, and you take care."

"You too. Bye!"

I hung up, feeling lighter, once again full of hope that he may grow from this experience like I had. A few months later a major event distracted me from worrying about my friendship with Andrew. My nephews lost their father to a heart attack. My heart ached, struggling to understand all that what was happening, but staying focussed and strong for my family. At the same time this was all going down, Andrew called.

"How are you?" he asked, his tone indicating he expected my usual upbeat response.

"Actually, I'm not that good!" I said, tears forming.

My head was foggy from sleepless nights.

"Why what's been happening?"

"Well, my sister's ex-husband just died. It's so sad for my nephews."

The lump in my throat made it hard to speak. The boys were only just entering their teens.

"Oh I'm so sorry! That's really bad news."

There was an uncomfortable silence. I had nothing else to say.

"How about I come over and cheer you up tonight, we'll have dinner?"

My heart skipped a beat; I still had strong feelings for him.

"Um, okay that sounds nice. How about I cook?"

"That sounds lovely," he said. "I'll see you later!"

A few hours later he sent me a text to cancel, saying he had a long day and was tired, and I responded accordingly.

"If you think this is how friends treat each other, you're not the kind of friend I need at all!"

He texted a humble apology but it wasn't enough. I'd had a rough time and needed someone around who would follow through on their commitments.

"Goodbye Andrew, I hope you get your priorities sorted soon!"

The next morning he sent me another text.

"Good morning! Have you been for your morning walk?"

Not in the mood for this banter I said yes, already sitting at the café having my morning coffee and reading the newspapers.

"Well, how about I come over and we go for another one?"

I didn't respond, not believing for a minute he would show up when half hour later he arrived on my doorstep, two water bottles in hand.

"Okay, are we going for a walk or not?"

I was so surprised! We head out for an afternoon walk which ended with Thai dinner and wine. We talked about how much we had grown as people during the past year, and how busy we both were with trying to set up new businesses. He was curious about my research into sexual health coaching, but gave nothing away about what his new project was. I could be patient. The whole day was magic. We spent time together again the following week after work. Arriving armed with sushi and wine, he made me laugh.

Later that evening we finally got a little more intimate, then afterward he apologised for not being able to stay. The nerves in my belly threatened to sabotage my belief that this could be it. But he looked perplexed, almost emotional as he faltered momentarily before walking out the door. I was uneasy again, observing his eyes for clues. He hesitated. I could see he wanted to something, but didn't. Was he feeling the same way as me or was he about to disappear?

It was a warm, sunny morning a year later when I received the text I'd been waiting for. Losing my phone a week after our last meeting, I was afraid I would ever hear from him again. He never gave me his last name! My heart had ached each day, never giving up.

"Hello! How are you? I'm sure you're shocked to hear from me but I've been thinking of you for a while and wanted to say hi!"

"Hi!" I texted back. "What's happening? Are you still in Sydney? Married with kids?"

I held my breath, fearing the response, once again figuring that he may have ended up marrying that ex-girlfriend.

"Hey I'm just passing through your way, how about I drop in for a cup of tea!"

"Okay," I said, feeling a little better. "I'll see you soon!"

Manically I cleaned the house and changed into a long, flowing dress. What was I going to say? How would he look? During this time I had often taken a second glance at a familiar face across the street, wondering if it was him. He arrived twenty minutes later, and after a long hug we sat down outside on the balcony.

"Thanks so much for dropping by. How are you doing anyway?" I asked, prompting him to open up more.

He sat rigid, looking uneasy.

"Are you okay?" I asked.

He faced me, looking grim. My heart plunged. Was he sick again?

"Well, I promised myself after that horrible way I treated you, and after disappearing that you deserved to hear the truth."

His eyes went downward, reflecting the discomfort. My belly flipped; fear gripping me.

"I'm married. Have been for a number of years, and we've just had a baby. I'm sorry, I should've told you."

My eyes were stuck on his face, trying hard to fathom what I was hearing. The sudden pain through my chest was incredible, ridiculous even. He was married and yet still took my personal number? This cannot be happening. He was my friend then a lover. Why would he do that?

"Um, are you kidding me?"

How could I have avoided this? Hadn't I done everything right in order to make space for him?

"How could you have lied to me? I let you into my personal life - into my bed! I made space for you in my life, gave up sex work so that I could reserve myself for you and there was never any chance?! Did you think I was a play thing?"

He squirmed. "No, no not at all! We were on the verge of separating at the time I met you. Then the rest was unexpected – falling in love with you. I'm sorry but I do love you. I wish I had told you before, when all that mess was happening, but I was scared to tell you then."

He was rambling. My head was spinning. I stood up to go to the kitchen to make some more tea. What was I doing? I turned around just as he stood up, standing there facing me.

"You love me? Say it again, here and now. What did you say?"

He stood firm.

"Yes, I love you. I have for all this time. Not that it matters now I guess."

For a moment I weakened, bathing in the words I'd practiced hearing over and over again these past few years.

"Andrew, I fell in love with you the moment you walked through that front door nearly three years ago!"

His lips were on mine before I could finish. This could not be happening! I didn't sleep with married men in my personal life. But I had! How was I supposed to know that when he had lied? There were too many memories being replayed – all lies. I pushed him away.

"I thought you had judged *me*!"

"No, never." His eyes held mine again.

I believed him although I realised it no longer mattered. Now I was judging *him*. How could I resolve this? What was it I was feeling in this moment?

"Why come and tell me now?"

"I can't not see you anymore I've missed you so much!"

"Not enough obviously!" I said, trying to preserve some pride.

"Yes and no. No I guess not. I made a bad choice and I regret everything but I can be stronger. We can be friends…"

"Friends? You're a liar. And secondly, do you think I want to hear about your life, your wife and baby!?"

Was this man crazy?

"I want you to leave."

The shock on his face wasn't pleasant. He quickly looked down, then back up at me.

"I'm so sorry. Please, I love you and respect you totally but I don't know what to do. I want to be with you."

My desire for a child was becoming an obsession; hormones peaking more as I grew older. His news hurt way more than I could have imagined. As I stood there I knew my ego was struggling to justify a more positive outcome, but there wasn't one. He was someone else's husband and a father to a child that wasn't mine. This was his story, and I didn't have to buy into it. I could be free to start again. What on Earth was I meant to be learning from all this?

Love is not enough.

The voice I tried so desperately not to hear kept repeating this.

"I've made so many mistakes and I have so many regrets about you and me…"

"Everyone makes mistakes, Andrew. I've been an expert in fact, but I've learned that there is no mistake that doesn't have a reason; a lesson or a chance for growth. Your actions have consequences – own up to them."

His eyes softened then he leaned forward and held me close. "It's so hard. I always loved your smell when we first met."

Holding him at a distance, the anger began to swell. "You have made choices, Andrew. Now you can either stick by those or accept your mistakes as lessons and resolve to fix this. What are you going to do?"

Our eyes met again, momentarily searching for answers that were nowhere to be seen. In my heart I still hoped he could come up with a solution that included me but I knew this wasn't going to happen.

"I don't know. Our marriage isn't good, but I came from a broken home so I can't leave our baby."

My heart sunk, making me feel desperate for space. I needed him out of my energy field where the pull was sending me into a confused state. Knowing what to do was so hard. I took a deep breath to steady myself.

"Goodbye Andrew."

His eyes held mine before we walked in silence to the front door where he turned around to face me for the last time. My heart could not take any more, of this I was certain. My ego wished to create a story in order to stay attached to the heartache but I didn't want that to happen. I deserved a whole man; not a wounded one who was unable to show up ready to be with me!

"You will be fine and I wish you and your family well."

Chapter 14

Identify Yourself

etrenched at Christmas much to Eva's surprise and my detriment, I panicked. There was no way I was going back into the sex industry, and as such I chose to remain unemployed, taking the time to hibernate, meditate and seek further tantric teachings for my own integration. Contacting the local prominent School of Tantra, I asked some questions about securing work, but realised I was way too fragile to allow strangers into my auric field. Energetically a lot of healing was taking place at a deep cellular level, with my body reclaiming its right to be free. No touching without love was its message, and I listened

As another new year rolled around, I continued to look for work whilst doing further research for my book which was cathartic, helping to stem the fear and alleviate stress that came from observing debt as it quickly stacked up. With two mortgages on the Gold Coast, taking cash withdrawals out on my credit card at the ATM was my clever way of paying for any excess expenses. Renting out my spare room afforded additional financial support but otherwise, I kept my head down and just got on with life.

It was during this transition when I told my closest friends about Jewel. In survival mode, my heart was so raw I figured that any negative response would simply confirm that they didn't really care about me. Nor did I feel concerned that they may not understand why I chose this path when there were moments I had no idea myself. Was this path chosen for me, I often wondered? If so, could I change direction? It was possible – but the more I tried the harder my life seemed. I only had to recall my move to Queensland to understand that. Maybe it was time to follow the path of least resistance, and set myself free?

When Eva and I caught up on her lunchbreak, I lost it completely, breaking down in tears. We were walking through the Botanic Gardens when she asked me about Andrew and how it was all going. I hadn't told her anything about what happened between us before. Bent over in self-imposed misery, I felt compelled to get the bigger secret out. It was choking me. I could no longer breathe.

"Oh my God, what's wrong?" Eva asked, kneeling down beside me.

"I'm such a failure, Eva. I'm a mess! My life it's one big lie! I should never have gone away with him!"

"Why, what happened? I thought you really liked this guy, and you knew him really well right?"

I thought about that for a moment, trying not to become hysterical. Did I know him that well? Do we ever know anyone that well? Did any of my friends know who I was? Of course they didn't – how could they? I could barely keep track of who I was myself. My life was a lie. With this in mind there was no more denying anything. I looked at Eva and wondered what made me feel so afraid of speaking up? With humility already looming large, any retribution from friends would be warmer than this icy cold feeling of despair.

"I was an escort. I sold sex for money all those years ago when we were in college. I went back to it when I returned. That's how I met Andrew, so how could he take me seriously – I was just sex! He said he didn't judge me, but of course who was I kidding?!"

The shock on Eva's face was quickly removed, replaced with a look of compassion. I wasn't expecting that, but then again I wasn't expecting anything at all. I was empty and tired from carrying such a heavy burden for so long.

"Oh my God! Are you okay? I did wonder how you managed to have such a good life!"

We kept walking through the park, looking ahead. Eva was still talking to me, so my life wasn't over yet. Was she going to wake up in a moment and realise what I had said?

"You know, Eva. I did have a great life. It was a high class experience. Not at all like most people might imagine."

It wasn't my intention at all to justify the experience. I found myself yet again being aware of how much more control I had within that role. Outside, when dealing with my feelings and trying to trust them, I was hurt. Relationships seemed so difficult.

I shared this with Eva as she became more curious to know what it was like for me.

"Were you safe? I mean, oh my God! All those men?"

I stopped walking.

"Eva, there weren't that many. That's the other thing. I saw the same men every week for years. Sometimes they even drove me bloody nuts, like anyone's boyfriend or lover does. They're real people too Eva, like me! They treated me really well – better than Andrew did!"

Sharing my secret proved that there was no judgement, only more love and understanding of my overall plight. My friends all embraced my coming out, confirming what many of them had often wondered, just like Eva, how I had managed to live so well when working only a few days a week. There was the occasional, 'why didn't you tell me you needed money, sweetie? I would never have judged you!' to 'good for you girlfriend! I have other friends who've worked, and why not hey?' which confirmed to me that everyone had secrets.

I invited Sally over for dinner, sitting outside with a bottle of wine where we chatted until I felt it was the right moment to tell her.

"Sal, I've been going through a tough year as you know, and I'm feeling a little happier but think it's time I shared something with you."

"Oh? What, love? There's nothing you can't tell me. What is it?" she said, grabbing the bottle of wine to top up her glass.

"Well." I moved my chair closer to hers so that I could speak softly. The neighbours downstairs were outside in their courtyard. "I worked for a few years as an escort, and it was great so I've figured there's no point to keeping it a secret anymore."

I had expected Sally to be the most relaxed about my confession, but she wasn't.

"What? Oh my God you of all people. Why? Are you okay?" Her eyes were wide as she skulled from her glass, leaning over me to grab the bottle and top up yet again.

I was confused. "It's all good. It was sometimes great sex!" I said, thinking this would comfort her, but it didn't.

"But it's paid. I mean that's prostitution! How horrible for you!"

I leaned back, scowling a little.

"I'm not judging you. It's just... are you okay?"

I had a well-rehearsed response. "Sal! I took an opportunity to utilise my sexual freedom, that's at all - a biz transaction from metering out sexual service for money."

I waited for her reply.

"Well, love. It's just that you're being fucked - used! What a risk!"

I found myself getting annoyed.

"Don't you think that I knew *not* to be fucked? Yes, it may be considered a risk, but I was always in control. I started off in a very controlled, safe environment. I felt more 'fucked' as you say, in the real world – out here!"

Sally didn't look convinced.

"Listen Sally. Women have allowed an element of propaganda to flourish in terms of how we view ourselves. We've grown up fearing that men will view us as sluts and whores' if we are sexually expressive, but we women don't support each other enough in diffusing such a man-made myth. I learned so much about myself during this experience. If anything it taught me about empowerment."

"Yes I see what you mean, but still we all want to be in love." Sally offered nervously.

Had I offended her?

"Sal, what I'm saying is this. Due to my relationship failures I was fearful of falling in love so I avoided it. But I still wanted sex. I'm not saying it was all rosy in that role, sure. But I got to explore my body, and at the same time I felt safe about keeping my emotional investment out of it. Oh, and I got treated really well!"

"Yes, yes I see what you mean," Sally said, grabbing the empty bottle. "But still, being paid for it?"

"That was the best part to begin with, giving me the motivation to stay in the industry for so long. Think about it, Sal. Where sex is concerned, wouldn't you have preferred a man paying that much attention to you, loving you up and occasionally giving you the best orgasm of your life without the added confusion that comes from forming an attachment? Here, I've got champagne," I said, walking back into the kitchen.

When I returned, I was already a little tipsy but more determined to speak up. I wanted Sally to understand something that I knew she hadn't experienced.

"Sal, I saw the same men every week for years and knew more about them than I understood about my own ex-husband or Greg for that matter. Also did you know that in many cultures, women of abundant sexual energy were in fact respected as Goddesses?"

She smiled. Sally was notorious for sexual abundance – her list of conquests long.

"Sounds fucking fair to me! Here, give me the champers, love!"

The bottle was taken from my hands as I sat down.

"Yes well, I'm doing more research for my book now that I have so much time, and it just so happens that throughout the ages there has been much written about sexual energy being the soul's source to divination. Think Indian culture and yogic practice which in itself embodies Tantra."

Looking over at Sally I could see she was more intrigued.

"So how's the book going?"

I laughed.

"Slow. The more I talk about my experience, the more everyone wants me to write a juicy tell-all but I want to focus on the reality, and highlight the magic of Tantric sex."

"I've heard about Tantra but never bloody had a decent enough partner to try it out. What's it like, then?" Sally asked.

"It's like a meditation where we are able to open energy through our chakras. Do you know about these channels?"

Sally was quite esoteric in nature, and nodded yes.

"Yes, well these can embody pure love and deep spiritual connection leading to a kundalini experience as it is referred to. In most cases I can see why some clients felt this energetic force between us and considered my service a form of therapy, although I didn't know it at the time."

I thought about this some more as Sal slowly processed my words. What would bring my point home?

"Sal, there were no booty calls with these blokes. They booked in an hour or two, and always called every week without fail, and without ever breaking my heart!"

For the first time ever, Sally was speechless.

I had hit my mark.

After opening up to a few friends I became more determined to make myself heard. What were the other factors relating to our perception of the sex industry that I was determined to clarify? Prostitution had a negative connotation, and yet when I looked up on the internet under sex therapy there were a lot of listings for people looking to refresh their sexual potential, without strings attached yet these arrangements were considered acceptable! It was a fascinating insight into what can be finely disguised and perpetrated in our society. To be a naughty housewife or join an 'affair' club was okay, but who really knew what was going on?

Further discussions with close girlfriends revealed that some had settled for less than what they had always wanted in a man. Another friend not too convincingly confessed to being ok with maybe one day falling in love with her partner she met on RSVP. A couple of friends shared that they had ambled along for decades surviving in a relationship that anyone else may consider profoundly unusual.

One friend with two children at high school had a lover with whom she met up with every Christmas break when her husband travelled overseas to visit family. It was something she looked forward to every year! She didn't want to change the family dynamics, and this arrangement worked. Her marriage was a happy one. The amount of women I met through friends who were entangled with married men, believing that he would leave his wife, was astounding! It became apparent to me that the options were endless depending on what we're prepared to settle for in order to be in relationship.

The statistics were stacking up, proving human relations were not so easy to cultivate in the manner of a conservative, fulfilled long term monogamous relationship we all aspire to achieve. I was amazed to learn about my friend Petra's attempts to get back out there on the playing field after her divorce by signing up to a sex only site. With two toddlers to take care of, she had no time for love, but was mad keen on getting her sexual needs met. She didn't flinch at my revelation of Jewel but I was shocked to hear hers!

"How can you do this, meet strangers for sex after chatting on line late at night?" I asked.

Petra sat there calmly. "It's easy! Sure it's a risk but everyone's doing it. That's the fun!"

I recalled during the early years of sex work watching the client numbers drop drastically with the advent of internet dating, hearing talk from girls and clients how much easier it was to spend the same money and get all the benefits of a) dinner b) conversation and c) probably the whole night of free sex.

Internet daters had become much savvier hence 'sex only' sites were fast becoming the place in cyber space for such connection. The world of professional sex became more latent for the average sex fiend/fanatic as women's sexual confidence began striding into the social norm.

At the end of the day I thought, who are we to judge how someone manages their sexual cravings, as long as it makes them happy and is practised safely? I asked my friend to promise to let me know when she met any of these blokes and where, which was fortunate because one became a stalker when she decided not to continue their liaison, ending once the police were called in! This made me think more about the lack of education as young women entered riskier domains in their quest for a relationship, be it for sex or love.

When I bumped into my friend Becky at the local café that week, she invited me over for dinner where I proceeded to share the intimate details of my transition and alternative life.

"Oh darling," she said. "We all go through stages in life where we make choices. You did what you had to do. Are you okay?"

Well aware of how such a response was a preamble to feelings of discomfort around my choice, I wondered if speaking up was beginning to overcloud my empathy at times, having witnessed some friends tensing up when we were out in a group in case I mentioned my sex work past.

"Yes, I really am okay!"

"But what about the risk, are you seeing a counsellor?"

"Yes I do check in on a regular basis with my therapist, and Becky I know this sounds bizarre but I never felt at risk. I'm writing about all this so people will understand more."

Becky wandered around behind the kitchen bench where she was preparing our lunch.

"Yes but do you understand that for the average person this doesn't seem like normal behaviour. You could've been raped or worse, murdered!"

On one level I could accept that she was right, but on another, as I thought again about my female friends and what I had observed in their behaviour, I was strong enough in my convictions to support my point of view.

"Well yeah, you're right it's not a normal job, but I'll argue it's a less targeted area for violence. If anything, a rapist is a criminal. Rape is a crime about power and violence – not sex! It happens to women who are unprepared, putting themselves in danger zones like walking down dark alleys, going out with men they don't really know, marrying someone they barely like. It happens when we don't feel empowered. I was empowered. I felt strong and very aware of my environment and actions. It is not a hunting ground for that type of man, love!"

She looked at me, I could tell, with a mind running through all the scenarios, preparing appropriate response.

"And Becky, let me say this. I think that by letting ourselves fall in love we take on the riskiest act of all. Every day someone somewhere is getting hurt out in the world. Even me."

I told my sister about Jewel during a telephone chat one afternoon after another challenging day of interviews with employment agencies. I was a little flustered to start, however she listened patiently as I stated that as a single forty something woman with a string of lovers I'd made mention of, it just so happened that they were also paying for the privilege of my time. I reiterated that they didn't own me, nor was it about love or always seedy dirty sex – okay maybe occasionally depending on our mood. Yet again I joked, reinforcing gently that I was an independent soul who happened to be grateful for the chance to take up such an option as escorting so late in life.

My sister laughed momentarily before commenting, "If you ever needed more money or support, why didn't you say?"

"Well, now that you mention it. Can you pay the council rates this year?" I said, waiting for her to baulk. She didn't.

"Yes of course I will! You can ask me for anything. I will pay for everything until you get back on your feet!"

I knew I had the greatest sister. My heart soared.

"Thanks for this. It won't take me long, I'm sure!"

"You know, I'm a bit disappointed you felt like you couldn't share this with me. We've never keep secrets from each other."

I had expected this. Some of my friends had also been a little disheartened about not knowing me so well.

"Please, I want you to really understand this; it was a persona, like being an actress. When I was with you and the boys or with my friends I wasn't acting. It was me. That life was such a deeply ingrained secret harboured in a way to protect my then fragile ego from self-judgement. Please believe me when I say that there was never any lie intended. You of all people have known all along who I really am."

There was a moment's silence.

"Yeah, I do know who you are. And I think you're amazing, so strong! Just like dad always says."

"Really? He says that?"

"Yes, all the time. You've always been here for me and the boys, and we all know how much you care. I love you, we all do!"

My heart expanded as the tears welled, and for the first time I could remember I allowed myself to cry tears of relief. I allowed my sister to hear me, to understand the depth of my emotions as I gave myself permission to relinquish control. Revealing that I had feelings was terrifying but I knew it was time. I had been my worst critic and biggest judge, but not anymore.

Over a period of a few months I had caught up with and told everyone who mattered, but I couldn't let my story go for a little while longer because it felt like a betrayal. Not being quizzed or have anyone angry at me or even disgusted, I felt some disappointment. Eventually I realised what this was about. Having kept such a secret for all those years only for it to lose its power meant I no longer had a story to hang on to. It was time to create a new one for myself. I felt ecstatic to be mentally free, but it was also unfamiliar, making the leap forward a scary one! How is it that we easily wallow in the difficulties of our past and pine for the possibility of a brighter future when by simply being in the present we may enjoy our lives?

Once I got this, Jewel was honoured with a ritual of letting go, a mantra spoken as I burned incense to clear the energy. She had become fully integrated in a way that honoured her purpose, allowing me to move on into the next phase of my life.

Chapter 15

Discipline Seeks Divine Intervention

My first draft was finished within months. Soon I was faced with another challenge – what to do with it? Although comfortable talking about my life as an escort to anyone within my personal reach I had no intentions of revealing myself in the greater public domain. It became my mantra to remind friends that although my experiences were interesting, my writing process was cathartic, and not worthy of great expectations for publishing. I wanted to own my work, presenting it to the public in a way that honoured my journey.

When discussing this proposal to a couple of writer friends they informed me that they had published their own work, so I signed up to do an e-book publishing workshop to learn more. This was where I met Lydia, a woman with whom I felt a wave of familiarity; her demeanour so pleasant that we began to chat after class. She had written a story, one of sex and debauchery based upon her life just like mine. Lydia revealed that she was a disciplinarian and my curiosity piqued.

"What's a disciplinarian?" I asked.

"Well, I'll give you the website to go check it out, but basically my clients are those that like to be humiliated and caned."

Checking out the site, once again I was educated on the diversity of sexual preference and desire. After the course ended, Lydia and I lost touch for a while, shooting each other an occasional text. A few years passed before she called to ask how my writing was going.

"I haven't had much enthusiasm, lately to be honest. I don't even know what it all means anymore, just something to occupy spare time I think?"

"Everything okay?" she asked

Unable to secure work as a therapist, I was employed by a non-profit organisation again.

"Yes and no. I'm broke! This job does not pay well and I can't stand the long commute anymore!"

"Oh really? Last time I heard you were pleased to be back in the workforce."

"I was! But it's not where I'm meant to be."

"So what are you going to do?"

I sneaked out into the foyer to continue chatting. Working in partitioned office space made it impossible to have a private conversation; my team environment conducive to work productivity only. So much for boosting morale!

"Well, actually I've resigned, and after next week I have no idea!" I said, trying not to acknowledge the panic rising. My ulcers had begun playing up again.

"Could you go back to sex work?"

I hesitated before answering.

"Hmm, yes I suppose that's my calling, isn't it?"

"You don't sound too sure about that."

"I'm not. I don't want to but it's so much better than this!"

"Well, if you want, I have a client who would love to have someone watch as he is being humiliated. He's a big client of mine actually. A banker from Europe, he comes over once a year for a three day dungeon and caning plus spanking session. He's got a lot of money and is quite happy to pay for additional assistance if I say you're okay. He trusts me. What do you think? Interested?"

My mind was already folding the idea over. What harm could it do? It sounded like a far better plan than the one I was cooking up.

"Yes for sure!" I answered, wondering if I could really sit in on such an act. Even though I had seen a lot of crazy and unusual things during the years, now that I had been out of the industry for a while, it was a little daunting.

Two days later I called in a sickie and caught a train to Lydia's house where she greeted me at 9am.

"Oh, welcome! Are you ready?" she asked, chuckling a little.

I laughed, walking through the door as she stood aside to let me in. The house was seated on a ridge overlooking a valley covered in dense forest.

"Oh wow this is such a gorgeous spot! I love this place!"

Walking past a solid oak coffee table and cowhide throws I stepped down into the sun room which gave me a better view of the undulating garden. Floor to ceiling glass ran the whole way along the house, a balcony covered in pots and hanging birdseed bowls where parakeets were landing to feed. It was a stunning hideaway; obviously very effective in keeping the noise at bay.

"Okay, come through to the kitchen and I'll make you a cup of tea while we go through the day's session. You ready?"

Lydia, much taller in stilettoes, moved gracefully toward the kitchen where I followed. Her full head of blonde hair cascaded down the back of her gorgeous navy silk blouse.

"Ready?"

"Oh, yes I'm ready!" I said, pulling out a chair by the kitchen bench.

"Okay, what we're going to do is greet him pleasantly to start. Then actually, um, I might just greet him first and you can get changed into some high heels in the room up there."

She pointed to the mezzanine level behind me.

"Ok."

"Then I will call you to come out. Now be prepared. I will have him dressed in an apron and stockings, nothing else."

Her eyes met mind. I didn't flinch.

"Rightio. No worries," I said, trying hard to keep a straight face.

Lydia laughed.

"I know it's a new world for you, but don't worry you'll have fun! I will lead and all you will have to do is watch. Okay? And we will call you Miss Danielle."

"Okay, done!"

Twenty minutes later the doorbell rang and I dashed upstairs to wait. Five minutes later I was called.

"Miss Danielle, we're ready for you to come out and see this very naughty boy!"

Teetering on heels, making my way down a couple of steps I glanced ahead to see what looked like a rag doll hanging over a chair. Inside I was chuckling. Lydia watched me approach, talking me through.

"Okay then Miss Danielle," her eyes twinkled, flicking over to the bare white bum I could see. "Have a look at this naughty boy's bottom, will you?"

I couldn't help but look. It was raw! There were welt marks across the lower part, the fleshy saggy bum not pretty in contrast to the frilly knickers pulled down around his knees. Was this really happening?

"Say hello to Miss Danielle then."

"Hello Miss Danielle," a man's voice proffered.

Where was his face? Bending over a little I saw him briefly as he lifted his head in acknowledgement. Looking back at Lydia for direction, she could see I was fine.

"Okay then. I gave him a warning whip, but maybe you could give him the cane if you think he deserves it?"

Again her eyes looked deep into mine, signalling whether I was ready. I was.

"Yes absolutely Mistress Belle, I believe I am!

Slowly Lydia walked around to me, standing by my side.

"See here, the table laden with all our favourite canes? There's also a whip and a paddle. So, Miss Danielle, which one would you like to choose today?" Mesmerised by the display, I couldn't help but wonder how this could be considered sexually satisfying to these men, but then again I had stopped asking questions a long time ago, having sourced many answers that would be given reference in my writing. People did things - stupid things, wrong things whatever, but as long as it wasn't hurting anyone else I no longer cared.

"Give me the paddle," I said, taking the biggest piece from the collection.

"Good choice then. Master Frederick hates, absolutely *hates* the paddle, don't you Frederick?"

"Yes Mistress Belle!" The little scared voice shared.

Standing back as Lydia showed me how to line up the paddle along the butt cheeks of this strawberry white bum, I took in the situation once again. This middle aged man, an international banker, was barely hanging onto the stool he was bent over, wearing a pink tutu, tights and frilly knickers. So, he had millions of dollars and this was how he wasted it? Banks, having earned mega interest off all our hard earned cash were paying these wankers big salaries to squander in such style?

I took the paddle.

"Ready Miss Danielle? How many whacks hey Frederick? Shall we say five to begin?"

She nodded at me, mouthing 'are you okay with five?'

I nodded back, yes.

"Yes Mistress," he said.

"No, you say *yes* to Miss Danielle."

"Yes, Miss Danielle!"

Lydia led me into position sideways, bringing my arm up, heavy wooden oak paddle in hand. She nodded again for me to begin. Slamming the paddle hard against the flesh, the sound reverberated, a thwack followed by his flinching as cheeks wobbled and reddened.

"That will teach you to ever fuck with me!"

Lydia's face contorted with shock.

"Ooh, Miss Danielle's not happy at all! Are you okay Miss Danielle?"

Andrew came to mind. So too did the banks who had been chasing me for late payments when I was struggling with my mortgage during these last few years. All of the world's bankers were now in this room, bent over the chair with poor Frederick.

"Yes Mistress Belle, I've never felt better!"

Lydia looked concerned, idling toward me a little just as I whacked him again, already coming up for the third time, gaining momentum as I swung.

"You've been really bad, Frederick. And you really have to pay!" The paddle resounded; his cries getting louder.

Lydia quickly came over to relieve me of the paddle before I went for swing number six.

"I think we're done, don't you Frederick?"

He didn't move, barely whispering.

"Yes please Mistress. I promise I won't ever be naughty again!"

I smiled at a nervous looking Lydia who could see how much I was beginning to like this gig.

Later that night when talking to my sister, I gave her an account of the day's proceedings and together we laughed our heads off.

"I do hope you gave him an extra whack for me after that hard year we had!"

"I certainly did," I said. "Absolutely, in fact I thought of you just as his legs began to buckle."

It felt so good to be happy again, proving that things were looking up, although it would've been nice to share this with my friend Jay.

When I first returned to Sydney, Jay and I had caught up at an inner city bar. Waiting, I realised I was nervous. Contemplating his reaction to my year that was, I wondered why I was so concerned? I had failed to mention that I was back in the sex game. Could I trust him not to judge me? It was time to find out. Jay of all people already had a head start, hence while sitting there sipping a very expensive glass of champagne (probably a dead give-away) I finally told him, after I ordered another bottle of Veuve.

"Hey Jay, how's it all going for you?" I asked, feet tapping the base of the tan poufe-like couch.

Swigging vodka he dribbled a little on his chin before answering enthusiastically.

"Yep, just got back from India. Business is doing well! And you?"

"Oh yeah, it's been hard. Still sending off resumes but I'll get there. Anyway, while I've had so much time I thought I may as well write some more. You know, stuff about sex etc."

Jay's head jolted upright and he giggled his usual funny sound.

"Cool!"

That's Jay, I thought. He was never overly flustered by anything I said, and given I'm not one to postulate; I asked him the big question.

"So, what are you doing for sex these days?"

He leaned back, enjoying my familiar direct approach. Without flinching, he happily divulged the truth, telling me he had frequented the place where we'd met and had sex with some of the other girls there. A strange conversation was unfolding. After all these years I had never asked. We never talked about how we met and yet there I was getting all skittish and curious.

"Ok, yep. Can I ask you then, why didn't you ever try to have sex with me?"

This comment caught him a little off guard, vodka splashing his black triangle goatee beard. It seemed I had opened up a can of worms hence turning a somewhat usual catch up into an interesting evening, with me finding out a whole lot more about my friend.

"Because we've always been close as friends and I've got other tastes."

"What do you mean *other* tastes?"

More champagne was ordered as I sat there listening to Jay telling me he much preferred a bit of the kinky and dominant stuff.

"Hmm sounds interesting. What's that all about?" I asked, noting the tangent.

Leaning back, Jay didn't hesitate to explain.

"Well, there's a group, and we get together every so often. The women are submissive and I'm one of the dominant blokes."

"Jay! And I thought I was the one with the big, naughty secret sex life?"

Jay laughed. "We call types like you 'vanilla'."

"Vanilla? But I've not ever stayed in any normal position. And it's paid!" I retorted, confused.

"Kink is, well. Here, let me show you the website."

Jay continued to tell me what was involved as images of people clad in leather gear and bondage scenes popped up on his iPhone. I was blown away.

Just when you think you know someone.

Giving me an update on his monthly dominant parties, I was very intrigued.

"How about coming along to one? You can hang around and no-one will touch you."

For a moment I actually contemplated the idea, possibly thanks to the second bottle of champagne kicking in.

"Jay, I just couldn't. I'm too private – and vanilla, like you said. And on that note, I've been seeing a few clients again."

"Good!" he said, not flinching. "There's nothing wrong with that. You gotta do what you gotta do. But as long as you're ok?"

I was surprised that he wasn't disappointed in me for falling back. Why was I so intent on believing myself worthy of judgement? Why did I feel guilty for this choice? He made me feel ok about my choices, which was why I loved him. There was nothing in it for him, he just cared about me.

"Yes. Yes and no," I answered, feeling the emotion welling up behind my eyes. Looking down at my feet I continued. "I would much rather be doing something else though. Anything actually. I'm over it."

"What else have you been doing then?"

"It's a nightmare at the moment to get a small business started. But I'm determined to start doing some life coaching so I'm hunting for extra daytime work." I looked sideways, aware of feeling a bit despondent.

We smiled at one another once again, me appreciating my friend for being so laid back and more able to rationalise than I was.

"Good," he said, giving me a squeeze. "Now, what are you?"

"What on earth do you mean?" I quizzed, sipping on my fourth or fifth glass.

My drinking had increased during this time I was well aware. After tonight another visit to a weekend health retreat was in order.

"Well, are you dominant or submissive in bed?"

"What? Are you serious? I'm not going to tell you what I get up to in the bedroom!"

"No, no. Not in details!"

I stared at my friend as this new concept sunk beneath soggy brain cells. Trying not to grin like a schoolgirl I took a deep breath.

"Well, I'm always in control. A bit grumpy even," I said, thinking of a client who was running late once. "I missed out on my morning coffee because he wanted to see me before 9am, only to arrive at ten. He nearly got slapped hard, but not until after I had his money."

"Well, you too are a dominant personality; in control," Jay stated in a tone that reminded me of Simon. I wondered what he would make of all this?

"Hmm, yep I guess that's so! How do you, your crowd know what to choose?" I chuckled ridiculously.

Jay talked openly about how the group gained pleasure from freely indulging their fetish; the pleasure was mutual, often in favour of the women in terms of orgasm.

Wow, well there you go!

Feeling tired, I opened up a little more.

"I think I've got all my bases covered these days thanks. I met someone who makes me feel quite orgasmic."

"What do you mean? Who's this then?" he asked, eyes quizzing me.

"Um, I think I've had enough to drink. You hungry?"

Jay looked for the waiter, ready to pay for the bill.

"I'm always hungry," he joked.

We left our conversation there.

A year later Jay came over for dinner and I felt comfortable enough to tell him more about my feelings for Andrew. Shortly after he surprised me by proposing via text that we go out on a date, but I declined. Then I lost my phone and never heard from Jay again.

After my ex brother in law's funeral my sister asked to be left alone for a while so that she and the boys could grieve. I had to accept I couldn't be of more help, nor could I burden my parents who were coming to terms with dad's prostate cancer diagnosis and treatment plan. When my flatmate left, putting more financial pressure on me, I became despondent and withdrawn. In the meantime, still facing my own grief regarding Andrew, the heartache wouldn't ease, sending me into a downward spiral where recovery seemed impossible.

Gradually I put one foot in front of the other, planning each step carefully in order not to fall apart. Hadn't I soaked up enough New Age affirmations to disable such self-destructive patterns? I was happy one minute – suicidal the next.

"What is my true purpose?" I asked the Universe or whoever was listening. I was experiencing another Dark Night of the Soul; terminology given by lecturers for when we disconnect from spirit, losing sight of the meaning of life. My mind was foggy, my body overwhelmed with fatigue once again, triggering anxiety. How could I overcome this? I wasn't happy, each day pulling myself through while trying not to obsess about Andrew, torturing myself constantly with random thoughts and angry outbursts.

Moving through the muck and trying to survive was incredibly challenging. Every night for months I cried myself to sleep, the next day dragging myself off to work where I felt even less inspired. This was a rude existence – not a life at all! Did I really want to continue living like this? I was feeling pushed, pulled, empty and alone. Eventually I felt myself give up, my heart slowing to a pace that made it seem so easy to rest if I wanted to. A glow was activated within the region of my forehead, making me feel light.

My spirit was breaking down.

I sat up immediately, changing my mind. In that moment I knew it was time to get out there and carve a life that suited me. I had tried to conform, but why? I needed to feel my heartache and let people know I wasn't ready to let go, accepting also that it was time I stopped resisting the pull toward a more unconventional lifestyle.

The next morning my sister phoned with an edge to her voice.

"Are you okay?" she asked.

"Yes, why?"

"Well, I woke up hysterical after a nightmare. I dreamed you died! Are you sure everything's fine?"

Her intuition amazed me; our connection acute.

"Yes I am now, actually. I've decided to quit today to start my own business - back in the sex industry again!"

Chapter 16

The Power of Sexual Energy & Intuitive Evolution

I asked for divine guidance, reclaiming energy as my direction became clear. I needed to expand my heart and trust that I had choices, although the first one was hard to make. After much thought, I had decided to contact a few clients, asking them to support me through this transitional period so I could create my own therapeutic business. They agreed, happy to participate and see me exclusively at a premium rate.

Next was a decision I found a little more challenging.

Having always maintained that I would never work from my own bed, I reminded myself that loyalty to such a mantra had set me up for disappointment. Never say never, as they say. After all, it was just a bed and I would adjust. Besides, my soul was still my own. The sacredness of this piece of furniture had already been tainted by a lie.

A visit to an energetic healer helped me begin the painful process of releasing Andrew. There was an attachment that wouldn't shift; a past life agreement that had now been met. Apparently I had learnt the lessons necessary to access my higher purpose. Insights came through meditation as my plans unfolded easily. Slowing down, sinking into meditation each evening helped me redraw my energetic boundaries, keeping me vigilant for the next sign which came when I bumped into a friend I hadn't seen in quite a while.

Wandering around aimlessly one morning, I was surprised to see Sherri at the local supermarket. She looked exactly the same and said I did as well, which prompted our chat about Scarlett's; laughing about the day she had first met me at the back door. It seemed like a life time ago, and I suppose it was. No longer was I that brazen yet cautious, untrusting person she'd first met.

Sherri informed me that Scarlett's had closed down, thanks to the internet age and lack of long term vision by new management to maximise loyalty, so she was out of work and searching for something different to do. She asked if I'd kept in touch with Emilee, which I hadn't, but then few months later when having my morning coffee I saw Emilee walk into the café.

"Emilee!" I said, standing up.

Her face looked surprised as she stopped by the counter.

"It's me, Taryn! How are you?"

As her eyes softened she smiled.

"Oh my God you haven't changed a bit! I'm good thanks, how are you?" she asked, coming over to give me a hug.

"I'm really well. I can't believe this! I was only talking about you recently when I bumped into Sherri!"

Emilee pointed to a seat. "Shall we sit and have a quit chat? I'm just working part time at a charity here while I'm finishing a master's degree so I haven't got much time."

"Sure, no worries!" I said, aware she was always great at prioritising and minimising emotional connection.

"So, what are you up to these days?" Emilee asked, dropping her handbag down by the table leg.

It was hard to believe we had once juggled naked knees under tables in the company of wealthy men. I recalled our harbour experience eating seafood. Did that really happen?

"Ah well, I'm seeing a couple of my old favourite regulars, not that they're that old. One's about fifty and the other is thirty but it's a mistress arrangement while I try to get my coaching and counselling business up and running. I'm meditating and practicing Tantra as well to keep myself in balance."

Emilee stared at me and smiled.

"Wow counselling hey? That sounds great. Well good for you! I have a few friends who've continued to work. They're more like you; more emotional nurturers. Not like me!"

I never thought of myself as a nurturer.

"They also bring their Tantra into the practice, soothing their clients with tantric massage."

I moved in closer.

"Tantra massage. What's that?"

She looked at me quizzically. "Don't you massage your clients?"

"No, not at all unless they ask me to. They usually massage me! I'll ask them and maybe I can explore the practice."

"Yes do! You'd be great at that," she said, glancing at her watch. "Oh look I have to go, but let's catch up for dinner one night so we can relax and chat more."

She stood up, grabbing her bag to get her mobile phone.

"What's your number?"

"Yes here I'll give it to you, and also shall I tee up a time with Sherri too? We can all catch up then."

"Yes that would be great! Okay, let's do that. Maybe next month shall we? Just let me know what works for Sherri too."

Handing me her phone, I typed in my number for her. "There you go."

"Thanks! It's so lovely to see you." Emilee stood up and gave me a hug. "Take care."

I learned a lot more about boundaries with this new arrangement, two bachelor boys creating a challenge I hadn't foreseen. Although Iggy and Joshua each spent two hours with me every week equalling four hours of professional time, this often expanded with their messaging afterwards which prompted a great deal of management.

Diplomacy was key when they regularly texted after 9pm. Bored and lonely, their delicate ego's went into a spin if I didn't reply, triggering responses reflecting their issues around rejection and low self-esteem. I could sense the beginnings of detachment in their written response, taking due diligence on my part to alleviate this through gentle dialogue.

They were both pivotal in expanding my knowledge on the psyche of men only partly covered in classes about relationship dynamics. Being mindful of their inherent insecurities helped strengthen my business acumen to make sure I didn't allow co-dependency to set in. Finally I understood Emilee, realising that this was what had kept her so well adjusted and successful for so long.

The mistress arrangement was great for cash flow as I got serious about what I was going to create. When proposing to Iggy that he experience one of my tantric therapeutic sessions, he declined, telling me that had seen a Goddess on the Central Coast, and just didn't get the whole body orgasm thing.

"There was no sex at the end, either. She just burned lots of incense and did some chanting. It was relaxing though!" he said.

"What about a massage then, what did that entail?"

He smiled.

"Well, you already integrate quite a lot of that practice when we're together, so it's just that the Tantra stuff gets too heavy; bit too deep for me, really."

I smiled politely, accepting that Iggy had no inclination for personal growth or relational development. Joshua was easier to talk to about the concept however he was less than responsive about the idea.

"Yeah, sure it sounds good but I don't get it. It seems like a waste. Not that it would be a waste of time with you!" he quickly added.

Momentarily defeated, I looked at him and reminded myself that some people were simply not ready to expand along a path of enlightenment, nor did they wish to change their routine. Sex was intimate enough for these men, along with heartfelt conversations like friends. Embracing any deeper connection was a terrifying concept given that they would have to know themselves more and surrender to change.

"It's a deeper experience, Josh. And you get to have a more delicious orgasm for a whole lot longer!"

His eyes glazed over. I had lost him, making me see I would have to do a lot of research in order to pitch this to potential clients. The plan was to educate them about the powerful healing experience of sex when coupled with coaching, counselling and Tantra. The next question was how could I pull everything together in a way that would work for me? I needed a business model that would succeed this time around.

It had to be authentic, reflecting the integrity and sheer hard work of this modality. Wary of various rub and tug massage venues around, some providers posed as Tantric Goddesses. On-line research provided me with enough insight into the massage component ritual, never taught in my studies with Sophia. Then there were the more conservative fully clothed group facilitated events which I would eventually suggest my much younger clients attend.

By the time 2011 rolled around I no longer felt it necessary to hide behind a persona, ready to step out into the public forum with social media and a website using my own name and credentials. More sure about my direction, I no longer feared judgement from my peers.

Combining sex work and Tantric services attracted a curious audience.

Next I had to figure out how to incorporate sexual therapy without alienating these men, many sex work clients disappointed to discover that I wasn't offering full service. Like Joshua and Iggy they just didn't understand how male ego spurned their drive and sexual arousal, keeping them from expanding with greater orgasmic growth.

I had to support many men who feared showing such vulnerability. Releasing the notion that physical action is required in order to sustain sexual arousal is the male ego driven to control an outcome. Ego attachment is the platform upon which many sex work clients operate from. However once orgasm is reached, they are done; a superficial physical experience based upon stroking the waves of pleasure as they quickly peak.

Tantra encourages a person to surrender, imperative in order for the physical body to shift into energetic vibration, the masculine and feminine polarity being central in ascertaining equilibrium therefore heightened orgasmic sensations brew.

I wanted to take these men further, more deeply into the ecstasy and fulfilment they could reach within the realm of Tantric mastery. In my role as an escort no personal boundaries were crossed, nor were there any discussions about sexuality or performance unless the client instigated it. With Tantra, where I could introduce cues such as gentle touching at the heart centre and base of the spine, some men began to experience the connectedness which raised their deeper vibrational flow.

Yab Yum, the most popular position where a man and woman are sitting opposite each other, often the woman on his lap, makes it easy to hold each other's gaze while supporting the spine. Once energy stirs, it may peak and resonate with one's partner, heating up the base chakra region where kundalini energy may reside. Moving this up through the body with gentle sweeping motions, some of the energy may exit through the crown chakra on the top of the head, noted for being the gateway to ultimate consciousness – the Universe, God, Shiva or The Divine, depending on the Tantric methodologies one embraces.

Shiva (Universe) and Shakti (Goddess, Mother Earth) energies move more freely through the introduction of dance. Tantra is 'to weave and expand' as in consciousness and harmony – sexual divinity being the intention for us here on earth. 'Brahma', which means sacred, reminded me it was time to get back into my yoga practice in order to keep attuned.

In the early months many of the faces were familiar. I began seeing old clients from early escorting days who could barely manage an erection, saving money by taking up this far less expensive option for naked foreplay. There was no sex, of course but to these men who knew nothing about Tantra they didn't really care. It was such an eye opener as I wondered how those beautiful goddesses had managed to survive. This more divine authentic offering made us more available to narcissists.

Within six months I was ready to launch Tantra Sydney, promoting myself as a tantric sex coach and relationships counsellor, infusing Tantra and energetic healing as part of the bodywork experience. Some men were intrigued by the idea that Tantra may help with erectile dysfunction or premature ejaculation, often discovering through our session that they were highly stressed, sometimes lacking self-worth. Men came in to explore post-operative care after a radical prostatectomy which has left them wondering how to return to sexual intimacy if they no longer can get or manage an erection. There is still sensation, and in some cases men may find that their penis and perineum, an area between the penis and scrotum, is more sensitive allowing for creativity and confidence to return as we explore options for them to practice later at home.

Opening up to me in a more therapeutic setting, concerned about dry orgasms after a prolonged sexual foreplay, I witnessed the relief as men learned that this was not abnormal. In the few seconds after ejaculation men lose a great deal of energy along with the semen. Whilst ejaculation may feel great it's more for procreation and not necessarily as orgasmic as Tantra can be, the energy resonating through the whole body for much longer. Often if there are other disturbing factors revealed to me, I recommend they see a medical professional for a check-up and appropriate practitioner advice if under psychiatric care.

Women who can't orgasm may discover through somatic bodywork that this could be due to past emotional abuse from an ex-husband or a very traumatic birthing experience. Chakra balancing helps clear this trauma trapped within the lower spine at base chakra level.

Gradually I was in the flow, more relaxed about the business side and ready to introduce myself to fellow tantric practitioners. I learned to trust the industry I was fast becoming part of, grateful for referrals which often led to ongoing therapeutic sessions with men who showed aspects of repressed grief or pain around relationship issues.

One pattern was evident from a therapeutic perspective. Even though the initial decision to come see a Tantric practitioner was driven primarily by sexual issues closely linked into relationship problems, these clients often displayed fear around love and intimacy. Often rejected, or worse, sexually or emotionally abused I remain congruent as they revisit events that stir the pain, bringing it to the surface where healing can occur.

Incorporating cognitive behavioural therapy helps clients recognise inherent psychological patterns. I may engage Gestalt methods, helping them to understand more about the self as a sexual, physical and spiritual human being, with a body-centred approach imperative in order to lead them beneath the many layers of trauma and belief systems that have been incorporated, often remaining stuck for years. Helping a client become aware of why a relationship may have failed helps them to gain perspective and empowerment. The next stage is to encourage acceptance in a way that allows them to heal and move on.

Once I began to advertise further afield, those who were ready to step onto the path of self-discovery or in need of deeper healing began to contact me. These were people who knew they had a block but didn't know where to start asking for help. They weren't looking for sexual gratification in order to keep the ego in check, but instead seeking guidance, recognising that certain things were no longer working in their life. Many informed me that they had lost a wife or partner to disease and weren't looking for anything other than some form of intimacy that didn't involve sex. These men needed to be held, often embracing me in a hug when I give them the space for grief to be released.

Tantra incorporates many of the basics that are fundamental in in sustaining human life.

Being transparent and fully present, I guide clients using pranayama (breath work techniques) into a deeper state of relaxation. Stillness, visualisations and energetic intuition supports my healing practice. Based upon this therapeutic model, I may observe self-depreciating dialogue or disowned parts, aware that there are some men who feel overwhelmed when I bring it to their attention. Unimpressed if believing their issue is simply related to current sex issues, some people choose to remain stuck, not ready to confront their discomfort when I suggest we look at other events. Usually this is the case when there are childhood issues never dealt with. These may range from abuse to absent fathers or disappointing events that have stayed with them.

Upon informing one client that the energy I felt around his heart was a little heavy, cool to my touch which indicated to me there was a block, I asked him if he had experienced any disappointments or heartache here. He hesitated, resistant at first to divulge anything which is often the case when pain keeps a person paralysed. His tone then became angry as he began telling me his story.

"I'm fine and I have a big, kind heart my friends always say. You should ask my wife! I was married for ten years - gave that bitch everything until she left me eighteen months ago!" He looked at me, anger brewing in his eyes. "Took up with my best mate so there you go - I lost two people who I thought I could trust!"

I stood there quietly, watching as his body softened after sharing this with me. His eyes met mine, looking momentarily relieved.

"That's big! So I can understand why you haven't been able to move on. It's too soon."

"I'm ready – I'm over it now! Life's hard, just gotta get on with it don't we?"

He was in no way ready to begin a new relationship given that there was anger still stuck in his gut. His heart was also closed down.

"What do *you* have to offer a new relationship?" I asked.

He stared at me blankly before replying, "I'm wealthy and I have a good heart like I said. I always take women out and spend lots, giving them a good time!"

"Why do you feel that wealth makes you more lovable? Don't you think you are enough?"

He looked at me with slight disdain. "Women always want something. My wife had everything. Can't win, really can we?" He said, trying to coerce a little pity.

"It's not about winning. It's about loving yourself and being happy again. Then you'll attract someone who wants to be with you!"

He left, and never returned.

Only when we are ready to let go of grudges are we able to attract a partner to build a healthy relationship with. Men can become co-dependent in a long term relationship, often struggling post separation to re-examine their needs and dating style.

Although many of us seek intimacy in our relationships, the reality of relating to one person intimately on a daily basis is hard for most people to sustain. I inform my clients that this can be cultivated through establishing mutual codes of conduct and building trust, understanding that it takes commitment and respect. Being clear and honest to ourselves about our needs will ensure we set up our relationship for longevity. I encourage independence and strength in acknowledging where a union has faults and why.

Sometimes the very act of forgiving a relationship for its failure gives us the capacity for retrospection, acceptance of our part and the opportunity to move on. If we don't heal or evolve then we cannot create a clean slate upon which to draw up the next healthy stage of a relationship – or allow a new one to begin.

I was inspired to offer education to couples on how to nurture their partnership. Relationship counselling and tantric coaching practice supports them to discover what it is they desire and how to clearly communicate their needs.

Wanting vs. Meeting One's Own Needs

We all want to be loved, or to be in love, and expect our partners to be faithful but in truth we need to ask ourselves the difficult questions. Are we putting our needs first and foremost? Are we fulfilled enough to be open and comfortable, transparent with our partners? These were the lightning bolts I threw in when speaking with a couple who stared blankly at me, stating that they were indeed happy with everything in their lives.

A few weeks later the bloke popped back to see me, openly admitting that in truth he felt 'hemmed in' by his relationship. He loved his partner but something was missing. He wanted more experimental sex, not just lovemaking every now and then. He felt like it was wrong to ask his partner for such things. I reiterated that he needed to trust in his feelings enough to communicate with her, exploring together their deeper issues so that they could both gain from growing an honest relationship.

Fear may tip some into finding other avenues of sexual expression. In this situation it's for both parties in the relationship to explore the lack of balance, supporting one another through learning and recognising what constitutes intimacy for each of them. Once re-evaluation occurs, the next step is to ensure that self-esteem is restored and any past resentments or wounds are healed.

Other matters relating to intimacy often stem from couple's saying that they don't have enough time. Either too busy with work, or the kids are central to their day, I suggest to everyone who is serious about keeping their relationship alive that it's worth the effort to *make* time to play! Clients tell me they are bored, but what I hear is that they've become lazy and tired. Get creative and surprise each other. Explore each other's bodies slowly and engage more sensually without sex being the main goal. Intimacy doesn't always need to be expressed through penetration. It's created by feeling mutual desire and being fully present with one another in mind, body and spirit, giving precedence for subtle, loving energy to flow easily.

Learning Tantra helps revive connection, as I point out to my desperate clients. There's no need for too much physical exertion if you can simply sit and stare into each other's eyes. I suggest they tell each other what they really like about their partner every day, any time - even if it takes one whole minute. This initiates the practice of mindfulness as both begin to see each other again – sometimes for the first time even, breathing each other in. Gentleness and stillness with one another leads to a more relaxed state of mind that allows the energy to return to the base of the spine often opening up the space for sex!

Sex and sentiment doesn't need to be abandoned, nor does it have to be a conservative rule that intimate moments occur at night when a couple lay together in bed. A quick bonk may take place in the kitchen, maybe because the dishes got done by a partner without being asked. Women tell me that this small task does indeed raise their libido! Many married men will happily sneak out in the afternoon for a play, so why not be available for a dirty afternoon rendezvous at lunchtime or before the kids get out of school?

Sex drive can always be ramped up when we seductively plan or impulsively indulge in such things. Men often say to me that they would respond more if they felt wanted and not just expected to perform because they're the husband, provider or father.

Understanding why sex drives are different helps in finding new ways to harness the energy when it's there. Escape to the mountains, take a sickie and send the kids somewhere (I'm thinking your mother's or at a friend's place where they're safe of course) for a day.

Healthy and loving relationships deserve as much attention if not more than any other part of our lives.

Women like to feel needed and listened to, supported and loved. Some women begin to rely upon a partner for their happiness if they themselves feel discontent. Addressing our relationship as a partnership, I believe we would benefit from organising a meeting every so often to ensure that our needs are being met and that the business is running well. I recommend being vigilant in sensing how each other is feeling by talking openly and putting needs into perspective regularly.

It takes a lot of courage for a person to do this, but by denying our feelings they become hidden, possibly manifesting as risky behaviour. If a man speaks to me about the lack of sexual intimacy with his wife, telling me that the issue has been raised with her only to be shut down, I suggest marriage counselling for them both. Marriage counsellors are specialists in this area, yet I'm finding that many men will see me at the same time that this taking place simply because they feel more able to voice their sexual frustrations. They are afraid of upsetting their wives, meaning there is little chance of resolution.

A somatic energy session helps to source where the shift in power has occurred, uncovering a stage in life that may have fostered passive response. Once identified and resolved, the fear may be alleviated and insecurity around change will no longer exist. Confidence sparks enthusiasm as we redefine ways of communicating in a marriage that may support it to survive!

Sex is not only about pro-creation but re-creation too.

Epilogue

Writing has been cathartic, helping to confirm that I am indeed on the right path. Had I not fallen ill with adrenal fatigue, my spiritual healing wouldn't have taken place. Faced with psychological studies and my own therapy, this process of introspection has supported my growth, parallel to that of my many clients.

It's hard to believe I was once so insecure, a pattern set up from an early age. As a young person who witnessed addictive behaviours and experienced abuse that made me feel unsafe, I was unsure of how to assert myself or create boundaries around intimate relationships. Heartache fuelled my desperation to be empowered, with sex work validating me in more ways than I could ever have imagined. I'm so grateful to those who nurtured my self- esteem as I regained my confidence.

Some people still hold misconceptions about the sex industry and I'm reminded we all have discretionary rights. I declare my history with honour for the insight that it has provided. Most ask me questions like 'do black men really have big penises' and 'wow, so how I do I give good head?' I would never ask them such questions, nor would I want to know unless we're engaged in a professional therapeutic session. Then there's the classic belief of all times, 'My God you must've made a shitload of money!' to which I reply, "Well, no. But it was far better to have the occasional dud bonk and get paid at that stage in my life."

Those who visit for Tantric sessions are quite different in their needs. By participating in these healing experiences I understand more fully the role I had played in the demise of my own marriage and relationships. Through Tantra I radiate my true nature, feeding a re-emergence of my identity with positive energy. As my focus became clear I was able to forgive. I don't blame the people in my life for anything, nor do I regret one single thing. Except for those in our society that deviate and inflict abuse, generally the people that we love don't intentionally set out to hurt us. We feel hurt therefore we react, responding with feelings of anger and resentment. If we're able to acknowledge this, then we can focus on the love once shared. To separate ourselves from another is not to un-love but to move forward and love again. In accepting this for myself, my struggle was over.

Attachments create suffering, locking us in to a false sense of belief. Expectation spurns disappointment, creating resistance to positive growth. Duality is key as we a seek balance of our own feminine and masculine, yin yang forces providing a platform for healthy energies to flow. Life is all about change. We reshape our lives from birth right up until death, and relationships are part of the establishment in order to keep us connected in this lifetime. Greed and negativity has tipped the scales, therefore we need to become more conscious around our values as this is the turning point in alleviating suffering. Once we learn to relinquish materialistic desires, old beliefs and attachments, replacing them with expansive unconditional love, there is no suffering to be had.

We all have the power to change our story once we trust ourselves enough to take the first step. The expansive nature of Tantra allows spirit to enter the room whilst ego takes a back seat; exhausted or never really present. Those seeking my support are following a higher purpose as they pursue their desire to live a more fully integrated sexual and sensual life. I admire everyone who begins this process, when they call or email seeking advice. It's a responsibility and a passion for me to be able to assist people in exploring new options, their own story underpinning what needs to find a voice.

It is my intention to encourage future generations to explore sex and embrace its healing qualities. As we coexist, seeking intimacy and wanting to belong, it is vital that we value the power of sexual energy, not only as a biological driver but as a gift. Giving ourselves permission to mindfully practice pleasure helps balance resonance, connecting us with divinity.

Life is challenging, but it can also be very rewarding once we choose to live with purpose. In order to achieve a healthy relationship we need to make ourselves happy first by knowing what our purpose is and being able to love without fear.

Discovering this to be my life's purpose, I'm so grateful to have persevered so that I may continue to enjoy the journey, and support others along the way!